TELL ME THREE THINGS

Also by Julie Buxbaum

What to Say Next

Hope and Other Punch Lines

Admission

Year on Fire

TELL ME

THREE THINGS

JULIE BUXBAUM

EMBER

Text copyright © 2016 by Julie R. Buxbaum, Inc.
Cover art copyright © 2016 by Getty Images
Hand lettering by Erin Fitzsimmons

All rights reserved. Published in the United States by Ember, an imprint of Random House Children's Books, a division of Penguin Random House LLC, New York. Originally published in hardcover in the United States by Delacorte Press, an imprint of Random House Children's Books, New York, in 2016.

Ember and the E colophon are registered trademarks of Penguin Random House LLC.

Visit us on the Web! GetUnderlined.com

Educators and librarians, for a variety of teaching tools, visit us at RHTeachersLibrarians.com

The Library of Congress has cataloged the hardcover edition of this work as follows:
Buxbaum, Julie.
Tell me three things / by Julie Buxbaum.
pages cm
ISBN 978-0-553-53564-8 (trade hc) – ISBN 978-0-553-53565-5 (library binding) –
ISBN 978-0-553-53566-2 (ebook) – ISBN 978-0-399-55293-9 (intl. tr. pbk.)
[1. High schools—Fiction. 2. Schools—Fiction. 3. Moving, Household—Fiction.
4. Stepfamilies—Fiction. 5. Grief—Fiction. 6. Los Angeles (Calif.)—Fiction.] I. Title.
PZ7.1.B897Tel 2016
[Fic]—dc23
2015000836

ISBN 978-0-593-56720-3 (tr. pbk.)

Printed in the United States of America
10 9 8 7 6 5 4 3 2 1
2022 Ember Edition

For my E and L:
I love you
to the moon and back
and back and back.
Ad infinitum.

CHAPTER 1

Seven hundred and thirty-three days after my mom died, forty-five days after my dad eloped with a stranger he met on the Internet, thirty days after we then up and moved to California, and only seven days after starting as a junior at a brand-new school where I know approximately no one, an email arrives. Which would be weird, an anonymous letter just popping up like that in my in-box, signed with the bizarre alias Somebody Nobody, no less, except my life has become so unrecognizable lately that nothing feels shocking anymore. It took until now—seven hundred and thirty-three whole days in which I've felt the opposite of normal—for me to discover this one important life lesson: turns out you can grow immune to weird.

To: Jessie A. Holmes (jesster567@gmail.com)
From: Somebody Nobody (somebodynobo@gmail.com)
Subject: your Wood Valley H.S. spirit guide

hey there, Ms. Holmes. we haven't met irl, and I'm not sure we ever will. I mean, we probably will at some point—maybe I'll ask you the time or something equally mundane and beneath both of us—but we'll never actually get to know each other, at least not in any sort of real way that matters . . . which is why I figured I'd email you under the cloak of anonymity.

and yes, I realize I'm a sixteen-year-old guy who just used the words "cloak of anonymity." and so there it is already: reason #1 why you'll never get to know my real name. I could never live the shame of that pretentious-ness down.

"cloak of anonymity"? seriously?

and yes, I also realize that most people would have just texted, but couldn't figure out how to do that without telling you who I am.

I have been watching you at school. not in a creepy way. though I wonder if even using the word "creepy" by definition makes me creepy? anyhow, it's just . . . you intrigue me. you must have noticed already that our school is a wasteland of mostly blond, vacant-eyed Barbies and Kens, and something about you—not just your newness, because sure, the rest of us have all been going to school together since the age of five—but something about the way you move and talk and actually don't talk but watch all of us like we are part of some bizarre National Geographic documentary makes me think that you might be different from all the other idiots at school.

you make me want to know what goes on in that head of yours. I'll be honest: I'm not usually interested in the contents of other people's heads. my own is work enough.

the whole point of this email is to offer my expertise. sorry to be the bearer of bad news: navigating the wilds of Wood Valley High School ain't easy. this place may look all warm and welcoming, with our yoga and meditation and reading corners and coffee cart (excuse me: Koffee Kart), but like every other high school in America (or maybe even worse), this place is a freaking war zone.

and so I hereby offer up myself as your virtual spirit guide. feel free to ask any question (except of course my identity), and I'll do my best to answer: who to befriend (short list), who to stay away from (longer list), why you shouldn't eat the veggie burgers from the cafeteria (long story that you don't want to know involving jock jizz), how to get an A in Mrs. Stewart's class, and why you should never sit near Ken Abernathy (flatulence issue). Oh, and be careful in gym. Mr. Shackleman makes all the pretty girls run extra laps so he can look at their asses.

that feels like enough information for now.

and fwiw, welcome to the jungle.

yours truly, Somebody Nobody

....

To: Somebody Nobody (somebodynobo@gmail.com)
From: Jessie A. Holmes (jesster567@gmail.com)
Subject: Elaborate hoax?

SN: Is this for real? Or is this some sort of initiation prank, à la a dumb rom-com? You're going to coax me into sharing my deepest, darkest thoughts/fears, and then, BAM, when I least expect it, you'll post them on Tumblr and I'll be the laughing-stock of WVHS? If so, you're messing with the wrong girl. I have a black belt in karate. I can take care of myself.

If not a joke, thanks for your offer, but no thanks. I want to be an embedded journalist one day. Might as well get used to war zones now. And anyhow, I'm from Chicago. I think I can handle the Valley.

....

To: Jessie A. Holmes (jesster567@gmail.com)
From: Somebody Nobody (somebodynobo@gmail.com)
Subject: not a hoax, elaborate or otherwise

promise this isn't a prank. and I don't think I've ever even seen a rom-com. shocking, I know. hope this doesn't reveal some great deficiency in my character.

you do know journalism is a dying field, right? maybe you should aspire to be a war blogger.

....

To: Somebody Nobody (somebodynobo@gmail.com)
From: Jessie A. Holmes (jesster567@gmail.com)
Subject: Specifically targeted spam?

Very funny. Wait, is there really sperm in the veggie burgers?

....

To: Jessie A. Holmes (jesster567@gmail.com)
From: Somebody Nobody (somebodynobo@gmail.com)
Subject: you, Jessie Holmes, have won $100,000,000 from a Nigerian prince.

not just sperm but sweaty lacrosse sperm.

I'd avoid the meat loaf too, just to be on the safe side. in fact, stay out of the cafeteria altogether. that shit will give you salmonella.

....

To: Somebody Nobody (somebodynobo@gmail.com)
From: Jessie A. Holmes (jesster567@gmail.com)
Subject: Will send my bank account details ASAP.

who are you?

....

To: Jessie A. Holmes (jesster567@gmail.com)
From: Somebody Nobody (somebodynobo@gmail.com)
Subject: and copy of birth certificate & driver's license, please.

nope. not going to happen.

....

To: Somebody Nobody (somebodynobo@gmail.com)
From: Jessie A. Holmes (jesster567@gmail.com)
Subject: And, of course, you need my social security number too, right?

Fine. But tell me this at least: what's up with the lack of capital letters? Your shift key broken?

....

To: Jessie A. Holmes (jesster567@gmail.com)
From: Somebody Nobody (somebodynobo@gmail.com)
Subject: and height and weight, please

terminally lazy.

....

To: Somebody Nobody (somebodynobo@gmail.com)
From: Jessie A. Holmes (jesster567@gmail.com)
Subject: NOW you're getting personal.

Lazy and verbose. Interesting combo. And yet you do take
the time to capitalize proper nouns?

....

To: Jessie A. Holmes (jesster567@gmail.com)
From: Somebody Nobody (somebodynobo@gmail.com)
Subject: and mother's maiden name

I'm not a complete philistine.

....

To: Somebody Nobody (somebodynobo@gmail.com)
From: Jessie A. Holmes (jesster567@gmail.com)
Subject: Lazy, verbose, AND nosy

"Philistine" is a big word for a teenage guy.

....

To: Jessie A. Holmes (jesster567@gmail.com)
From: Somebody Nobody (somebodynobo@gmail.com)
Subject: lazy, verbose, nosy, and . . . handsome

that's not the only thing that's . . . whew. caught myself
from making the obvious joke just in time. you totally set
me up, and I almost blew it.

....

To: Somebody Nobody (somebodynobo@gmail.com)
From: Jessie A. Holmes (jesster567@gmail.com)
Subject: Lazy, verbose, nosy, handsome, and . . . modest

That's what she said.

....

See, that's the thing with email. I'd never say something like that in person. Crude. Suggestive. Like I am the kind of girl who could pull off that kind of joke. Who, face to face with an actual member of the male species, would know how to flirt, and flip my hair, and, if it came to it, know how to do much more than kiss. (For the record, I do know how to kiss. I'm not saying I'd ace an AP exam on the subject or, you know, win Olympic gold, but I'm pretty sure I'm not awful. I know this purely by way of comparison. Adam Kravitz. Ninth grade. Him: all slobber and angry, rhythmic tongue, like a zombie trying to eat my head. Me: all-too-willing participant, with three days of face chafing.)

Email is much like an ADD diagnosis. Guaranteed extra time on the test. In real life, I constantly rework conversations after the fact in my head, edit them until I've perfected my witty, lighthearted, effortless banter—all the stuff that seems to come naturally to other girls. A waste of time, of course, because by then I'm way too late. In the Venn diagram of my life, my imagined personality and my real personality have never converged. Over email and text, though, I am given those few additional beats I need to be the better, edited version of myself. To be that girl in the glorious intersection.

I should be more careful. I realize that now. *That's what she said.* Really? Can't decide if I sound like a frat boy or a slut; either way, I don't sound like me. More importantly, I have no idea who I am writing to. Unlikely that SN truly is some

7

do-gooder who feels sorry for the new girl. Or better yet, a secret admirer. Because of course that's straight where my brain went, the result of a lifetime of devouring too many romantic comedies and reading too many improbable books. Why do you think I kissed Adam Kravitz? He was my neighbor back in Chicago. What better story is there than the girl who discovers that true love has been waiting right next door all along? Of course, my neighbor turned out to be a zombie with carbonated saliva, but no matter. Live and learn.

Surely SN is a cruel joke. He's probably not even a he. Just a mean girl preying on the weak. Because let's face it: I am weak. Possibly even pathetic. I lied. I don't have a black belt in karate. I am not tough. Until last month, I thought I was. I really did. Life threw its punches, I got shat on, but I took it in the mouth, to mix my metaphors. Or not. Sometimes it felt just like getting shat on in the mouth. My only point of pride: no one saw me cry. And then I became the new girl at WVHS, in this weird area called the Valley, which is in Los Angeles but not in Los Angeles or something like that, and I ended up here because my dad married this rich lady who smells like fancy almonds, and juice costs twelve dollars here, and I don't know. I don't know anything anymore.

I am as lost and confused and alone as I have ever been. No, high school will never be a time I look back on fondly. My mom once told me that the world is divided into two kinds of people: the ones who love their high school years and the ones who spend the next decade recovering from them. What doesn't kill you makes you stronger, she said.

But something did kill her, and I'm not stronger. So go figure; maybe there's a third kind of person: the ones who never recover from high school at all.

CHAPTER 2

I have somehow stumbled upon the Only Thing That Cannot Be Googled: *Who is SN?* One week after receiving the mysterious emails, I still have no idea. The problem is that I like to know things. Preferably in advance, with sufficient lead time to prepare.

Clearly, the only viable option is to Sherlock the shit out of this.

Let's start at Day 1, that awful first day of school, which sucked, but to be fair probably sucked no more than every other day has sucked since my mom died. Because the truth is that every day since my mom died, she's still been dead. Over and out. They've all sucked. Time does not heal all wounds, no matter how many drugstore sympathy cards hastily scrawled by distant relatives promise this to be true. But I figure on that first day there must have been some moment when I gave off enough pitiful *help me* vibes that SN actually took notice of me. Some moment when the whole *my life sucks* thing was worn visibly on the outside.

But figuring that out is not so simple, because that day turned out to be chock-full of embarrassment, a plethora of moments to choose from. First of all, I was late, which was Theo's fault. Theo is my new stepbrother—my dad's new wife's son, who, *yippee,* is also a junior here, and has approached this whole blended-family dynamic by pretending I don't exist. For some reason, I was stupid enough to assume that because we lived in the same house and we were going to the same school, we would drive in together. Nope. Turns out, Theo's GO GREEN T-shirt is purely for show, and of course, he doesn't have to worry his pretty little head about such petty things as, you know, gas money. His mom runs some big film marketing business, and their house (I may live there now, but it is in no way *my house*) has its own library. Except, of course, it's filled with movies, not books, because: LA. And so I ended up taking my own car to school and getting stuck in crazy traffic.

When I finally got to Wood Valley High School—drove through its intimidating front gates and found a parking spot in its vast luxury car–filled lot and hiked up the long driveway—the secretary in the front office directed me to a group of kids who were sitting cross-legged in a circle in the grass, with a couple of guitar cases spread around. Like this was church camp or something. All *kumbaya, my Lord.* Apparently, that can happen in LA: class outside on an impossibly green lawn in September, backs leaned up against blooming trees. Already I was uncomfortable and sweating in my dark jeans, trying to shake off both my nerves and my road rage. All of the other girls had gotten the first-day-of-school memo; they were wearing light-colored, wispy summer dresses that hung off their tiny shoulders from even tinier straps.

So far, that's the number one difference between LA and Chicago: all the girls here are thin and half naked.

Class was already in full swing, and I felt awkward standing there, trying to figure out how to enter the circle. Apparently, they were going around clockwise and telling the group what they did with their summer vacation. I finally plopped down behind two tall guys with the hopes they had already spoken and that I might be able to take cover.

Of course, I picked wrong.

"Hey, all. Caleb," the guy right in front of me said, in an authoritative way that made it sound like he assumed everyone already knew that. I liked his voice: confident, as sure of his place as I was unsure of mine. "I went to Tanzania this summer, which was totally cool. First my family and I climbed Kilimanjaro, and my quads were sore for like weeks. And then I volunteered with a group building a school in a rural village. So, you know, I gave back a little. All in all, a great summer, but I'm happy to be home. I really missed Mexican food." I started to clap after he was done—he climbed *Kilimanjaro* and *built a school*, for God's sake, of course we were supposed to clap—but stopped as soon as I realized I was the only one. Caleb was wearing a plain gray T-shirt and designer jeans and was good-looking in a not-intimidating sort of way, his features just bland enough that he could be the kind of guy who I could possibly, one day, *maybe*, okay, probably not, date. Not really attainable, no, not at all, too hot for me, but the fantasy wasn't so outrageous that I couldn't revel in it for just a moment.

The shaggy guy sitting right in front of me was up next, and he too was cute, almost an equal to his friend.

Hmm. Maybe I'd surprise myself and end up liking it here after all. I'd have a great fantasy life, if not a real one.

"As you guys know, I'm Liam. I spent the first month interning at Google up in the Bay Area, which was great. Their cafeteria alone was worth the trip. And then I backpacked in India for most of August." A good voice too. Melodic.

"Backpacked, my ass," Caleb—Kilimanjaro-gray-T-shirt-guy—said, and the rest of the class laughed, including the teacher. I didn't, because as usual I was a moment too late. I was too busy wondering how a high school kid gets an internship at Google and realizing that if this is my competition, I'm never getting into college. And okay, I was also checking out those two guys, wondering what their deal was. Caleb, his climb up Kilimanjaro notwithstanding, had a clean-cut frat-boy vibe, while Liam was more hipster cool. An interesting yin and yang.

"Whatever. Fine, I didn't backpack. My parents wouldn't let me go unless I promised to stay in nice hotels, because, you know, Delhi belly and all. But still, I feel like I got a real sense of the culture and a great application essay out of the deal, which was the point," Liam said, and of course by then, I had caught on and knew not to clap.

"And you? What's your name?" said the teacher, who I later found out was Mr. Shackleman, the gym teacher SN warned me likes to stare at girls' asses. "I don't recognize you from last year." Not sure why he had to point so the whole class looked at me, but no big deal, I told myself. This was a first grader's assignment: what did I do with my summer vacation? No reason for my hands to be shaking and my pulse to be racing; no reason for me to feel like I was in the early stages of congestive heart failure. I knew the signs. I had seen the commercials. All eyes were on me, including those of Caleb and Liam, both of whom were looking with amusement and suspicion. Or maybe it was curiosity. I couldn't tell.

"Um, hi, I'm Jessie. I'm new here. I didn't do anything exciting this summer. I mean, I . . . I moved here from Chicago, but until then, I worked, um, at, you know, the Smoothie King at the mall." No one was rude enough to laugh outright, but this time I could easily read their looks. Straight-up pity. They had built schools and traveled to foreign locales, interned at billion-dollar corporations.

I had spent my two months off blending high-fructose corn syrup.

In retrospect, I realize I should have lied and said I helped paraplegic orphans in Madagascar. No one would have batted an eye.

Or clapped, for that matter.

"Wait. I don't have you on my list," Mr. Shackleman said. "Are you a senior?"

"Um, no," I said, feeling a bead of sweat release and streak the side of my face. Quick calculation: would wiping it bring more or less attention to the fact that I was excreting a massive quantity of water from my pores? I wiped.

"Wrong class," he said. "I don't look like Mrs. Murray, do I?" There were outright laughs now at a joke that was marginally funny, at best. And twenty-five faces turned toward me again, sizing me up. I mean that literally: some of them seemed to be evaluating my size. "You're inside."

Mr. Shackleman pointed to the main building, so I had to get up and walk away while the entire class, including the teacher, including fantasy-worthy Caleb and Liam, watched me and my behind go. And only later, when I got to my actual homeroom and had to stand up and do the whole summer vacation thing all over again in front of another twenty-five kids—and utter the words "Smoothie King" for the second time to an equally appalled audience—did I realize I had a large clump of grass stuck to my ass.

On reflection, the number of people who may have sensed my desperation? At least fifty, and I'm estimating on the low side just to make myself feel better.

The truth is SN could be anyone.

Now, a whole fourteen days later, I stand here in the cafeteria with my stupid brown sandwich bag and look around at this new terrain—where everything is all shiny and *expensive* (the kids here drive actual BMWs, not old Ford Focuses with eBay-purchased BMW symbols glued on)—and I still don't know where to go. I'm facing the problem encountered by every new kid ever: I have no one to sit with.

No chance of my joining Theo, my new stepbrother, who, the one time I said "hey" in the hall, blanked me with such intensity that I've given up even looking in his direction. He always seems to hang around with a girl named Ashby (yep, that's really her name), who looks like a supermodel midrunway—all dramatic gothy makeup, uncomfortable-looking designer clothes, blank wide features, pink spiked hair. I'm getting the sense that Theo is one of the more popular kids at this school—he fist-bumps his way down the hall—which is weird, because he's the type of guy people would have teased in Chicago. Not because he's gay—my classmates at FDR were not homophobic, at least not overtly—but because he's flamboyant. A little much about muchness. Everything Theo does is theatrical, except when it comes to me, of course.

Last night, I ran into him before bed and he was actually wearing a silk smoking jacket, like a model in a cologne ad. True, my cheeks were smeared with zit cream and I reeked of tea tree oil, looking like my own ridiculous parody of a pimply teenager. Still, I had the decency to pretend that it wasn't strange that our lives had suddenly, and without our consent, become commingled. I said my friendliest goodnight, since I can't see the point of being rude. It's not like that's going to unmarry our parents. But Theo just gave me an elaborate and elegant grunt, one with remarkable subtext: *You and your gold-digger dad should get the hell out of my house.*

He's not wrong. I mean, my dad's not interested in his mom's money. But we *should* leave. We should get on a plane this afternoon and move back to Chicago, even though that's an impossibility. Our house is sold. The bedroom I slept in for the entirety of my life now cradles a seven-year-old and her extensive American Girl doll collection. It's lost, along with everything else I recognize.

As for today's lunch, I considered taking my sad PB&J to the library, a plan that was foiled by a very stern NO EATING sign. Too bad, because the library here is amazing, so far the only thing I would admit is an improvement over FDR. (At FDR,

15

we didn't really have a library. We had a book closet, which was mostly used as a place to make out. Then again, FDR was, you know, public school. This place costs a bajillion dollars a year, a bill footed for me by Dad's new wife.) The school brochure said the library was donated by some studio bigwig with a recognizable last name—and the chairs are all fancy, the sort of thing you'd see in one of those high-end design magazines Dad's new wife keeps strategically placed around the house. "Design porn," she calls them, with that nervous laugh that makes it clear that she only talks to me because she has to.

I refuse to eat in the restroom, because that's what pathetic kids do in books and movies, and also because it's gross. The burnouts have colonized the back lawn, and anyway, I don't want to sacrifice my lungs at the altar of fake friendship. There's that weird Koffee Kart thing, which would normally be right up my alley, despite its stupid name: Why "Ks"? Why? But no matter how fast I get there after calculus, the two big comfy chairs are always taken. In one is the weird guy who wears the same vintage Batman T-shirt and black skinny jeans every day and reads books even fatter than the ones I tend to like. (Is he actually reading? Or are the books props? Come on, who reads Sartre for fun?) The other is taken by a revolving group of too-loud giggling girls who flirt with the Batman, whose real name is Ethan, which I know only because we have homeroom and English together. (On that first day, I learned he spent the summer volunteering at a music camp for autistic kids. He did not, in any way, operate a blender. Plus side: he did not give me one of those pitying looks I got from the rest of the class when I told them about my super-cool smoothie gig, but then again, that's because he couldn't be bothered to look at me at all.)

Despite the girls' best efforts, the Batman doesn't seem interested in them. He does the bare minimum—a half-hug, no-eye-contact brush-off—and he seems to shrink after each one, the effort costing him in some invisible way. (Apparently, there's a lot of hugging and double kisses at this school, one on each cheek, as if we are Parisian and twenty-two and not American and sixteen and still awkward in every way that matters.) Can't figure out why they keep coming back to him, each time in that bubble of hilarity, as if being in high school *is so much fun!* Seriously, does it need to be repeated? For the vast majority of us, *high school is not fun; high school is the opposite of fun.*

I wonder what it's like to talk in superlatives like these girls do: *Ethan, you are just the funniest! For reals. Like, the funniest!*

"You need some fresh air. Come walk with us, Eth," a blond girl says, and ruffles his hair, like he is a small, disobedient child. Sixteen-year-old flirting looks the same in Los Angeles and Chicago, though I would argue that the girls here are even louder, as if they think there's a direct correlation between volume and male attention.

"Nah, not today," the Batman says, polite but cold. He has dark hair and blue eyes. Cute if you're into that *I don't give a crap* look. I get why that girl ruffled his hair. It's thick and tempting.

But he seems mean. Or sad. Or both. Like he too is counting the days until he graduates from this place and in the meantime can't be bothered to fake it.

For what it's worth: 639 days, including weekends. Even I manage to fake it. Most of the time.

I haven't had a chance to really look without getting caught, but I'm pretty sure the Batman has a cleft in his chin, and there's a distinct possibility that he wears eyeliner, which, *meh*. Or maybe it's just the dark circles that make his eyes pop, because he looks chronically exhausted, like sleep is just not a luxury afforded to him.

"No worries," the girl says, and pretends not to be stung by his rejection, though it's clear she is. In response, she sits on another girl's lap in the opposite chair, another blond, who looks so much like her that I think they might be twins, and faux-cuddles her. I know how this show goes.

I walk by, eager to get to the bench just outside the door. A lonely place to eat lunch, maybe, but also an anxiety-free zone. No way to screw it up.

"What are you staring at?" the first blonde barks at me.

And there they are, the first words another student has voluntarily said to me since I started at Wood Valley two weeks ago: *What are you staring at?*

Welcome to the jungle, I think. *Welcome. To. The. Jungle.*

CHAPTER 3

It's not so bad here, I tell myself, now that I'm sitting on a bench with my back to the Batman and those bitchy girls, the cafeteria and the rest of my class safely behind him. So people here are mean. No big deal. People are mean everywhere.

I remind myself of the blissful weather. It's sunny, because apparently it's always sunny in LA. I've noticed that all the kids have designer sunglasses, and I'd get all snarky about people trying to look cool, but it turns out they need them. I spend my days all squinty, with one hand cupped over my eyes like a saluting Boy Scout.

My biggest problem is that I miss my best friend, Scarlett. She's my five-foot-tall half-Jewish, half-Korean bouncer, and she would have had the perfect comeback for that girl, something with bite and edge. Instead, I've only got me: me and my delayed response time and my burning retinas. I've been trying to convince myself that I can go it alone for the next two years. That if I need a boost, I can just text Scarlett and it will feel like she's nearby, not halfway across the country. She's fast on the trigger. I just wish I felt a little less stupid about how this place works. Actually, SN is right: I have lots of practical questions. I could totally use a Wood Valley app that would tell me how to use the lunch credit cards, what the hell Wood Valley Giving Day is, and why I'm supposed to wear closed-toed shoes that day. Maybe most importantly, who is off-limits for accidental eye contact. *What are you staring at?*

The flirting blondes now walk by my bench—guess their attempt to get Batman to walk was fruitless—and giggle as they pass.

Are they laughing at me?

"Is she for real?" the blonder girl mock-whispers to her only slightly less blond friend, and then glances back at me. They are both pretty in that lucky, conventional way. Shiny, freshly blown yellow hair, blue eyes, clear skin, skinny. Oddly big boobs. Short skirts that I'm pretty sure violate the school's dress code, and four coats of makeup that was probably applied with the help of a YouTube tutorial. I'll be honest: I wouldn't mind being lucky in precisely that way, being that rare teenager who has never stared down the head of a pimple. My face, even on its clearest days, has what my grandmother has always not-so-charitably called character. It takes a second, maybe a third look for someone to notice my potential. That is, if I have any. "Did you see that scrunchie?"

Oh crap. I was right. They are talking about me. Not only will I spend the next two years without a single friend, but all those *20/20* specials on school bullying will finally make sense. Somebody Nobody may be a prank, but he/she is right: this place is a war zone. I'm going to need my own personal "It Gets Better" video.

My face burns. I touch my finger to my head, a sign of weakness, yes, but also a reflex. There's nothing wrong with my scrunchie. I read on Rookie that they're back. Scarlett wears one too sometimes, and she won Best Dressed last year. I fight the tears filling my eyes. No, they will not see me cry. Scratch that. They will not *make* me cry.

Screw them.

"Shhh, she can hear you," the other one says, and then looks back at me, at once apologetic and gleeful. She's high with a vicarious bitch thrill. Then they walk on—sashay, really, as if they think there's an audience watching and whistling. I glance behind me, just to make sure, but no, I'm the only one here. They are swaying their perfect asses for my benefit.

I pull out my phone. Text Scarlett. It's lunchtime for me, but she's just getting out of school. I hate that we are far apart in both space *and* time.

Me: I don't fit in here. Everyone is a size 0. Or 00.

Scarlett: Oh no, don't tell me we have to do the whole U R NOT FAT thing. The entire basis of our friendship is that we are not the kind of girls who have to do that for each other.

We have never been the types who are all, "I hate my left pinky finger! It's just so . . . bendy." Scarlett is right. I have better things to do than compare myself with the unattainable ideals established by magazine art directors who shave off thighs with a finger swipe. But I'd be lying if I didn't admit to noticing that I'm on the bigger side of things here. How is that possible? Do they put laxatives in the water?

Me: And blond. Everyone is. Just. So. California. Blond.

Scarlett: DON'T LET THEM TURN YOU INTO ONE OF THOSE GIRLS. You promised not to go LA on me.

Me: Don't worry. I'd have to actually talk to people to go LA.

Scarlett: Crap. Really? That bad?

Me: Worse.

I quickly snap a selfie of me alone on a bench with my half-eaten peanut butter and jelly sandwich. I smile instead of pout, though, and label with the hashtag #Day14. Those blondes would pout, turn it into an *I'm so sexy* picture, and then Instagram it. *Look how hot I am not eating my sandwich!*

Scarlett: Lose the scrunchie. A little too farm girl with that shirt.

I pull my hair loose. This is why I need Scarlett here. Maybe she's the reason I've never been teased before. If we hadn't met at the age of four, I'd likely be an even bigger dork.

Me: Thanks. Scrunchie officially lost. Consider it burned.

Scarlett: Who's the hot guy photobombing you?

Me: What?

I squint at my phone. The Batman was looking out the window just as I took my shot. Not photobombing exactly, but captured for posterity. So it turns out Blond and Blonder did have an audience after all. Of course they did. Girls like that *always* have an audience.

My face flushes red again. Not only am I a big fat loser who eats lunch alone with an unironic scrunchie in her hair, but I'm stupid enough to get caught taking a selfie of this wonderful moment in my life. By a cute guy, no less.

I check the little box next to the picture. Hit delete. Wish it were that easy to erase everything else.

CHAPTER 4

"T. S. Eliot's '*The Waste Land*.' Anyone read it?" asks Mrs. Pollack, my new AP English teacher. Nobody raises their hand, myself included, though I did read it a couple of years ago, in what now feels like a different lifetime. My mom used to leave poetry books strewn around our house, as if they were part of some unspoken scavenger hunt, a scattering of convoluted clues leading to I don't know what. When I was bored, I'd pick up the books off her nightstand or from the pile next to the bathtub and randomly flip them open. I wanted to read wherever she had highlighted or scribbled illegible margin notes. I often wondered why a certain line was marked with faded yellow.

I never asked her. Why didn't I ask her? One of the worst

parts about someone dying is thinking back to all those times you didn't ask the right questions, all those times you stupidly assumed you'd have all the time in the world. And this too: how all that time feels like not much time at all. What's left feels like something manufactured. The overexposed ghosts of memories.

In "The Waste Land," my mother had underlined the first sentence and marked it with two exuberant asterisks: "April is the cruellest month."

Why is April the cruellest month? I'm not sure. Lately, they all seem cruel in their own way. It's September now: sharp pencils. A new year and not a new year at all. Both too early and too late for resolutions and fresh starts.

My mother's books are packed up in cardboard boxes and getting moldy in a self-storage unit in Chicago, their paper smell turned damp and dusty. I don't let myself think about that or about how all matter disintegrates. About how all that highlighting was a waste.

"It's a four-hundred-thirty-four-line poem. So that's what, like, four hundred thirty-four tweets?" Mrs. Pollack gets a laugh. She's young—maybe late twenties—and attractive: leopard-print leggings, leather peep-toe wedges, a silk tank top that shows off her freckled shoulders. She's better dressed than I am. One of those teachers who the kids have all tacitly agreed to root for, maybe even to admire, since her life doesn't seem so far out of our reach. She's something recognizable.

On my first day, she introduced me to the class but didn't make me stand up and say something about myself, like the rest of my teachers had done. Considerate of Mrs. Pollack to spare me that indignity.

"So, guys, 'The Waste Land' is hard. Really, really hard. Like, college-level hard, but I think you're up for it. Are you up for it?"

She gets a few halfhearted yeses. I don't say anything. No need to let my nerd flag fly just yet.

"Nuh-uh. You can do better than that. Are you up for it?" Now she gets full-on cheers, which impresses me. I thought the kids here only got excited about clothes and *Us Weekly* and expensive trips to pad their college applications. Maybe I've written them off too quickly. "Okay, here's how we're going to do this. You're going to partner up into teams of two, and over the next two months, on a weekly basis, you are going tackle this poem together." Oh no. No. No. No. You know the only thing worse than being the new kid in school? Being the new kid who needs to find a partner. Crap.

My eyes bounce around the room. Theo and Ashby are in the front, and it's a given that Theo will not help a stepsister out. The two blondes who made fun of me earlier are sitting to my right. Turns out their names are Crystal (blond) and Gem (blonder), which would be hilarious if they weren't nasty. Look left. The girl next to me wears cool big black Warby Parker frames and ripped jeans and looks like the kind of person who would have been my friend back home. But before I can think of a way to ask her to team up, she's already turned to the person next to her and done the whole *let's be partners* thing without exchanging a word.

Suddenly, the whole room is paired up. I look around, try not to seem too desperate, though there is a pleading in my eyes. Will I have to raise my hand and tell Mrs. Pollack that

I don't have a partner? *Please, God, no.* Just as I bend my arm, ready to raise it in defeat, someone taps my shoulder from behind with a pen. I breathe a sigh of relief and turn. I don't care who it is. Beggars and all that.

No. Way.

The Batman.

My stomach does an embarrassing squeeze. He gives me a little nod, like Theo's guy nod, but this time, there's no mistaking it: he's clearly asking me to be his partner. His blue eyes are piercing, almost violating, like he isn't just looking *at* me but *inside* me too. Measuring something. Seeing if I'm worth his time. I blink, look down, nod back, give him the slightest smile as a thanks. I turn forward again and use all of my willpower not to put my hands against my cheeks to cool them down.

I spend the rest of class wondering why the Batman picked me. Maybe I look smart? And if I look smart, does that mean I look dorky? I mentally scan my outfit: plaid button-down, Gap jeans cuffed up, my old beat-up Vans. My Chicago uniform, minus the heavy jacket. Nothing too telling there, especially now that I'm scrunchie-free. My first instinct is that, for whatever reason, he's just doing a good deed. I must have looked pathetic, wildly scanning the room for a willing face, especially after he saw me getting bitched out by Gem earlier and embarrassing myself on the first day of school. Even Ken Abernathy, who according to SN has a farting problem, found a partner immediately.

When the bell rings and we're all packing up our laptops—of course I'm the only one here without a fancy, slim computer—the Batman stops at my desk, stares me down again with those killer eyes. Am I just imagining that they have a sociopathic hint to them? He can't be that mean. Picking me was actually a nice thing to do. I don't remember taking the time to befriend a new kid back home. Hot and nice. That. Is. So. Not. Good.

I realize just in time that I need to stop staring and speak up.

"So do you want to exchange numbers or something?" I ask, and hate the nervous lilt in my voice that makes me sound way too much like the girls who gather around him at lunchtime. It's just that I haven't really spoken much in weeks. Scarlett and I mostly text. My dad has been so busy looking for a new job and spending time with his new wife that we've barely seen each other. He's not my favorite person right now anyway. I don't like this new version of him, distracted and married to a stranger, forcing me into an unrecognizable life without a say in the matter.

And that's it. The sum total of people left in my world.

"Nah. I'll just do the assignment and put both of our names on it." This guy doesn't wait for my okay. He just nods again, like I've said yes. Like he asked and I answered a question.

Right. Maybe not so nice after all.

"But—" But what? *I was looking forward to being your partner? I like your serial killer eyes?* Or worst of all: *Please?* I don't finish speaking. Just look back down at my leather book bag, which I thought was cool until I got here and realized everyone else's was a fancy French brand that you hear about in rap songs.

"Don't worry. You'll get an A."

Then the Batman walks out so fast that it's almost like I

imagined him there. Some perverse version of a superhero. And I am left alone to gather up my stuff, wondering how long it will be till someone talks to me again.

Me: It will get better, right? Eventually, it will get better.

Scarlett: I'm sorry I'm not the type to lower our discourse to emoji use since you totally deserve a smiley face right now. Yes, it will get better.

Me: Ha. It's just. Whatever. Sorry to keep whining.

Scarlett: That's what I'm here for. BTW, that email you forwarded? My guess: TOTALLY A SECRET ADMIRER.

Me: You've read too many books. I'm being set up. And stop YELLING AT ME.

Scarlett: No way. I didn't say he was a vampire. I said he was a secret admirer. Most def.

Me: Wanna take bets?

Scarlett: You should just know by now that I'm always right. It's my one magic power.

Me: What's mine?

Scarlett: TBD.

Me: Thanks a lot.

Scarlett: Kidding. You are strong. That's your power, girl.

Me: My arms are v. toned from stress-eating ALL the cookies. Hand to mouth. Repeat 323 times. Hard-core workout.

Scarlett: Seriously, for a second, J? Just because you're strong doesn't mean you shouldn't ask for help sometimes. Remember that. I'm here, ALWAYS, but you might want to take up that offer from someone local.

Me: Whatever. Ugh. Thanks, Dr. Phil. I miss you!

Scarlett: Miss you too! Go write back to SN. NOW. NOW. NOW. Now tell me the truth? Anyone at your school unusually pale?

To: Somebody Nobody (somebodynobo@gmail.com)
From: Jessie A. Holmes (jesster567@gmail.com)
Subject: Conjuring my spirit guide

Okay, I call mercy. You're right. This place is a war zone, and I could use some help. So I'm going against my gut here and just hoping I can trust you. Are you still game for just a few questions? (And if this is Deena, you win. You got me.)

....

To: Jessie A. Holmes (jesster567@gmail.com)
From: Somebody Nobody (somebodynobo@gmail.com)
Subject: at your service, m'lady

> now you got me curious about this Deena chick. why is she out to get you? the offer still stands.

....

To: Somebody Nobody (somebodynobo@gmail.com)
From: Jessie A. Holmes (jesster567@gmail.com)
Subject: I'm virtually curtsying.

> The Deena story isn't particularly interesting. Stupid high school girl stuff. Speaking of which: you said that there was a short list of people I should befriend? Not to sound too desperate, but some guidance would be appreciated on that front.
>
> What's up with WV Giving Day and what will happen to my toes if I leave them exposed?
>
> Do those weird lunch cards come preloaded with $$ or what?

....

To: Jessie A. Holmes (jesster567@gmail.com)
From: Somebody Nobody (somebodynobo@gmail.com)
Subject: toes chop suey

> start with Adrianna Sanchez. she's shy, so she won't approach you first. But she's cool and smart and secretly funny once you get to know her. I don't know why, but I feel like you two could be good friends.
>
> community service day with Habitat for Humanity. it involves hammers, hence closed-toe shoes. your Vans should be fine. they're cool, by the way.

31

nope, not preloaded. machine outside the caf takes only tens and twenties and credit cards.

Huh. Maybe this SN guy knows me better than I thought. Adrianna Sanchez is the girl with the oversized Warby Parker glasses who sits next to me in English class. The one who reminds me of my friends back home. I blush a little at his Vans compliment. I'm such a sucker.

To: Somebody Nobody (somebodynobo@gmail.com)
From: Jessie A. Holmes (jesster567@gmail.com)
Subject: The One Percent

Credit cards? For real? Is everyone here rich?

To: Jessie A. Holmes (jesster567@gmail.com)
From: Somebody Nobody (somebodynobo@gmail.com)
Subject: come for a ride on my G4.

honestly? we have a couple scholarship kids, but this place costs mad bank, as i'm sure you know. it is what it is.

Spelled out in black-and-white: Reason #4,657 why I don't fit in here. My dad's not a film marketing mogul, whatever the hell that is; he's a pharmacist. Back home we were far from poor. We were what I knew as normal. But no one had their own credit cards. I shopped at Target or Goodwill with saved-up cash, and we wouldn't just buy a five-dollar coffee without first doing the unfortunate math and realizing that the drink cost almost an hour's worth of after-school pay.

My parents were never much interested in money or

clothes or any of the fancy-pants crap that's ubiquitous here. I wasn't the kind of kid who asked for designer stuff—it was never really my style, and even if it had been, I'm pretty sure my mom would have given me a lecture. Not just because we couldn't afford more than the occasional splurge, but because my mother considered name brands and decorative stuff wasteful. Silly stuff for silly people. She was much more interested in using whatever money she and my dad saved to travel to interesting places or to donate to good causes. *Experience over things,* she used to say, and then talk about some social science study she had read that definitively proved money doesn't buy happiness. I wish I could say I always agreed with her—I remember one fight we had over a two-hundred-dollar dress for the eighth-grade dance—but now I'm proud of how I was raised, even if it means I'm even more of a stranger in a strange land at this school.

Suddenly, my gratitude toward the Batman turns to fury. How dare he hijack my grade? Unlike the rest of the loaded kids here, I'm hoping to get a scholarship to college. I can't just trust his promise of an A. And what if Mrs. Pollack found out we didn't work together? When I enrolled, I had to sign an honor pledge. Technically, this could be counted as cheating and go on my permanent record.

Tomorrow I will have to gather the courage to talk to the Batman and tell him that we need to work together or I'll have to ask Mrs. Pollack for a new partner. I hate that I have five hours of homework and still need to find time to get a part-time job. I hate that Scarlett is not here. I hate Theo, who just came home and, though I was sitting right there in the living room, didn't even have the courtesy to say, "Hey, how was your day?" I even hate my dad, who, I decided after my mom died, is easier to love than to pity, for bringing me here, for leaving me to fend for myself. Even he is nowhere to be found.

My mom used to get mad when I used the word "hate." She thought it was an ungrateful, overly entitled word, and no doubt she'd be furious at me for using it in reference to my dad. But then again, she's gone, and he's married to someone else now. Pretty sure none of the old rules still apply.

To: Somebody Nobody (somebodynobo@gmail.com)
From: Jessie A. Holmes (jesster567@gmail.com)
Subject: And now an understatement

> Hey, Spirit Guide. Not to sound unappreciative or anything, but can I just say: YOUR SCHOOL SUCKS.

To: Jessie A. Holmes (jesster567@gmail.com)
From: Somebody Nobody (somebodynobo@gmail.com)
Subject: tell me something I don't know.

> preaching to the choir. now please stop yelling. you're giving me a headache.

CHAPTER 5

"Home, sweet home," Dad said the first time we walked into his new wife's house, and he spread his hands wide, as if to say *Not too shabby, right?* If our house in Chicago was low-ceilinged and squat and tough, what I thought of fondly as a wrestler of a house, this one is the prom king: tall and shiny-toothed and the effortless winner of everything. White couches. White walls. White bookshelves. It's bad enough she's paying my tuition. Now I'm terrified to add stain damage to my running tab.

No, not quite home, sweet home. It feels weird to complain about living in something out of *MTV Cribs,* and yet, I miss our house, which Dad sold to the Patels the first day we put it on the market. Aisha is now sleeping in my old room, which has been stripped of my vintage movie posters, and collage of book covers, and pictures of Scar and me making silly faces. Here, I'm tucked away in one of the many extra guest rooms, all of which are decorated so as to keep you from overstaying your welcome. I now sleep on an antique-style daybed—the sort of thing fit for a 1950s pinup girl to show off her garters, and not so much meant for, you know, actual sleeping. The en suite bathroom is equipped with monogrammed Tuscan soaps that look too expensive to touch, much less use. And the walls are decorated with the kind of abstract art that looks like the handiwork of a third grader. My only addition to the room, besides Bessie, my childhood stuffed cow, is a tiny photo of my mother and me from when I was about eight or nine. My entire body is wrapped around her thigh, like I'm a baby monkey, even though I was already too old for that sort of thing. She's looking down at me. There's love and amusement in her eyes, adoration and fear in mine. I still remember the moment it was taken. I was afraid of a new babysitter, convinced, for some reason, that if my mom walked out the door, she'd never come back.

"Don't you love it?" my dad asked of the house, after he had carried my life in two duffel bags up the sweeping staircase to "my room." He was so happy and excited, like a kid who had done good and wanted a treat, that I couldn't let him down. He had turned helpless when my mom got sick. One day she was healthy, the captain of both of our lives, the one who organized everything, and then suddenly she was not. The diagnosis: stage four ovarian cancer. She became too weak to walk across the room, much less navigate the intricacies of the day-to-day: meals, rides, keeping us stocked in toilet paper.

Sapped and exhausted, my dad lost both weight and hair,

as if it were him, not her, who was having the chemo and ra-
diation. As if he were her mirror image. Or conjoined twin.
One of them unable to function without the other. It had been
just over two years (747 days, I count them), and I couldn't help
but notice that only recently had he started to put back on the
weight, to look more solid. Again, finally, a man, the *dad,* not
the child. For months afterward, my dad would ask me questions that made clear he had no idea how our daily lives actually worked: Where do we keep the dustpan? What's the name
of your principal? How often do you get checkups?

My dad worked full-time, and when he wasn't working,
he was busy negotiating with the insurance companies, dealing with the mountains of doctors' bills that kept coming and
coming, so cruel after the fact. Instead of bothering him, I borrowed his tired credit card. Set up auto-ship for paper towels
and toilet paper, kept a grocery list, bought us granola bars
and instant oatmeal in bulk. Because I hadn't yet gotten my
driver's license that first year, I ordered bras online. Tampons
too. Asked the Internet all the questions I would have asked
my mother. A sad virtual substitute.

We made do. Both of us did. And for a while there, we were
so busy holding things together, I almost forgot how things
used to be. How all three of us used to be conjoined. When I
was little, I'd climb into bed between my parents so we could
make our daily Jessie sandwich. We were a happy unit; three
seemed a good, balanced number. Each of us had our defined
roles. My dad worked and made us laugh. My mom worked
too, but part-time, and so she was point person, the family
soother and the glue. My only job was to be their kid, to be
their good egg, to bask in their constant stream of attention.

It's been 747 days and still I have not yet learned how to talk about any of this. I mean, I can talk about how I bought the toilet paper, how we were broken, how *I* was broken. But I still haven't found the words to talk about my mom. The *real her*. To remember who she was in a way that doesn't make me keel over.

I don't know how to do that yet.

Sometimes it feels like I've forgotten how to talk altogether.

"It's amazing, Dad, really," I said, because the new house is amazing. If I was going to be held captive by a wicked stepmother, surely there are worse places I could have ended up than living in the pages of *Architectural Digest*. I wasn't going to complain about its utter lack of homeyness—and not even homeyness specific to me, but homeyness in general—or the fact that I felt like I had moved into a museum filled with strangers. That would sound petty. Anyhow, we both knew that that wasn't the problem. The problem was that Mom wasn't here. That she would never be anywhere again. When I thought about that for too long, which I didn't, when I could help it, I realized it didn't matter much where I slept.

Certain facts tend to render everything else irrelevant.

We once were three strong, and now we were something altogether different. A new, unidentifiable formation. A cock-eyed parallelogram.

"Call me Rachel," Dad's new wife had said the first time I met her, which made me laugh. What else was I going to call her? Mother? Ms. Scott? (Her maiden name. Actually, not her maiden name. Her previous married name.) Or even more ridiculous, her new name, *my* mother's name: Mrs. Holmes? In my head, she remains Dad's new wife; it's a futile

38

exercise to try to get me used to the idea. *Dad's new wife. Dad's new wife. Dad's new wife.* Talk about three words that don't fit together.

"Call me Jessie," I said, because I didn't know what else to say. The fact that she existed at all had come as a surprise. I hadn't even realized my dad had started dating. He had been traveling a bunch—pharmaceutical conventions, he claimed—and I hadn't thought to question him, even though he had never before taken a work trip. I figured he was using work the same way I was using school: as a way to forget. I was excited to be home alone for those weekends. (Did I take advantage and throw big parties, where kids sipped beer from red Solo cups and left piles of vomit on our lawn? Nope. Scarlett slept over. We made microwave popcorn and binge rewatched old seasons of our favorite shows.)

Then one day my dad came home and said this whole thing about having fallen in love and I noticed he had a new ring on his finger. Cold and shiny. Silver: a bitter medal. Apparently, somehow, instead of going to Orlando to learn more about Cialis, he had eloped to Hawaii with a woman he met on the Internet in one of his bereavement support groups. At first, I thought he was joking, but his hands were shaking, and he was half smiling the way he does when he's nervous. And then came the long, terrible speech about how he knew this was going to be difficult, a new city, switching schools and all— this was the part he said fast, so fast that I made him repeat it to make sure I had heard him right. This was the part when I first heard the words "Los Angeles."

A step up, he said. An *opportunity*. A way to get us out of "our rut." Those were other words he dared to use: "our rut."

I hadn't realized we were in a rut. "Rut" seemed way too small a word for grief.

He was tan, his cheeks pink from three days on a beach. I was still pale from the Chicago winter. My fingers probably smelled of butter. I didn't cry. After the shock wore off, I cared a whole lot less than I thought I would. Sometimes, when Scarlett says I'm strong, I think she really means I'm numb.

Rachel is one of those teeny-tiny women who somehow use their voice to take up a lot space. She doesn't speak so much as announce things. *Call me Rachel! Tell Gloria if you want to add anything to the grocery list! Don't be shy! She's a whiz in the kitchen! I can't even boil an egg! Pilates kicked my ass today!*

I find her exhausting to be around.

Today's announcement: "Family dinner!" Until now, I've mostly avoided sitting down with everyone at the dining table. Rachel's been busy working late on a new film—an action-hero slash sci-fi feature called *Terrorists in Space*—that she promises is "going to kill it at the box office!" On nights my dad's not out to business dinners with Rachel—"Schmoozing is key!" she likes to pronounce—he's been glued to his computer looking for a new job. Theo goes out a lot too, mostly to Ashby's house, where they steal her mother's Zone Delivery meals.

I tend to eat in my bedroom. Usually peanut butter and jelly that I've bought myself, or ramen with an egg. I don't feel comfortable adding to Gloria's shopping list. Gloria is the "house manager," whatever that is. "Like family!" Rachel pronounced when she introduced us for the first time, though in my experience family members don't wear uniforms. There also seems to be a cleaning crew and a gardener and various other Latino people who are paid to do things, like change lightbulbs or fix toilets. "Guys, get down here! We're all having dinner together, whether you like it or not!"

This last bit is said half jokingly, like: *Ha-ha, isn't it funny that you two don't actually want to be doing this? Sharing a house. Eating together. Life is hil-larious.*

Maybe I hate her. I haven't decided yet.

I peek out of my bedroom, see that Theo is making his way downstairs. He's wearing a huge pair of headphones. Not a bad idea. I grab my phone so I can text Scarlett while we eat.

"Seriously, Mom," Theo says, his ears still fully covered, so he talks even louder than usual. These people have no sense of volume control. "Do we really have to play happy family? It's bad enough that they *live* here."

I look at my dad, roll my eyes to show that I'm not bothered. He gives me a tiny smile when Rachel isn't looking. If Theo is going to be a bad sport, I'll do the opposite. Play perfect child and make Rachel even more embarrassed about her spoiled brat. Pretend I'm not angry that my dad has brought me here, that he hasn't even bothered to ask how I'm doing. I've mastered the game of Pretend.

"Looks delicious. What is this?" I ask, because it does look good. I'm getting tired of ramen and PB&J. I need some vegetables.

"Quinoa and a mixed seafood stir-fry with bok choy," Rachel announces. "Theo, please take off your headphones and stop being rude. We have some exciting news."

"You're having a baby," Theo deadpans, and then laughs at his own joke, which is not at all funny. Oh no. Is that even a biological possibility? How old is Rachel? Thank you, Theo, for adding one more thing to my biggest fears in life list.

"Very funny. No. Bill got a job today!" Rachel grins, as if my dad has just accomplished an amazing feat: done a triple backflip right in front of us and stuck the landing. She's still in her work clothes—a white blouse with a jaunty bow tie and black pants with a satin stripe down each side. I'm not sure why, but she always seems to wear stuff that dangles: ties, tassels, charms, scarves. Her blunt-cut brown hair is blown straight, and its perfection ages her, despite her tasteful Botox. Too many sharp lines. I'll grant her this, even though I'm not much in the mood to grant her anything: Rachel's enthusiasm is generous. My dad's salary is probably only a little bit more than what she pays Gloria. Still, I'm relieved. I can now ask for an allowance to hold me over until I get my own part-time job.

"Let's toast!" she says, and to my surprise pours both Theo and me each a small glass of wine. My dad doesn't say anything and neither do I; we can play sophisticated and European. "To new beginnings."

I clink my glass, sip my wine, and then dig into my stir-fry. I try not to make eye contact with Theo; instead, I text Scarlett under the table.

"I'm so excited. Didn't take long, darling!" Rachel smiles at Dad, squeezes his hand. He smiles back. I look at my phone. I haven't gotten used to seeing them together, acting all newlywed-y. Touching. I doubt I'll ever get used to it.

"Where will you be working?" I ask, mostly because I hope my talking will make Rachel take her hand away from Dad's. It doesn't work.

"Right down the street from your school. I'll eventually

run the pharmacy counter at Ralph's," my dad says. I wonder how he feels about Rachel making multiples of what he makes, whether it's emasculating or attractive. When I objected to her paying for my school, my dad just said, "Don't be ridiculous. This is not up for negotiation."

He was serious. None of it was up for negotiation: his marriage, us moving, Wood Valley. Before my mom died, I lived in a democracy. Now it's a dictatorship.

"Wait, what?" Theo asks, and finally takes off his headphones. "You are *not* working at Ralph's."

My dad looks up, confused by Theo's belligerent tone.

"Yeah. The one on Ventura," my dad says, keeping his own voice conversational, light. He's not used to belligerence. He's used to me: passive-aggressive. Actually, mostly passive, with the occasional storm of snappiness. When I rage, it is alone, in my room, sometimes set rhythmically to music. "Good benefits. Dental. I'll be a pharmacy intern for a while, since I need to take an exam to practice in California. So I'll be studying for my CPJE while you guys study for your PSAT. But, you know, it's paid, not like an *internship* internship. I'll be doing the same thing I did back in Chicago while I get certified."

My dad stutters a nervous laugh and wears that half smile. He's babbling.

"You got a job at the supermarket near *my* school?" Theo yells.

"At the pharmacy counter. I'm a pharmacist. You know this, right? He knows this?" my dad asks Rachel, now completely bewildered. "I'm not bagging groceries."

"You. Have. Got. To. Be. Kidding. Me. Mom: Are you serious?"

"Theo, slow your roll," Rachel says, and puts her hand out. *Who are these people?* I think, not for the first time. *Slow your roll?*

"As if I'm not humiliated enough. Now my friends are going to see him working at the supermarket with one of those lame little plastic name tags?" Theo throws his fork across the room and stands up. I can't help but notice the splash of soy sauce on the white dining room chair, and resist the urge to find some Shout. Or is that Gloria's job? "Give me a break. It's hard enough without this shit."

Theo storms off, all ridiculous stomp and huff, like a four-year-old. It's so overblown that I'm tempted to laugh. Did he learn to throw fits like that in theater class? Then I see my dad's face. His eyes are sad and hollow. Humiliated.

"Language!" Rachel says, even though Theo is long gone now, and also sixteen.

When I was little, I used to love to play pharmacist. I'd dress up in one of my mom's aprons and use the empty bottles my dad brought home to dispense Cheerios to my stuffed animals. Until my mother died, it never occurred to me to be anything but proud of my dad, and even then, my doubts were only about his survival skills, not his professional ones. I actually like the idea of him behind the counter at Ralph's, just down the road from school. I miss him. This house gives us too many rooms to hide in.

Screw Theo and his rich friends; we didn't have dental in Chicago.

My father is an optimist. I doubt he realized it would be this hard, or maybe, when it was just the two of us flattened in our wrestler's house, he thought: *There's no way California could be any harder than this.*

"I can't not take the job because he's embarrassed?" My dad says it like he's asking Rachel a question, and again I find I have to look away. But this time it's not to spare me, but to spare him. "I need to work."

Later, I sit outside on one of Rachel's many decks. Stare at the hills, which cocoon the house with their fairy lights. Imagine the other families out there, finishing up their dinners or soaking their dishes. If they're fighting, their fights are likely familiar, old habits rubbing each other raw in spots already grooved. In this house, we are strangers. Nothing like a family at all.

Weird too to think about how things used to be here, before my dad and I arrived, before Theo's dad died. Did they all sit down to dinner together, like my family did?

I have my phone with me, but I'm too tired to text Scarlett. Too tired even to see if I have another email from SN. Who cares? He's probably just another entitled little shit, like everyone else at Wood Valley. He's already admitted as much.

The screen door opens and closes behind me, but I don't turn to look. Theo plops down into the lounge chair next to mine and takes out a set of rolling papers and a bag of weed.

"I'm not an asshole, you know," Theo says, and begins to roll his joint with tender precision. Fat and straight. Elegant work.

"Honestly? You have given me no evidence to the contrary," I say, and then regret it immediately. Couldn't I have just said *Yes, yes you are.* Or *Leave me alone.* Why do I sometimes talk like a sixty-year-old? "Won't your mom see you?"

"One hundred percent sanctioned, legal, and medicinal. Got a prescription from my shrink."

"Seriously?" I ask.

"No joke. It's for my anxiety." I can hear the smile in his voice, and I find myself smiling back. *Only in California,* I think. He holds the joint out toward me, but I shake my head. My dad has had enough trauma for one day. He doesn't need to see his Goody Two-shoes daughter smoking up with his new stepson. For a pharmacist, he's surprisingly conservative about pharmaceuticals. "Anyhow, I think she'd be relieved it's just a joint. A kid from school died last year. Heroin OD."

"That's awful," I say. There was a ton of drug use at my old school. Doubt the stuff they take here is any harder, probably just more expensive. "I wonder what *his* prescription was for."

Theo shoots me a look. It takes him a moment to realize I'm kidding. I tend to make jokes at inappropriate times. Go darker than I probably should. He might as well learn that about me now.

"You know, in any other situation, I could see us being friends. You're not that bad. I mean, Ashby could have a field day giving you a makeover, but you already have the raw material. And I can tell you're kind of cool in your own way. Funny." Theo looks straight ahead, delivers his backhanded compliments to the hills. "Your dad sucks, though."

"And you *are* kind of an asshole," I say. "For real."

Theo laughs, shudders at some invisible wind. It cools down at night here, but it's still too hot for the scarf he has knotted around his neck. He takes a hit, long and hard. I've never smoked pot, but I can see the appeal. I can feel him unwinding next to me, sinking deeper into the chair. The glass of wine has loosened me too. I wish Rachel had offered me a second. That's a gift I wouldn't have refused.

"Yeah, I know. But do you have any idea how much shit I'm going to take at school because of him? Jesus Christ."

"I don't feel sorry for you."

"No, you probably shouldn't."

"This sucks for me too. All of it. Every single minute of every single day," I say, and once it's out, I realize just how true it is. *Dad, you were wrong: it could be worse. It is so much worse.* "I had a life back in Chicago. Friends. People who would actually *say hello to me* in the halls."

"My dad died of lung cancer," Theo says, apropos of nothing, and takes another long hit. "That's why I smoke. Figure if you can run twelve miles a day and get cancer anyway, I might as well live it up."

"That's the stupidest thing I've ever heard."

"I know, right?" Theo puts out the joint, carefully saves what's left for later. He stands up and looks me straight in the eye. No trace of his temper tantrum left. "Hey, for what it's worth, I'm really sorry about your mom."

"Thanks," I say. "Sorry about your dad."

"Thanks, I guess. By the way, can you please start eating the food in the kitchen? Gloria keeps bugging me about you. She said all that ramen is going to make you *guapo.*"

"The ramen is going to make me handsome?"

"*Gordo. Gorda.* Whatever. It's going to turn you into a big fat fatty fat fatty. All right, my community service is done for the day."

"Wow, still an asshole," I say, but this time I let my smile

47

seep into my voice. Theo is actually not that bad either. Not great, but not that bad.

"So I'm probably still not going to talk to you at school," he says, and for one fleeting second, I wonder if he could be SN.

"I figured as much," I say, and he gives me one quick guy nod before turning his back on me to go inside.

CHAPTER 6

To: Somebody Nobody (somebodynobo@gmail.com)
From: Jessie A. Holmes (jesster567@gmail.com)
Subject: I'm out of clever titles.

> Ever feel like your life is one long nightmare and you just keep hoping you wake up, but you never do?

....

To: Jessie A. Holmes (jesster567@gmail.com)
From: Somebody Nobody (somebodynobo@gmail.com)
Subject: Sleeping Beauty

> ummm, yeah. things that bad?

....

To: Somebody Nobody (somebodynobo@gmail.com)
From: Jessie A. Holmes (jesster567@gmail.com)
Subject: More like drama queen

> No. Not really. Sorry. Just feeling a bit self-pitying tonight. Never should have written.

....

To: Jessie A. Holmes (jesster567@gmail.com)
From: Somebody Nobody (somebodynobo@gmail.com)
Subject: my fortune cookie advice

> nah, no need to apologize.
>
> you know, they say how happy you are in high school is indirectly proportional to how successful you will be in life.

....

To: Somebody Nobody (somebodynobo@gmail.com)
From: Jessie A. Holmes (jesster567@gmail.com)
Subject: In bed

> Yeah? Well, then yay for me, because that means I'm going to be CEO of the whole effin' world.

....

To: Jessie A. Holmes (jesster567@gmail.com)
From: Somebody Nobody (somebodynobo@gmail.com)
Subject: Re: In bed

> nope. I will.

....

It's midnight now. I lie in bed and listen to the unfamiliar noises outside. California even *sounds* different. Apparently, there are coyotes in these hills, plus wildfires and mudslides to worry about. This place is always on the verge of an apocalypse.

I can't just lie here and wait for sleep or tomorrow to come, whichever happens first. My brain is spinning out. A cup of tea. That's what I need. Something warm and comforting. Chamomile has the same flavor in Chicago or LA. So I pull off the covers and put on my bunny slippers—the ones my mom gave me for my thirteenth birthday—even though the bunnies are kind of creepy now that they're each missing one eye, and I head downstairs, taking each step carefully so as not to wake anyone.

In the dark, the kitchen feels far away. I need to cross the long living room to get there, and I'm scared of knocking something over. I walk slowly, arms outstretched, and that's how I'm standing when I first see them: like a cartoon sleepwalker.

My dad and Rachel sit close together on the couch in the den off to the side, a single reading light turned on above them. They can't see me, thank God, because I'm now hiding behind a pillar. I feel embarrassed stumbling upon them like this and a little stunned too, since I can see that they are not merely strangers who decided on a lark to elope. They look like a real married couple.

This is intimate, and not in the way it was at dinner, when Rachel put her hand on my dad's, a gesture that on reflection seemed more for Theo's and my benefit. Now they are bent together, forehead to forehead, and there's a photo album I've never seen before open on their laps. Must be Rachel's. Is she showing my dad her *before* pictures? Her dead husband? Pictorial evidence that this house used to be filled with a functional family? I can't hear what Rachel is saying, but there's something about the hunch of her shoulders and the way my dad reaches up and touches her face—cups it between his palms, like it's something precious and easily shattered—that tells me she's crying. He might be too.

My heart pounds, and I feel sick to my stomach. I imagine the photos on her lap. Maybe there's one of Theo, age five, being swung in the air between his parents. We have that picture in our *before* album. My mom on the right, my dad on the left, me in the middle, caught right at magic liftoff. I am smiling so big you can see that I'm missing a tooth. Did my dad show Rachel our pictures? Hand over everything—our entire history—just like that?

My eyes fill with tears, though I fight them. I'm not sure why I feel like crying. Suddenly, everything feels irrevocably broken in that way it can in the middle of night when you are alone. In that way it can when you are watching your father comfort his new wife. In that way it can when you too are hurting but there's no one there to comfort you.

I walk backward, a silent moonwalk, a trip that feels so much longer going back than it did coming. I pray that they don't see me, pray that I can get away before they start kissing. I *cannot* watch them kiss. When I finally get to the stairs, I force myself to go up slowly and noiselessly, one at a time. I force myself not to run away as fast as my creepy bunny slippers will take me.

CHAPTER 7

Day 15: better and worse and maybe better. Sun still shines with relentless aim and glare. My classmates are still fancy-pants, and the girls still somehow look more mature than me, more confident. As if sixteen years adds up to more out west than it does where I come from.

The humiliation begins early, in class. *Good,* I think. *Bring it on. Let's get this over with.* Maybe I am my dad's daughter after all. An optimist.

"The Gap is so pleb, don't you think?" Gem asks her wonder twin, of course in reference to my jeans, though I have no idea what she means. Pleb, short for "plebian"? As in my pants are those of the common folk? Well, yes, yes they are. As are my Costco undies, which I'm tempted to pull down so she can kiss my ass.

The anger sharpens my wits, makes me want to advance rather than retreat. I will not engage with these girls. I'm not strong enough for that. But I will turn to Adrianna, who is sitting next to me, because, screw it, no time like the present to make an ally. I ignore my burning face, refuse to turn to see if the Batman overheard anything, and pretend I don't notice that anyone was talking about me.

"I like your glasses," I say, just a tad above a whisper. Adrianna blinks a few times, as if deciding about me, and then smiles.

"Thanks. I ordered them online, so I was a little nervous." There is something about her tone, quiet, like mine, that's inviting. Not overly loud, not that teenage-girl voice that everyone else seems to use to demand notice. She has brown hair tied back in a bun that looks purposely messy, big charcoal-lined brown eyes, and bright red lipsticked lips. Pretty in the aggregate, the sum somehow adding up to much more than each individual part. "You really like them?"

"Yeah. They're Warby Parker, right? They make neat stuff." I hear Gem and Crystal giggle in front of me, maybe because I used the word "neat." Whatever.

"Yup." She smiles and gives me an *ignore them* look. *Bitches,* she mouths.

I smile and mouth back, *I know.*

After class, I gather the courage to tell the Batman that we're going to have to de-partner, that I'm not willing to risk breaking Wood Valley's honor code just because he doesn't know how to play well with others. I am feeling brave today, empowered by having introduced myself to Adrianna and by not cowering before the blond-bimbo squad. Or maybe it's that for the first time since I moved to LA, I ate something other than peanut butter on toast for breakfast. Regardless, I will be immune to the Batman's cute-boy voodoo.

Not my type, I tell myself just before I march up to his usual spot by the Koffee Kart.

Not my type, I tell myself when I see him in all his black-and-blue glory, as tender as a bruise.

Not my type, for real, I tell myself when it turns out I have to wait in line behind a group of girls who are traveling five strong, like lionesses, one the obvious leader, the rest her similarly dressed minions. All the type to skin you alive and suck on your bones.

"E, tell me you're coming on Saturday," the leader, a girl named Heather, says, not at all dismayed by the Batman's dismissive hug or the fact that he keeps glancing down at his book. Not Sartre today. *Dracula,* actually, which is both awesome and seasonally appropriate reading, considering we are nearing Halloween.

Not my type, not my type, not my type.

"Maybe," he says. "You know how it is."

Generic words arranged in such a way as to say absolutely nothing. Impressive in their nothingness. I'm not sure I could say less in as many words, even if I tried.

"For sure, Ethan," one of the other girls says. Her name is Rain or Storm. Maybe Sky. Definitely something meteorologically related. "So, like, yeah, we'll see you then, then."

"Yeah," he says, and this time he just gives up the act completely. Starts reading right in front of them. His energy sapped.

"Okay, well, bye!" Heather smiles her best smile—perfect

teeth, of course, since LA is the land of the porcelain veneer. I Googled "veneers" last night and found out they cost at least a thousand dollars a tooth, which means her mouth cost five times more than my car.

"Bye-ee," the other girls say, and finally walk away. The Batman looks relieved that they're gone.

"Can I help you?" he asks, like I'm the next customer at a drive-through. I remember our English project, and how he just assumed I could be railroaded like everyone else.

"So 'The Waste Land' . . . ," I say, and tuck my hands into my back pockets, trying to look casual. "If you don't want to work together, that's fine. But then I need to tell Mrs. Pollack and find another partner. I'm not just going to let you do the work."

There, I said it. That wasn't so hard. I breathe out. I feel lightheaded and shaky, but nothing that can be seen from the outside, I hope. My mask firmly still in place. Now I wish he could just hand me my Happy Meal and end this thing.

"What's the problem? I told you I'll get an A," he says, and leans farther back. He owns that chair even more than I own my lunch bench. He stares at me again. His blue eyes look almost gray today: a Chicago winter sky. Why does he always look so tired? Even his hair looks tired, the way it sticks up in random little peaks and then folds down, as if bowing in defeat.

"That's not the point. I can get an A on my own. I don't need to hand in your work," I say, and cross my arms. "And anyway, it's against the honor code."

He looks at me again, and I see the faintest hint of a smirk. Better than a dismissal, I guess, but still obnoxious.

"The honor code?"

Screw him. He's probably the son of some famous actor or

director, and he doesn't have to worry about his place here. Or getting into college. He's probably never even heard the word "scholarship" before. Would have to look it up.

"Listen, I'm new here, okay? And I don't want to get kicked out or in trouble or whatever. And it's junior year, so it all counts. So I don't really care if you think that's dorky or stupid or whatever."

"Or whatever," the Batman says. Another inscrutable smirk. I hate him. I really do. At least when Gem and Crystal make fun of me, it's for things that I can tell myself don't matter. My clothes, not my words. I hear my mom in my head, for just a second, since her voice has mostly evaporated—water to air, or maybe disintegrated, dirt to dust—but for one easy second, she's right here with me: *Other people can't make you feel stupid. Only you can.*

"Or whatever," I say again, like I'm in on the joke. Like he can't hurt me. I bite back the sudden tears. Where did they come from? *No, not now. No way.* I take a breath, and it passes. "Seriously, I'll just find another partner. Not a big deal."

I force myself to look him in the eye. Shrug like I don't give a shit. Make it sound like I too have people lining up to talk to me, like the lionesses do for him. The Batman looks right back at me, shakes his head a little, as if trying to wake up. And then he smiles. Not a smirk. Nothing mean or cruel about it. Just a good old-fashioned smile.

He doesn't have porcelain veneers. He does have a cleft. His two front teeth are slightly crooked, veer just a tiny bit to the right, as if they've decided perfection is overrated. I don't think he wears eyeliner. I think he was just born like that: his features enunciating.

"Okay, let's do it," he says.

"Excuse me?" I am distracted because his smile transforms his face. He turns from beautiful, moody teenager to a goofy, slightly awkward one in an instant. I can almost see him at thirteen, vulnerable, shy, not the same person who holds court at the Koffee Kart. I bet I would have liked him better then, when he read Marvel comics instead of Sartre, when he didn't wrangle with all the hard questions and come out the other end sad or angry or tired or whatever it is he is.

I definitely like him better smiling.

"Let's tackle 'The Waste Land' together. *April is the cruellest month* and all that jazz. Not my favorite poem, but it's seminal," he says, and puts his bookmark in *Dracula* and closes it, like that's that. Decision made. Here are your Chicken McNuggets with extra honey mustard. *Pleasethankyouyou'rewelcome.*

"Okay," I say, because reading him makes me slow. I'm the tired one now. His smile is like unlocking a riddle. *How does an imperfection make him seem even more perfect? And did he just use the word "seminal"? Is he sad or angry or just sixteen?*

"Do we really have an honor code here?" he asks.

"We do. It's ten pages long."

"Learn something new every day. We haven't officially met yet, have we? I'm Ethan, Ethan Marks."

"Jessie," I say, and we shake hands like real adults: no fist bumps or faux cheek kisses or guy nods. His fingers are long and slender and solid. I like them as much as his smile. Like touching them even more. "Holmes."

"Nice to finally meet you, Jessie." He pauses. "Holmes."

Day 15. Definitely better.

• • •

Later, in gym, I walk the track with Dri—she says that's what her friends call her, because Adrianna has "too many reality-show connotations"—and we laugh as we count the number of times Mr. Shackleman tries to surreptitiously adjust his balls. It's Dri's game. SN is right: she's funny.

"I can't decide if he's itchy or trying to hide his boner from watching the Axis of Evil run," she says. Gem and Crystal have lapped us three times now, not breaking a sweat, not even breathing hard. They look so good, I can't help but watch them too.

Mr. Shackleman doesn't look much older than the high school boys, except he already has a beer gut and a small bald patch on the back of his head. He wears gym shorts and blows a shrill plastic whistle more than necessary.

"Are they twins?" I ask about Gem and Crystal.

"No," Dri laughs. "But they've been best friends, since, like, forever."

"Have they always been so, you know, bitchy?" I hate the word "bitch." I do. Using the B-word makes me feel like a bad feminist, but sometimes there is no other word.

"Not really. You know how it is. Mean girls get mean in seventh grade and they stay that way until your ten-year reunion, when they want to be best friends again. At least, that's what my mom says."

"It's funny how high school is high school everywhere," I say, and smile at Dri. Try not to feel uncomfortable at the mention of moms, like it didn't set off an invisible flare in my chest. "I mean, this place is completely different than where I come from, but in some ways it's exactly the same. You can't escape it."

"College. So close and yet so far away," Dri says. She's

nothing like Scarlett, who is brash and unafraid of anything or anyone—contrary to what she claims, she's the brave one of our duo—and yet, I have a feeling Scar would like Dri. Would guide her along, like Scar has done for me all these years.

"A friend told me recently that how happy you are in high school is indirectly proportional to how successful you'll be later in life," I say, testing the theory that maybe SN is Adrianna, which I'd definitely take over SN being Theo. Maybe she was just too shy to reach out on her own. I study her face, but there isn't even a twitch of recognition.

Nope, not her.

"I don't know. Hope so." She reaches into her pocket and pulls out an inhaler. "Sorry. I'm allergic to the outdoors. And the indoors. And everything else. I know it makes me look like a tool, but not breathing looks worse."

Once we are better friends, I should tell her she has nothing to be sorry for. No self-deprecating qualifier necessary. And then I laugh to myself, because even though she is two thousand miles away, Scar is right here too. Because that's exactly the kind of thing she would say to me.

CHAPTER 8

Theo is wearing jeans that are so tight it looks like they are thigh tattoos, and a sleeveless leather vest. I'm pretty sure he approaches getting dressed as an act in costuming. Today he's a buff and surprisingly hot Hells Angel.

"Look at you checking out my guns," he says, and opens the fridge. He takes out two fancy pressed juices and throws me one. "Here. This will keep you from getting rickets."

I'm perched on one of the kitchen stools, reading. This enormous house tricked me once again: I thought I was home alone. Had I known Theo was here, I wouldn't have left my room with my exfoliating clay mask on. Not my best look, costume or otherwise.

"What the hell is this?" I take a swig of juice, which is

green and cloudy and, it turns out, revolting. I fight my gag reflex.

"Kale, ginger, cucumber, and beet juice. Probably should have started you with one more fruit-heavy. Forgot you aren't an advanced juicer."

"An advanced juicer? Really? You know that sometimes talking to you is like watching a reality show," I say. "It's amusing only because it can't possibly be real."

"This is all real, baby." Theo again flashes his impressive muscles.

"Not too shabby," I say, referring to his arms. "I dig the biker look."

"Biker? I was going for rocker."

"That too."

"But healthy, muscular rocker, not strung-out, skinny rocker, right?"

"Definitely the former."

Theo looks relieved, and for the first time, I see that maybe he isn't all confidence all the time. Now that I know what to expect, I take another sip of my juice. There is something oddly virtuous about its grossness. I can't decide if I love it or hate it, which, it turns out, is exactly how I feel about Theo.

"Are you going to Heather's party tonight? It's going to be insane. Her dad and his new girlfriend are in Thailand, and he has this huge mansion in the Hills. They have mad bank."

Wait, SN used the expression "mad bank" recently.

Doesn't mean anything, I tell myself.

Those words are common enough, right?

I look at Theo, point to my mask.

"What do you think?"

"Oh no. Please don't make me have to take pity on you and take you with me," Theo says.

"What a lovely invitation, but no thanks. I have homework to do."

"Don't believe you. It's Saturday night."

"I have nothing to wear."

"That I believe. But I bet we could rustle something up."

"Seriously, appreciate the pity and all that, but maybe next time?"

"Your loss," he says, and jumps off his stool and attempts to fist-bump me. "Don't smoke all my weed while I'm gone."

To: Somebody Nobody (somebodynobo@gmail.com)
From: Jessie A. Holmes (jesster567@gmail.com)
Subject: Saturday night

Are you at Heather's party?
....

To: Jessie A. Holmes (jesster567@gmail.com)
From: Somebody Nobody (somebodynobo@gmail.com)
Subject: almost Sunday morning, actually

Maybe. Are you?
....

To: Somebody Nobody (somebodynobo@gmail.com)
From: Jessie A. Holmes (jesster567@gmail.com)
Subject: Not really. T-2 hours.

If you were there, wouldn't you know whether I was too?
....

To: Jessie A. Holmes (jesster567@gmail.com)
From: Somebody Nobody (somebodynobo@gmail.com)
Subject: fine. you win. Saturday night.

don't get all sly on me. Heather's parties are HUGE.

....

To: Somebody Nobody (somebodynobo@gmail.com)
From: Jessie A. Holmes (jesster567@gmail.com)
Subject: You gave up so easily.

You're the one who likes to be all sly.

....

To: Jessie A. Holmes (jesster567@gmail.com)
From: Somebody Nobody (somebodynobo@gmail.com)
Subject: I like that you can have . . .

does this count as our first fight? ;)

....

To: Somebody Nobody (somebodynobo@gmail.com)
From: Jessie A. Holmes (jesster567@gmail.com)
Subject: ???

OMG, did you just emoji me?

....

To: Jessie A. Holmes (jesster567@gmail.com)
From: Somebody Nobody (somebodynobo@gmail.com)
Subject: . . . two conversations at once.

technically it was an emoticon. and you countered with
an "OMG," so i'm pretty sure we're even. not to get all
early '00s on you, but shall we IM? this refreshing my email
every two seconds is annoying. though I will miss your
subject lines . . .

....

Me: Done.

SN: ahh, this is so much better.

Me: Right? Right. Though not to get too crazy futuristic on you, but we could text. That's how normal people communicate.

SN: and give up my anonymity? no thanks. so, Saturday night. or almost Sunday morning. whatever. at the party or no?

Me: No. You?

SN: I was. not anymore. now just sitting in my car thumb-talking with you. wait, did that sound dirty? not my intention. unless you liked it.

Me: I'm just going to ignore you.

SN: please do. this whole anonymous thing makes me a little silly.

Me: The anonymous thing IS silly.

SN: is it? i'm not so sure. irregardless, that's how it goes.

Me: Irregardless is not a word.

SN: smarty-pants. I stand corrected. actually, I sit corrected.

Me: You are a dork, and I mean that in the best way possible.

SN: things any better on your end? you were all in the bell jar earlier in the week. I was worried.

Me: Definitely better. Thanks for checking. How 'bout you? Things good?

SN: yeah, fine, I guess. not having the best year.

Me: Know how that goes.

SN: do you? hope you really don't, but suspect you do. you have sad eyes.

Me: I do? And when have you seen my eyes?

SN: I haven't. not really. and I mean more your brow. you have a sad brow.

Me: I have no idea what to do with that information. Botox?

SN: and the Chicago girl goes LA. but nope.

I stop writing. Feel my brow with my hands. I do have a tendency to knit my eyebrows, have always done it. My mom used to warn me that I was going to get a permanent wrinkle if I kept it up, just like she had. But hers was an exclamation point right in the middle of her forehead. It exuded enthusiasm, maybe even joy. Not worry.

Do I look sad all the time? I hope not. I don't want to be the sad girl. That's not who I am. Actually, that's not true. This is truer: that's not how I want to be known.

SN: you still there? something I said? for the record, I like your brow just the way it is.

Me: Just thinking. Sorry.

SN: ahh, don't do that. you might hurt yourself.

Me: So tell me about the party. #vicariouspartygoer

SN: meh. it was a typical high school party, except it had some famous dj I've never heard of and Heather's dad has a cool house, and everyone was pretty wasted.

Me: You?

SN: nah, I'm driving. didn't feel like Ubering it. anyhow, knew I didn't want to stay too long.

Me: Just made your appearance.

SN: I don't know. I just find it all so . . . stupid or boring or something.

Me: I know what you mean. In Chicago, it was the same thing, but you know, instead of a super-fancy house and famous DJ, it was the bowling alley. But yeah, still . . .

SN: stupid and boring. but that's not it exactly. I mean small. it all feels small and unimportant.

Me: And yet vitally important to everyone else, and, dare I say it, maybe even a tiny bit important to you, which is even more embarrassing in its own way. Am I making sense?

SN: totally. fwiw, this feels important: talking to you.

Me: Yeah?

SN: yeah.

CHAPTER 9

Before my mom died, Scarlett and I used to talk about the concept of the *perfect day*. What would have to happen—from the moment we woke up to the moment we went to sleep—to make that day better than all the others before it. We didn't dream big. At least, I didn't. My focus was mostly on the absence of things. I wanted a day during which I didn't stub my toe or spill on my shirt or feel shy or awkward or unattractive. I wouldn't miss the bus or forget a change of clothes for gym. When I looked in the mirror after lunch, there wouldn't be food in my teeth or something in my nose.

Sure, it wasn't all omissions. I'd sprinkle in a first kiss, though I couldn't have told you who—some nameless, faceless guy who in the fantasy made me feel comfortable and known and also pretty. Maybe I imagined eating my mom's pancakes for breakfast before school, which always came in the form of my initials long after I was too old for that sort of thing because it turns out you are never too old for that sort of thing. And her veggie lasagna for dinner. I loved her veggie lasagna.

Nothing crazy.

Who knows? Maybe it would have been pizza day at school. Our school had surprisingly good pizza.

A perfect day didn't have to include a fantasy trip to the Caribbean or skydiving or hugging someone's leathered back on a motorcycle, though all of that and more was of course on Scarlett's list.

But I've always liked simple things.

Now, on the other side of *everything*, I can't wrap my head around a perfect day. Now, without my mother, what could that even look like?

I think back to before, *before before before*, and they all seem like perfect days. Who cares about a stubbed toe or the hint of a booger in my nose? I had a mother, and not just *insert generic mother here*, but *my mother*, who I loved in a way that not everyone gets to love their mom. I mean, I know on some level, everyone *loves* their mother because of the whole *she is your mother* thing, but I didn't love my mom just because she was my mother. I loved my mom because she was cool and interesting and warm and listened to me and continued to make me pancakes in the shape of my initials because somehow, even though I didn't, she always understood that I'd never be too old for that sort of thing. I loved my mom because she read the entire Harry Potter series out loud to me, and when we were finished, she too wanted to start all over again.

If there's one thing I've learned in the last two years, it's that memory is fickle. When I read Harry, I can no longer hear my mother's voice, but I picture her next to me, and when even that fails, I imagine the weight of someone against me, an arm against my arm, and pretend that's enough.

I loved my mom because she was mine.

And I was hers.

And that belonging-to-each-other thing will never happen for me again.

Perfect days are for people with small, realizable dreams. Or maybe for all of us, they just happen in retrospect; they're only now perfect because they contain something irrevocably and irretrievably lost.

CHAPTER 10

"Sorry, we only hire Starbucks-experienced baristas," the guy at Starbucks tells me when I inquire about an after-school job. He looks like he's in his early twenties and spends most of his milk-steaming money on hair-modeling clay. "This is a serious job. We take it very seriously."

"Wait, what?" I ask, because now he mouths words I can't quite make out.

"Sorry, just practicing my lines." He shows me a script he has hidden under the counter. "Have an audition later. I'm really an actor."

Coffee Guy, whose name—if his tag is to be believed—is actually Guy, smiles, but it's an insincere smile, the kind that looks like it's doing you a favor.

"I just did a guest bit on that new show *Filthy Meter Maids*."

"Cool," I say, wondering if the polite thing would be to say he looks familiar. He doesn't look familiar. "So how did you become a Starbucks-experienced barista if they only hire Starbucks-experienced baristas? Chicken, egg, right?"

"Huh?"

"I just mean, how'd you get the job?"

"Oh, right. I lied."

"You lied?"

"I said I'd worked at Starbucks before. For years."

"And they believed you?" I think about going home, editing my résumé, adding a line—*Starbucks Oak Park, 2013–2014*—and coming back tomorrow. But then I picture my first day as a faux-experienced Starbucks employee. No doubt I'd scald myself or get yelled at by frustrated customers. People are nasty before they've had their coffee.

"I guess I'm a very good actor." Coffee Guy smiles again, and now it seems he's saying three things all at once. The words he's speaking out loud, the ones he's practicing from under the counter, and the unspoken ones his smile can't help but say, which is *You're welcome*.

After Starbucks, I get shot down at the Gap, the pressed juicery, a gluten-free vegan bakery, and Namaste Yoga. I am almost ready to give up hope when I notice a tiny bookstore called Book Out Below! tucked next to a designer kids' clothing store. No help wanted sign, but still worth a shot.

Immediately, the smell of books greets me, and I feel at home. This is what my house in Chicago used to smell like: paper. I cross my fingers in my pocket and say a quick prayer as I make my way through the stacks to the desk in the back.

Normally, I would take my time, run my hands along the spines, see if there's anything that catches my eye to possibly borrow from the library later. But what I need right now is a job, not more reading material. As it is, even without any semblance of a social life, I'm up late every night trying to keep up with homework and PSAT studying. And though I desperately needed the caffeine today, I couldn't even buy a Diet Coke from the stupid Wood Valley caf. (SN was right. The credit card machines have a ten-dollar minimum. I have $8.76 to my name. I was going to ask my dad for money this morning, but Rachel was there, and I couldn't bear the thought of her reaching into her wallet and handing me a twenty.)

"Can I help you, dear?" the saleswoman asks me, and seeing her face makes me realize that since moving here, I haven't seen a single person with wrinkles until now. The women in LA all have taut skin, the kind pumped full of injectables that render them ageless, just as believably forty as seventy. This woman, on the other hand, has bobbed gray hair and crisscrossed lines at her lips and wears the sort of linen tunic they sell in expensive hippie stores. She's probably the same age as Rachel, though they could be different species. Where Rachel is hard, she's soft.

"Hi, do you happen to be hiring?" I ask, and hear Scar in my head: *Channel your inner goddess. Be confident, strong, undeniable.* Scar's favorite word is "undeniable," actually, which tells you everything you need to know about her. My favorite word, on the other hand, is "waffle." Both a delicious breakfast food and a verb.

The woman eyes me carefully, takes in my Vans and my ratty scarf and my leather motorcycle jacket and my hair, which is pulled up into a messy loop on top of my head. Maybe I should have gone more professional, not that I own a suit or anything. I even had to borrow clothes from Scarlett for my mother's funeral. Ruined her favorite blazer by association.

"That depends. Are you a book person?" the woman asks.

I put my bag down on the counter and open it. Take out the six books I checked out of the library last week. When we moved, I got my library card. Figured it was the one thing that was guaranteed to be free.

"This is what I'm reading now. 'The Waste Land' and *Crime and Punishment* are for school, but the rest are for fun."

"You're reading a nonfiction book about Nazi Germany for fun?" she asks, pointing to *The Lost* by Daniel Mendelsohn.

"I wanted to mix it up. It looked interesting. It's about a guy trying to learn about what happened to his family."

"Huh. Book three of an apocalyptic YA series, which shows you are willing to follow through. Oooh, and some old-school Gloria Steinem. I like it. Eclectic taste."

"I've always been a reader. It's in my DNA," I say, and hold my breath.

"Here's the thing," she says, and I can already hear the apologetic start of a rejection.

No, I need this to go my way.

"Please. Listen, I don't need a ton of hours, unless you need someone for a lot of hours, and then I can need them. What I mean is, I'm flexible. I'm available any day after school and on weekends. I love books, I love your store, even its punny name, though I'm not sure about the exclamation point, and I just think this would be a good fit. Me. Here. I have a résumé if you need it."

I take out my pathetic résumé, which is filled with baby-sitting references and a short stint at Claire's selling barrettes to snotty seven-year-olds and, of course, my illustrious two years at the Smoothie King. My after-school activities (yearbook, newspaper, photography club, Spanish club, poetry club), my GPA at FDR, and a short section titled Interests and Hobbies: Reading. Writing. Mourning. (Okay, that's not on there, but it should be. I'm a champ at that.)

I had to change the font to 16-point Courier so my résumé would take up a whole page.

"Where do you go to school?"

"Wood Valley?" I say it like a question. Damn you, nervous uptalking. "I mean, I'm a junior there? I just moved?"

"My son is at Wood Valley too. He's a senior. Do you know him? Liam Sandler?"

"Sorry, I'm really new. I don't know anyone yet."

"I like you," she says, and her smile is the opposite of Coffee Guy's. Reassuring, not self-affirming. "Let me talk to Liam. He's been complaining that he wants more time off to practice with his band. If he wants to give up his hours, they're all yours."

"Thanks so much. My number's on there, so just call me. Whenever." I'm hesitant to leave even though it's obvious I should go. My fate is now tied to some Wood Valley senior who wants more time to bang on his drums. I hope he wants to practice every afternoon and every weekend.

I want to move out of Rachel's house and move in here, sleep under the stacks and make Cup-a-Soup from the water cooler in the corner. I want this gray-haired woman to talk books with me and help me with my homework. I want her to tell me I'll do okay on the PSATs even though I don't have a tutor twice a week like Theo does. I want her to tell me everything is going to be okay.

And if not all that, I at least want her to give me a discount.

I gather my books and walk toward the door, head down. Pull out my phone to text Scar.

Me: Send positive vibes. Perfect bookstore=perfect job. Me want it badly.

Scarlett: Better than making smoothies with your bff?

Me: Not even close. But if I must be a loner, best to be surrounded by imaginary friends.

Scarlett: Miss you, lady.

Her words make me feel lighter, and I find myself smiling at my phone. I am not alone. Not really. Just geographically isolated.

Don't walk and text. That's my first thought when I find myself on the floor of the bookstore, right on the threshold, holding my throbbing forehead. I see stars. Not the celebrity kind my dad promised when he tried to get me excited about moving to Los Angeles, but the cartoon kind that signal a concussion. I have no idea how I got here. Why it hurts to turn my head, or how my knees buckled, or why I feel perilously close to crying for about the millionth time since I moved to this place.

"Are you okay?" a voice asks. I don't look up, not yet, because I think if I move my head I might throw up, and that's the only thing that could make this any worse. Humiliation has not kicked in, and I'd like to stave that off for as long as possible, not compound it. "I didn't see you there."

"Clearly," I say, and suddenly I'm eye to eye with a guy about my age, who has squatted down to check out the damage to my face. He has longish dirty-blond hair and dark brown eyes and a hint of a pimple on his chin. A much better-looking version of Adam Kravitz: the boy next door. Sweet and distracted and probably smart and kind to his mother and will grow up to invent something like Tumblr. The kind of guy you'd probably want to kiss—especially if he made you laugh—and whose hand you definitely wouldn't mind holding. I blink, notice his shaggy hair again. I know him from somewhere.

"What was that?" I ask.

"That was Earl." He motions to a large object he is carrying on his back.

"Earl?"

"My guitar," he says.

"Your guitar is named Earl?" I ask, which is probably the least relevant question to the matter at hand. I should have asked for some ice or a bag of frozen peas, at the very least a Tylenol. I can already feel a lump forming.

"Yup. Are you sure you're okay? I whacked you hard."

"I'll live." He puts out his hand and helps me stand up, and I find I'm more stable on my feet than I would have guessed.

"I'm really sorry. Totally my fault." He pockets his

phone—maybe he was walking and texting too?—and puts his guitar down against one of the stacks. There's a WHVS sticker on his case. Ah, now I place him. Of course. He was witness to my very first, but not last, Wood Valley humiliation. The guy who interned at Google and traveled around India. He looks different in this context.

"Just thought of some lyrics and wanted to get them down before I forgot."

"Wait, you're Liam, right?" I ask.

"That depends on whether you're planning to sue me," he says. Now that I've put two and two together, I can see his mother in his face. The same generous grin. I wonder what kind of music his band plays. I bet it's something folksy, and that they're not half bad. Surely he *should* practice more.

"Nope." I smile.

"Well then, what can I do for you? I clearly owe you one."

I hear Scar loud and clear in my head: *Be undeniable.* And so I am.

"I got a job!" I announce when I get back to Rachel's later. I'm so excited that I have to tell someone, even if that someone is my disinterested stepbrother, who would never lower himself to do something as mundane as work. I find him on his bed, playing with his laptop. "And before you throw another fit, it's not at Ralph's. It's a place you and your friends will never, ever go. So don't you worry."

"I've never seen you so animated. It's kind of adorable," Theo says. "So where will I never ever go? Oh wait, let me guess."

He puts down his laptop and puts his hands to his head, as if he's thinking very hard.

"KFC?"

"Nope."

"The batting cages?"

"Nope. But I like this game."

"The ridiculously delicious pretzel place."

"Not even close."

Rachel sticks her head in the door, and I feel that squeeze in my stomach that always accompanies an interaction with her. I'm smart enough to know it's not really her fault, that my feelings toward her probably have little to do with the reality of who she is, but still, I can't help it. I don't want to know her, don't want this random person my father has inexplicably chosen to marry to be an integral part of my life.

"What happened? I heard happy squeals!" she says. She can't help herself; she looks from Theo to me and me to Theo, and her smile is so emphatic that I can see the fillings in the back of her mouth. She is almost thinking out loud: *Maybe this whole thing will work after all.*

"Nothing," I say, and when her face falls, I feel guilty. I don't mean to cut her down, but I just don't have it in me to give her this. To hand over the one good thing that has happened since I moved here.

"Sorry. I'll leave you guys to it!" she says, as always too loud, and continues down the hall. I wonder if I'll hear about this later from my dad, if she'll tell him that I was rude and he'll ask me to be nicer.

I should be nicer.

"All right, I give up. Tell your big brother," Theo says, not at all seeming to notice how I talked to his mother, or maybe not much caring.

"Ew, that sounds so wrong."

"I know, right? Okay, so where?"

"Book Out Below! You know, the bookstore?"

"Ah, how appropriate. But I actually have been there, if you must know. I am highly literate."

"I'm sure you are," I say, which is the truth. Theo recently beat me on a physics quiz, even though I know for a fact he didn't study the night before. The kid is smart. It seems, with the possible exception of Tweedledee and Tweedledumber, everyone at Wood Valley is smart, or at least motivated. Here it's cool to try, which is funny, because trying is why I wasn't particularly cool in Chicago. By the transitive property you would think I'd be cool here, but no. Then again, I casually reference things like the transitive property, so maybe there are other, more valid reasons for my lack of popularity.

"So, what the hell happened to your face?" Theo asks.

CHAPTER 11

Ethan: You. Me. "The Waste Land." Library. Friday 3:30. Work
for you?

Me: Sure.

Ethan: Cool beans.

How does he make something like "cool beans," perhaps
the dorkiest expression ever uttered, sound acceptable? Do I
write more to keep the conversation going? I'm better writing
than I am talking in person. Maybe this is my shot to show
who I actually am, not the weird loser I morph into around

people who make me nervous. Will I still have this bulbous bruise on Friday?

This is ridiculous. This is so not a big deal.

We are working on a project together.

He doesn't like you. You certainly do not like him.

Get over yourself, Jessie.

Grow up.

Scarlett: School sucks balls without you. I had to sit with Deena today and hear all about her gymnastics meet. How's your head?

Me: Swollen. Blue. I took your hat suggestion. Got alternately mocked and complimented.

Scarlett: If I were there, I'd give those two girls a knuckle sandwich.

Me: Not worth hurting your hands.

Scarlett: You okay? I worry.

Me: Don't. Fine. Making friends with Dri.

Scarlett: Just don't like her better than me.

Me: Never.

Scarlett: And how's Mr. Holmes?

Me: No idea. He's always with the stepmonster. Rather not deal.

Scarlett: Adam Kravitz wants to take me to homecoming.

Me: WHAT?!? Took you long enough to tell me. And?

Scarlett: We'll see.

Me: How'd he ask?

Scarlett: Text. But cute text. You know. He's shy.

Me: I bet he's a better kisser now.

Scarlett: I'll let you know. Maybe. You know he only asked me bc you're not here.

Me: Not true.

Scarlett: I bet we spend the whole time talking about how much we miss you.

Me: No way. Go forth and prosper.

Scarlett: Nerd.

Me: If I used the expression "cool beans," I'd sound like an even bigger nerd than I already am, right?

Scarlett: OMG. Seriously, unless you want to be bullied for-ever, DO NOT USE "COOL BEANS."

Me: Yeah, that's what I thought.

• • •

SN: nice hat.

Me: Thanks. Actually, that's kind of creepy. You know what I wore today, but I still have no idea who you are?

SN: jeans, a t-shirt, sneakers. same as yesterday and tomor-row. you missed nothing.

Me: Not the point.

SN: what happened to your head? do I need to beat someone up for you?

Me: You know, that's the second time today someone has of-fered to defend my honor. Makes a girl feel special. But no. Culprit was a guitar case.

SN: OUCH.

Me: Not my finest moment. I'm not usually that clumsy. Felt like a rom-com heroine, except it wasn't romantic or funny. And I hate that trope.

SN: sorry for delay. was looking up the word "trope." don't think less of me.

Me: Ha. I'm not a word snob. I just like them.

SN: me too. who else offered to defend your honor? do I need to beat him up?

Me: ☺ No. My best friend from home. Scarlett.

SN: I like her.

Me: Is it weird for me to say that I think you actually would?

SN: Nope.

Me: How was your day?

SN: fine. just some stuff on the home front.

Me: Want to talk about it? Or write about it, I should say?

SN: not really. just my mom. she's . . . going through a tough time.

Me: Yeah. I know how that is.

SN: going through a tough time? or having a mom who is?

Me: Both, actually.

86

Me: Well, sort of.

Me: It's complicated.

SN: me too. it's all f'ing complicated.

Me: Hey, what's your favorite word?

SN: why.

Me: Just thought it was something I should know about you.

SN: no, I mean my favorite word is why.

Me: It's a good word. Why.

SN: right? right. a word and a whole question. and yours?

Me: Waffle.

SN: huh. a great breakfast food. and of course dictionary .com reminds me that it also means "to speak or write equivocally."

Me: exactly.

SN: i think one day we should eat waffles together.

Me: equivocally yes.

· · ·

Next day at lunch I sit with Dri and her friend Agnes, who is probably her Scarlett. I'm still too new here to see where this table fits into the high school hierarchy. It seems none of my old rules apply. Back in Chicago, the athletes, who gathered Saturday nights in the bowling alley parking lot to sit in open hatchbacks and drink cheap beer by the case and toss their empty cans at the Dumpster were the popular kids, and the theater dorks, who had ill-placed piercings and one silly streak of cotton-candy-colored hair, were, well, the dorks. Theo and Agnes wouldn't have even rated. Here, it's the opposite; theater is an actual graded class *and* an after-school activity, and both are considered cool.

Back home, I was neither athlete nor theater dork. Instead, I was in that middle clique that every school needs to function efficiently: the worker bees. We took the honors classes, ran the newspaper and the yearbook and the student government. Not popular, not even close, but at least indispensible. (Back at my old school, it was important to distinguish the worker bees from the straight-up nerds: the nerds were even less cool than the theater dorks, but they were too busy learning how to write code and nurturing dot-com fantasies to care.)

The truth is it doesn't matter to me where Dri and Agnes fit in, because this sure as hell beats sitting on my bench alone outside. Anything is a step up.

"I just think that if you're going to post that kind of nasty shit on Instagram, own it," Agnes says. I have no idea what she and Dri are debating, only that they each seem invested in their side of the argument. Agnes is a tiny girl with a dyed red bob, plastic-framed glasses similar to Dri's, and a nose that looks like someone pinched it too hard and it stuck. She's not beautiful, not necessarily even pretty, but cute. What happens when you take something full-sized and remake it in miniature.

Okay, I'll just admit something here. Something I've never told anyone, not even Scar. Whenever I meet someone new, I silently ask that inevitable catty girl question: is she prettier than me? The truth is, the answer is often yes, which I think makes my even asking the question in the first place a little less offensive. I know I am not ugly—my features all fall within the normal range (nothing grossly oversized, nothing too small), but I definitely look different from the girls here.

I imagine, or I *hope,* that one day I will be discovered—that I will actually be *seen*—not as a sidekick, or as a study buddy, or as background furniture, but as someone to *like,* maybe even to *love.* Still, I've come to accept that high school is not my forum. Bookish is not even on the list of the top ten things high school boys look for in a girl. I'm pretty sure boobs, on the other hand, rank pretty high.

If you must know: a B cup on a good day.

Agnes is probably an A but makes up for it by being adorable. That is, until she starts talking.

"Like, what do you think, Jessie? Am I right?" I wasn't listening. I was looking at all the other kids in the cafeteria, at all these strangers, thinking how intimate it felt to be sitting there together shoveling our food into our mouths. Wondering whether this place would ever start to feel familiar. And true, I was also watching Ethan, Ethan Marks through the window, sitting alone near the Koffee Kart, another book in hand, though I can't see the title. "If you're going to say something online, be prepared to say it to my face."

"Yeah, I guess," I say, a good waffle. They've saved me on more than one of these lost-in-thought occasions. I'm pretty sure I don't agree with Agnes, if only because she seems to be the type of girl to make all sorts of silly pronouncements. ("Mr. Greene is such a bitch. He said I plagiarized, just because I borrowed a couple of sentences from someone else's blog post. It's called *pastiche,* dude." Or "Only wannabes wear Doc Martens." Or "Jessie, you'd look so pretty with a little makeup.")

"Agnes, sometimes people are shy. She didn't say anything bad. She just said you hurt her feelings, which you did. Some people find it easier to write than to say it to your face," Dri says. She looks to me to back her up, and I wonder if my existence is a problem for her friendship with Agnes. Scar and I always sat alone at lunch. We weren't really interested in talking to anyone else. To be honest, I'm not sure how I'd feel if she had invited some new girl to sit with us. Dri not only invited me, but did so excitedly.

"Obviously, I don't know the full story, but I'm definitely like that. I'm so much more comfortable writing than saying things out loud. I wish I could live my whole life on paper." I consider telling them about Somebody/Nobody. I wish I could explain how "talking" to him is so easy the words flow in a way they never do when I have to talk out loud. I also wouldn't mind some help figuring out who he is. Then again, maybe I don't want to know. SN may be right: the not knowing is what keeps us connected. It would be so much harder writing to someone I knew I'd see the next day. And I wonder if it works the other way too. Even though he knows who I am, maybe not having to face me makes the conversation flow for him as well.

Of course, Agnes is wrong—words are no less courageous for having been written rather than spoken—and I'm all set to say that to her, out loud and with conviction, when I hear my name being yelled from across the cafeteria.

"Jessie!" At first, I assume the voice is calling someone else—on account of my having no friends at this school—but the voice is so insistent, and even vaguely familiar, that I look up. Shaggy hair and a smile.

"Hey, Jessie," Liam says, now next to our table, having jogged over with Earl again thrown over his shoulder. He pushes his bangs out of his eyes and then points to his forehead. "How's the wound?"

"Almost gone. But if you bring that guitar any closer, I'm going to have to get a restraining order," I say, which even to my own ears almost sounds like flirting. I blush. I don't know how to flirt. I always feel like an impostor. And I don't even want to flirt with Liam. He's kind of my boss.

"Ha. Listen, we're still on for training this afternoon, right? Expect to be there till closing."

"Sure. Thanks again for the job. I really appreciate it."

"No problem. Least I could do after maiming you." He smiles, then does this strange little arm-punch thing, which actually kind of hurts, and then hurries off, Earl flopping behind him.

"Shut the front door." Dri grabs my hand in a vise grip.

"How do you know Liam Sandler?" she asks. Her eyebrows practically touch her hairline. "No effin' way. Liam. Sandler."

"Relax. He's not Ryan Gosling." Agnes rolls her eyes at Dri. "I'll never understand what you like about him."

Dri ignores her. Waits for me to answer.

"I got a job at his mom's bookstore, basically because he hit me in the head with his guitar case. Embarrassing but true."

"And?" Dri says.

"And what?"

"And everything."

"And everything like . . ."

"What did he say? What did you say? Can you introduce me? Have you heard his band? Oh. My. God. Orgasmville."

"Ew," I say. "I mean, he's not bad, but really?"

"No, that's his band's name. Orgasmville."

"Seriously?"

"Yup. And he is. That. Cute. You *have* to see him onstage. I've been, like, in love with him for forever. He's never said a word to me. Not one. Until right now."

"He didn't technically say anything to you," Agnes informs her.

"He spoke in my vicinity, which is more than he's spoken to me in the last two years. I'll take it," Dri says, and tightens her grip on my hand. That hurts too. "Eeeeee!"

"He has a girlfriend," Agnes says, and I wonder about her need to piss all over Dri's parade. If Pete McManning, the senior Scar was obsessed with all of freshman year, had ever talked within her vicinity, I would have squeed right along with her, even though I never quite got Scar's interest in him. I can't handle a wispy mustache, even if it's for the hipster cause.

"Whatever. Gem can kiss my ass."

"He's dating Gem?" I ask, and realize just how much I have to catch up on. I know nothing about this school. Forget the honor code; there should be a book that chronicles all this stuff. So, Liam and Gem. Huh. If I had thought about it, I would have figured Liam might have a girlfriend, but I wouldn't have paired him with Gem. And not because she's hot—he's the type to have a beautiful girlfriend—but because she's nasty. I had him pegged as better than that.

"I know, right? It's the only thing I don't like about him," Dri says.

"Dri is, like, totally obsessed with him. Literally obsessed. She even took up the ukulele to get him to notice her. Hashtag fail."

"I went through a twee phase. Whatever," Dri says to me, and gives me a hug. "Arrgghh! You are now my favorite person in the world."

I smile. Pretend not to notice Agnes's dirty look.

SN: how's your day, Ms. Holmes?

Me: Not bad. Yours?

SN: good. been doing my homework in listicle form, because, you know, anything to make it more interesting.

Me: Do you think college will actually be better? For real?

SN: hope so. but then again, I just read about a guy who lost a ball in a frat hazing incident.

Me: Seriously? What is wrong with people?

SN: can you imagine wanting to be liked so badly that you'd give up one of your testicles?

Me: I can neither imagine having testicles nor giving one up.

SN: you won't let me use emojis, but an 'i heart my testes' one would be appropriate right about now.

Me: You know what I heart? Nutella. And pajama pants. And an awesomesauce book. Not necessarily in that order, but together.

SN: awesomesauce? 2012 texted and wants its word back. btw, do you eat the Nutella right out of the jar with a spoon?

Me: Used to. Now I share a kitchen with the Others, so I can't. Wanted to label it, but my dad said that would be rude.

SN: The Others?

Me: Stepmom and stepbrother. Do you have Others?

SN: nope. my parental structure is still intact. well, at least legally. they barely look at each other these days.

Me: Why?

SN: it's complicated.

Me: Do you think we'll ever get past "it's complicated"?

SN: no doubt in my mind, Ms. Holmes.

CHAPTER 12

Dri's plan is to live vicariously through me, which is a first, since no one has ever wanted to be me. Ever. I've been told to text if Liam says anything interesting. Actually, anything at all.

"You want to learn via text how to work the cash register?" I asked in all seriousness at the end of last period, just before I jumped into my car to go to my first shift at Book Out Below! I wasn't sure how deep Dri's obsession went, but as someone who has had my fair share of crushes, I understand the need for information. Details allow you to pretend that you actually know the person who you obsess over, even though you don't know them at all.

"You can skip that part. Unless he does something cute while explaining it. Then yes, text away," Dri said, fortunately understanding that I was not, in fact, making fun of her.

So far, Liam has said nothing worth memorializing, nothing really interesting at all. The cash register is the same model we had at the Smoothie King, so that shouldn't be a problem. Mostly, my job seems to be to sit behind the counter and stand up when I hear the bell on the front door announce a new customer. Judging by Liam's quick response time, it's clear that this will soon become a reflex.

"What kind of music does your band play?" I ask. I purposely don't say "Orgasmville," mostly because I don't think I can do it without blushing. The band's logo is a big vaginal-looking O, with a tongue through it. The Rolling Stones meets Georgia O'Keeffe. And, of course, the name is trying too hard. I give them no points for subtlety.

"I guess rock. Sort of. You know Lou Reed?" I nod, though I've only vaguely heard of him. I'm not one of those people who can play the music game, one-upping people via obscure band references.

"Like him. But modern. And maybe even better," he says, and smiles so that I know he's just joking. He's not cocky, like most of the senior boys, who take up too much space when they walk through the halls—all banging lockers and complicated handshakes and running commentary on the girls who are unlucky enough to pass by. Liam, despite swinging Earl, is a bit more contained, the kind of guy who might ask before kissing you.

Me: He compared himself to Lou Reed, but in a cute, self-deprecating way.

97

Dri: He's better.

Me: Groan.

Dri: Fine. Not better. Hotter.

"Who are you texting?" Liam asks, and I quickly tuck away my phone. I don't want to embarrass Dri, though, truth be known, I get the feeling he has no idea who she is.

"My friend Dri. Well, her name is Adrianna. But everyone calls her Dri," I say. He shrugs. Not interested. "She's cool. She was sitting at the lunch table when you came up today."

Again, no reaction. I wonder what he'd say if I told him that she knows his birthday, which colleges he's applying to, and his favorite cafeteria foods. That in her head, they have a complex and fulfilling relationship. No matter that it's purely one-sided. I think Dri might even prefer it that way. There are the girls like Gem and Crystal, fearless about guys and orifices and secretions, and there are the girls like Dri and me, who are terrified of rejection and mechanics and unfortunate angles. We realize just how far we still need to go till we can call ourselves women.

I may own my vagina, both in theory and in practice (we are on a first-name basis, Vag and me—Scar's idea, by the way, not mine; no, not even a little bit mine), but that doesn't mean I'm not terrified of its appetites. For a moment, I imagine Vag's almost-blank résumé. Sixteen years: closed for business. Hobbies and interests: cheesy romance novels, collecting information about Ethan, Ethan Marks.

Oddly enough, I have no problem imagining having sex with someone (say, Ethan, Ethan Marks), but it's not unlike imagining my Academy Awards speech. It's something I can perform perfectly in my head—with both charm and agility and just the right dose of modesty—but it's a speech that not only will never be delivered, but maybe shouldn't be. Will I, one day, be able to sleep with a guy and not feel horribly awkward and tortured and not wonder what it all means? I assume so. But right now, the thought of that sort of exposure seems unimaginable, and mostly, if I'm totally honest, nothing short of terrifying.

"So you're from Chicago, right?" Liam asks, and I wonder how he knows. We don't have any classes together, since he's a senior. Did his mom tell him? Is he Somebody/Nobody?

"Yeah. I just moved here," I say.

"How do you like it?" he asks. He gathers his hair into a ponytail and then sets it free, again and again. The movements so precisely the same each time, it's like watching a Vine.

"It's okay. Still adjusting, I guess," I say.

"Yeah?"

"Yeah," I say, and wonder if this counts as a scintillating-enough conversation to be reported to Dri. I wish I had more interesting things to say to Liam. My fear of saying something stupid often leaves me saying almost nothing at all. He doesn't seem to have much to say himself. "You know, still meeting people."

"I should introduce you to my girlfriend, Gem. She's cool as shit. She's a junior too."

"Oh, Gem. Yeah, I think we have a few classes together," I say, and I'm pretty sure I pull off the whole casual *I kinda know who your girlfriend is* thing. What I don't say: *Your girlfriend sucks.*

"Don't worry. It'll get easier. It's always hard to be new," he says. "Like, you know, my band. They were all together since, like, middle school, and I only joined last year. It was weird at first because of this whole crazy thing. But now they're like my brothers. You should come hear us play."

"Totally. Sounds like fun," I say, and I mean it, if only because I'll be able to bring Dri along and solidify our friendship.

Me: He says he was new to his band, but now they're his brothers.

Dri: Yeah. There was some Oville drama for a while. Sad story. But now they're all good.

Not sure how a high school rock band could have a sad story, but I'm sure I'll hear it in all its glorious detail from Dri later. I feel like the kids at Wood Valley have enough money to be immune from truly sad stories, but of course that isn't true. Not everything is for sale. I flash to my mom, bald and literally rotting from within, too weak even to squeeze my hand, and a wave of nausea hits me. It's always been easier to remember her sick, maybe because that was the most recent iteration or, more likely, just the most searing. I blink, and thankfully, the image is gone.

"We've got a gig in a few weeks playing a party. It's not a huge rager or anything. Just a chill time. You should come," Liam says, and I feel the lightness of anticipation; I may actually have something to do on a Saturday night. It would be fun to get out. "It's at Gem's house."

Oh. Yeah. So not going to happen.

Me: Invited me to a party they're playing in a few weeks. Was going to say we should go but—

Dri: WE HAVE TO GO!

Me: It's at Gem's.

Dri: So what? When Liam is around, Gem is a whole different person. Esp once she sees him talking to you.

Me: No.

Dri: Who cares what she says about your jeans? This is Oville. You'll love them.

Me: If I ever call them Oville, shoot me.

Dri: Cranky is not the same thing as charming, you know.

Me: Of this I am aware.

Dri: Good. It's settled, then. Get our your dancing shoes, because we are a-going.

"Is your music the kind of thing people dance to?" I ask Liam, seemingly out of nowhere.

"Huh?"

"Nothing," I say.

CHAPTER 13

Ethan, Ethan Marks is already in the library when I arrive. He's wearing his Batman T-shirt, of course, and is staring out the window, captivated, though I have no idea by what. All I can see is another cloudless sky, emptiness. His right hand massages his jaw, as if it's sore from all the talking he refuses to do. I wouldn't mind touching the rough texture of his cheek, feeling the knot where bone meets bone.

Did I just say that? Seriously? I take it all back. Sure, he's hot. But he's also kind of a jerk, and it's a waste of my time to have a crush on the one guy every girl in school wants. I don't have a shot.

Let's get an A in English and move on. I have stuff to do: work, school, PSATs. Things are finally starting to feel under control for the first time since we moved. I have a job, because: money. I have Dri, who is fast becoming a real friend, and SN too, who I IM throughout the day. SN and I mostly "talk" about stupid stuff, but it's fun having him in my pocket at all times.

"Hey," I say, and fold my legs under me. Casual, relaxed, as if I don't feel the least bit awkward. I'm not a terrible actress, it turns out. I almost believe me. When I look down and see a single brown hair sprouting from my ankle, though, it throws me off balance, and it takes all of my self-control not to yank down my jean cuffs. *Chill out. He's not looking at your ankles. Sudden moves make you look nervous.*

"Hey, Jessie." That smile is back, and his face opens up for just a second before it closes again. "Ready to do this?"

"Sure," I say, and I wonder if I'll ever be able to move beyond monosyllabic answers with this guy. Scarlett talks more when she's nervous—the adrenaline makes her witty, not slow—but my brain gets overwhelmed. Like I've stepped outside myself.

Ethan smells like lavender and honey. Fresh too, the opposite of that body spray all the boys in Chicago use, that horrible dome of chemical scent that would linger long after they walked away. Laundry detergent or cologne, I wonder? Does Ethan wash his shirt every night? Most likely he has his own Gloria to do it for him. Or maybe he has a Batman for every day of the week. And yes, I realize I'm starting to sound like Dri and her obsession with Liam, gathering details to mull over later.

Must. Stop. Now. I have a limited number of brain cells, and they're better saved for my PSAT prep app.

"You read any poetry?" he asks me, but not really. He asks the window. Ethan is looking at the Great Beyond again. He's somewhere else. Not like me most of the time, outside myself looking in, but outside himself completely. I recognize the look. There but not there. I've felt that way before: I'm physically present and accounted for, yet later, when I look back, I realize whole stretches of my day have been stolen. A body without a soul. Not unlike my mother, actually: there, somewhere—physically locatable, buried underground—but not there at all. Marked absent in every way that counts.

"Some," I say. *A single syllable. Again.* Good thing he's not listening. "I mean, yeah, I like poetry, and I read 'The Waste Land' a while back, but I didn't really get it, you know? It's like a mash-up of all these different voices."

"Totally. I Googled it, and apparently everything alludes to something else. It's almost like code," he says, and then looks at me. He's coming to again. Is he on something? Pot? Coke? Molly? Is that the sort of haze we are dealing with? But then he rubs his face, and I realize it's just good-old fashioned fatigue. This boy is tired. Why doesn't he sleep? What happens at night when he closes his eyes?

Stop it, Jessie.

I force myself to focus.

"Okay, let's start with the very first line: 'April is the cruellest month, breeding.' What does that even mean? I know it's poetic and kind of cool, especially the breeding part, but why April? Why is it crueler than any other month?" I ask.

"I don't know. But I kind of hate April," Ethan says, and then stops. He squints at me, almost angry. He didn't mean to say that. A slip, somehow. But about what? I don't get it. What does it even mean to hate April? I hated January in Chicago because it was effin' cold, but we're not talking about the weather here. He shakes himself out of it. "Do you like to walk? Why don't we do this walking?"

Ethan doesn't wait for my agreement, just gathers his books and his laptop, and so I follow him outside.

"I thought people in LA didn't walk," I say once I hear the school door close behind me. I always feel relief at that sound, another day done and survived. He slips on sunglasses, Ray-Bans, and now he's even harder to read because I can't see his eyes.

"I think better when I'm moving. It wakes me up. Want to hear what else I learned from Google?"

I nod, which is stupid because he's not looking at me.

"Sure."

"Eliot didn't originally start the poem this way. Ezra Pound told him to cut, like, forty-three lines or something. So the whole April thing was supposed to come later. And back then, presumably he had to literally cut and paste, with, like, scissors and stuff."

I close my eyes for a second and picture it, though I have no idea what T. S. Eliot looked like. But I imagine an old white guy with a monocle, a heavy pair of scissors, and a glue stick.

"I can't imagine writing without a computer," I confess. "When I use paper, it feels too . . . slow or something. My mind is faster than my hands."

"Yeah, me too. So tell me something else I don't know about you." He cocks his head to the side, and this time he is looking at me. I'm grateful for his sunglasses, that extra layer of protection. His gaze is too strong. This, surely, is one of the many things that keeps the girls coming to his chair, these little moments of connection dished out sparingly, like tiny gifts. Maybe he's intentionally stingy with them; too much and no one would ever leave him alone.

"I don't know," I say. "Not much to tell."

"I find that hard to believe."

"Okay, there's lots to tell, but not so much you would want to hear." *December, that's the cruellest month, I think. Dead mothers' birthdays and Christmas cheer. April too. The month of endings. And I like your Batman T-shirt and your scary eyes and I want to know why you don't sleep enough. When I close my eyes at night, I see last moments, impossible goodbyes.*

But I don't dream anymore. Do you dream? I miss it.

"So, what about you?" I ask.

"'Lilacs out of the dead land, mixing / Memory and desire, stirring / Dull roots with spring rain. / Winter kept us warm, covering / Earth in forgetful snow, feeding / A little life with dried tubers.'"

"You memorized 'The Waste Land'?" I ask. "For real?"

"Most of it, yeah. I read poetry when I can't sleep. I like to memorize it."

"Seriously?"

"Now I'm totally embarrassed. Stop looking at me like that," he says, but I'm the one whose face is red. I've been looking at him in, well, wonder. The guy reads poetry. For fun.

Swoon.

"I know it's weird."

He smiles, and so, so do I.

"No, that's really cool." I resist the urge to touch his

shoulder. *Who is he?* I am officially Dri. All I want are more details. "Dried tubers?"

"I know, right? Like what the hell are dried tubers?"

Later, I lie down on my day bed, prop my feet up on its curved edge. IM with SN.

SN: you've been quiet today. SO HOW WAS YOUR DAY. GO!

Me: Look at that. You do have a shift key. Day=not too bad. Yours?

SN: good, actually.

Me: Tell me three things I don't know about you. You know, besides your name and, well, everything else.

Heh. Apparently my afternoon with Ethan has left me braver. Reckless. When we said goodbye, next to my car, he put his hands in his jeans pocket, rocked back on his heels, and said, "Till next time." Till next time. Three words that sound good together like that. All in a row. Poetic.

SN: okay. (1) I make an amazeballs grilled cheese.

Me: Amazeballs?

SN: yup, so good it justifies the use of the word "amazeballs." (2) I went through a Justin Timberlake phase in 6th grade and called him JT. like "yo, what up, it's JT on the radio." yeah. it was bad. not my best year.

Me: I'll admit it: I'm still going through a Justin Timberlake phase. And 3?

SN: I don't know. may keep this one to myself.

Me: Come on. You keep everything to yourself.

SN: tell me three things and then maybe . . .

Me: (1) I have this whole weird theory of the universe that I don't actually believe but like to think about. Like we are something tiny and insignificant, like ants, to some larger, more complex species, which sort of explains all the weird random things that can happen, like hurricanes and cancer. OMG, I can't believe I just told you that. I've never said that out loud before. Not even to Scarlett. #embarrassed.

SN: that's a little weird, and yet possibly brilliant. #impressed

Me: I know, right?

SN: Google the Fermi paradox. will blow your mind. And 2 . . .

Me: (2) I have trouble remembering my times tables. I mean, I can do calculus and stuff, no problem, but basic math, not so much.

Me: Just Googled Fermi. How do you know that kind of thing off the top of your head?

SN: I dunno. just do. 3 . . .

Me: You only gave me 2.

SN: (3) I like you.

Me: (3) I like you too.

Crap. I did it again. Hit send without thinking. Who do I like? Who is this person? It's not a lie. I like his words. I spend my day looking forward to writing to him, hearing his thoughts on stuff. But to just come out and say "I like you" without knowing who he is, with this ridiculous imbalance—he knows who I am, probably where I live—is just plain stupid. I'm asking for some sort of cosmic smackdown. Can I take it back? How do I do that? Do I just let it lie, enjoy for a moment that a guy—and yes, I realize I say that hopefully, that he is an actual guy from Wood Valley and not some sort of joke, or something totally weird I hadn't thought of, like a cop who tries to catch child predators online or something—actually likes me? *Me.* I'm not sure that, other than maybe in sixth grade, when Leo Springer passed me a note that said *Let's go out!!!* and was then my boyfriend for approximately twenty-two hours because I forgave the excessive punctuation but not his excessive hand sweating, which I later felt bad about when it turned out he had a serious glandular issue, any guy has ever said anything like those words to me: "I like you." Screw it. I'm going to take a moment to revel.

No. This is too weird. I'm not reveling.

I'm freaking out.

Me: This is too weird. I don't even KNOW WHO YOU ARE. Let's dial it back.

SN: dial it back from "I like you"? okay, not sure what that means.

SN: I like you in my world means I think you're cool, whatever. relax, lady, i'm not proposing.

Me: Shut up. It's just. Forget it.

SN: it's just, what?

Me: Never mind. Seriously, forget it.

SN: come on. tell me.

Me: It's just weird that you know who I am and I don't know who you are. It's not fair.

SN: life isn't fair.

Me: Fine. Whatever. Gotta go.

I put my phone down for a second. I'm angry. Deflated. So he doesn't like me, he just thinks I'm cool. It wasn't like I was saying he thinks I'm the best thing in the world. It's just . . . It felt good to be liked, whatever that means.

SN: wait, stop. come back. I'm sorry.

Me: And?

SN: it's just that I like talking to you here. like this. I meant it. I do like you. irl, you make me nervous or something. it would just be different to actually talk-talk. and this works, right?

Me: Yeah. But . . .

SN: I'll give you three more things: (1) I like music and books and video games more than people. people make me awkward. (2) I used to sleep with a blanket when I was little, which I called . . . wait for it . . . Blanket, and okay, fine, I still do. (3) a year ago, I was a totally different person.

Me: Why? Who were you?

SN: happy. or happier. simpler. a bit more normal, if that's even a thing.

Me: And then . . .

A long beat. I wait.

SN: my sister died. suddenly. long story. and now. well, you know how it is.

Me: Yeah.

SN: your mom died, right? am I allowed to ask that?

Me: How did you

SN: Theo. I mean, he didn't tell me, but someone told me that you're his stepsister, so I sort of put it together. is it okay that I asked you that? I seem to have lost all sense of what you are allowed to say to people.

Me: Yes, it's okay. To ask, I mean. The fact of it is . . . well, not okay. I don't know. It's . . .

SN: yeah, it's.

Me: Right.

SN: how long ago?

Me: 765 days, five hours, twenty-two minutes. You?

SN: 196 days, one hour, three minutes.

Me: You count too?

SN: I count too.

I think about SN's sister. I don't know why, but I picture a twelve-year-old girl, pigtails, sick. But of course that's all in my imagination. I have too many questions: How old was she? How did she die? Then again, she's no longer here. That's what matters. The "hows" are, again, mere detail.

Later. Not now. Maybe I'll ask later.

SN: so yesterday, I saw a rainbow, and my annoying phone was dead from IMing with you, and it was almost like it didn't happen because I didn't take a picture. please tell me you saw it too.

SN: because sometimes I feel like I'm losing my mind. I want to know for a fact that it happened. you know that feeling?

I pause. Yesterday, on my way to work, it rained for no more than thirty seconds—the first rain I've experienced since moving here—and then the clouds shifted, and yes, SN is right. There was part of a rainbow, arched across half of the sky, so rainbowlike in its rainbowness it made me feel almost silly, like I lived in a cartoon. And I'm embarrassed to admit it, but for a second, I thought it was a message from my mom, or that somehow it *was* her, in a way that I could not and still cannot explain. I took a picture but didn't bother to Instagram it. I didn't want to seem like I was trying to be all free-spiritish, which I am not. In any way. Should I send it to SN?

Me: I saw it too.

    I find the picture on my phone. No need to even use a filter, because unlike absolutely everything else, it is perfect as is. Hit send.

· · ·

You have an IM from Liam Sandler.

Liam: Can you work tomorrow after school? Band practice.

Me: Sure.

Liam: You are a lifesaver. ☺

· · ·

Me: You ever realize how many of our day-to-day expressions are about death? Like someone just called me a lifesaver.

SN: yeah. since, you know . . . it's everywhere. dead meat. my mom's going to kill me. died and went to heaven. but the worst part? as soon as someone says it, they look at me all apologetically. like I'm going to be offended or freak out or something. so whose life did you save?

Me: Just taking an extra shift at work.

SN: that's nice of you.

Me: Not really doing it out of the goodness of my heart. Will do anything for extra cash.

SN: hmm . . . anything?

•   •   •

You have an IM from Ethan Marks.

Ethan: From Merriam-Webster: Tuber: "a short, thick, round stem that is a part of certain plants (such as the potato), that grows underground, and that can produce a new plant."

An IM from Ethan. Eight p.m. on a Thursday night. Which meant he was thinking about me, because you can't message someone without thinking about them first, right? Or maybe he was thinking about "The Waste Land," which isn't exactly the same as thinking about me, but close enough. The poem and I are now aligned. I'll take it. This is the sort of ridiculous analysis you engage in when you have a ridiculous crush.

Which I do not.

Me: Huh. Kinda makes sense. The whole feeding a new life part of the poem.

Ethan: But why are they dried?

Me: No idea.

Ethan: I like the word "tuber." Makes a good insult.

Me: ??? Example, please.

Ethan: Gem and Crystal? Total tubers.

Although I know Ethan heard Gem be rude to me that first time—he was, of course, the whole reason for the *what are you looking at?* fiasco that somehow set her off hating my guts—I didn't realize he hears all the crap she mutters under her breath in English class. Great. It's one thing to be mocked daily; it's a whole other thing when cute guys bear witness to it.

Today, the target was the stickers that decorate the back of my laptop. Scarlett made them for me for my birthday last year, and they are awesome. All the tattoos I would get if I were the sort of person who had the nerve to get tattoos, which I am decidedly not. Instead, I'm the kind of person who has spent hours debating said theoretical tattoos, despite my crippling fears of both needles and long-term commitment. Hence pain-less, temporary stickers: two Korean characters that Scarlett swears say "Best Friend"; the line *to thine own self be true,* written in Gothic script; and lastly, a snake, which was not on my list but which Scarlett added because she thought I should be more badass, even if only theoretically. Gem's brilliant take: "I bet that says 'loser' in Japanese."

Me: Total dried tubers. And thanks.

Ethan: For what?

Me: I don't know. Defending me, I guess.

Ethan: I didn't.

Me: Okay then.

Ethan: It's just that you don't seem like the kind of girl who needs defending.

• • •

Dri liked a photo of you and her on Instagram.

I click. Dri and I at the lunch table, Agnes just out of the frame. Was she cropped out? I can't remember. Maybe. Possibly. I think so. That shouldn't make me happy, but it does.

• • •

Scarlett: Not that you asked, but homecoming dress has been procured. FLUORESCENT YELLOW.

Me: You'll definitely stand out.

Scarlett: Don't need a dress to do that.

Me: How's Adam? Psyched?

Scarlett: Think so. Having major breakout issues. Not just little ones, but big-ass whiteheads. Takes all my willpower not to attack them with my nails.

Me: Gross.

Scarlett: Too bad that wouldn't count toward our community service requirement.

I'll admit it. I take a screen shot. Four conversations at once. Four different people who have something to say to me. True, one was about work, one was about a school assignment, one is with Scarlett, who doesn't count, and one is with someone I don't even know, but still, I'm going to count them all. Proof that maybe I'm starting to have something resembling a life again.

CHAPTER 14

SN: three things to kick off your morning: (1) I'm terrified of flying. I hate every second I'm on an airplane. man was not meant to fly.

Me: Don't love to fly but LOVE airports. Great people-watching.

SN: best hellos and goodbyes.

Me: Exactly.

SN: (2) I was a vegetarian for all of 8th and 9th grades, but I stopped because: bacon.

Me: Mmm. Bacon.

SN: (3) I spend way too much time playing video games. and you?

Me: Not so into video games.

SN: you: three things.

Me: Oh, right. (1) I generally don't like vegetables, but I hold a special place in my heart for the brussels sprout.

SN: mmm. with bacon.

Me: (2) I'm a night person. Mornings suck. Why does school have to start so damn early? WHY?

SN: then I'm honored you're talking to me before 8 a.m.

Me: Three cups of coffee. Gloria makes it strong. Have I told you about Gloria?

SN: ?

Me: The steppeople's house manager. I was skeptical at first. It's weird having someone who does all this STUFF for me. Don't tell, but now I'm kind of in love.

SN: independence is overrated. as is being able to list laundry under mad skillz.

Me: (3) I'm a lefty, but when I was about 12 I decided I wanted to be a righty instead, so I trained myself to be ambidextrous. But now I think it's cooler to be a lefty, so there's 3 months of my life I'll never get back.

SN: I'm a righty in all the things. ALL THE THINGS.

Me: Was that an attempt at innuendo?

SN: your use of the word "attempt" suggests that I failed.

Me: #innuendofailure

SN: I just said the word "innuendo" a bunch of times in my head and now its lost all meaning. innuendo. innuendo. innuendo. innuendo.

Me: Word ruined for me forever.

SN: ruinuendo.

Me: You are a dork.

SN: yes, yes I am. good that you find this out now.

CHAPTER 15

"It's literally just sex. I'm not sure why everyone makes such a big deal about it," Agnes says, and rolls onto her back on Dri's bed so her head is hanging off the edge and her bangs fall backward. She has a large forehead. The bangs, it turns out, are less about being hipster-cute and more tactical. It's Friday night, and instead of staying home with Harry Potter, I am here eating potato chips from a jumbo-sized bag, flipping through the Wood Valley yearbook, and chatting with Dri and Agnes, as if this is what I always do on weekends. And it doesn't feel too weird. When I start to get a little nervous that Agnes doesn't want me here, I remember that Dri invited me, even added a "come on, loser" when I said I might need to stay home and study. I chose to interpret her use of "loser" as affectionate.

"Since when are you an expert?" Dri asks, and throws a pillow at Agnes. "I don't care what you say. Technically, you're still a virgin."

"I am not! I totally technically lost my v-card," Agnes says with faux indignation. They sound like an old married couple who has had this particular fight before and neither cares how it turns out. The fun is in the fighting.

"Technically? What does that even mean?" I ask, and look at Agnes. "Please don't tell me you're one of those weirdos who, you know, count, um, oral."

"Course not. There was just a minor penetration issue," Agnes says, and giggles. "But it counts. It definitely counts."

I start laughing too, though I don't really get it.

"What the what?"

"Agnes was half penetrated. She got slipped a half peen."

"Half peen, that's hilarious," Agnes says, and soon we're all laughing so hard we have tears falling down our cheeks.

"Literally, I have no idea what that means. You have to tell me the whole story," I say.

"Okay, here's what went down," Agnes says.

"No pun intended," I say.

"Touché. So, last summer at drama camp, and yes, I know, cliché, blah, blah, but at least it wasn't prom. Anyhow, this guy Stills and I are hooking up outside my bunk, and we're on the ground, and I think, *Okay, let's do this.* I was kind of bored of the whole virginity thing, and so we get a condom, because safety first, right, and start to you know, have sex, with, you know, some penetration, and then all of a sudden he totally freaks out. Apparently, he's all into, and I quote, his 'bro J.C.' and wants to wait till marriage."

"No way," I say. "He actually said 'my bro J.C.'?"

"Yup. Humiliating on so many levels. So that's how I lost my virginity. It counts, right?" Agnes asks me, and I decide that maybe I've been too quick to judge her. She's funny and super honest and willing to laugh at herself. I get now why she and Dri are best friends.

"I vote yes," I say, because it's a hell of a lot closer than I've ever come to having a penis inserted into me.

"But Dri's right too. I totally got half peened. How about you?" Agnes asks so casually it's like she's asking what my favorite subject is.

"Not yet. I mean, I'm not waiting till marriage or anything like that, but, yeah, no real opportunity has presented itself," I say, which is the truth. What I don't say: that I wouldn't mind if it happened with someone I liked and found attractive and who liked me back. I assume I won't lose my virginity until college, because that's when it seems to happen for girls like me.

"Me neither," Dri says. "And to go back to my original point, I'm not saying it's some huge deal or anything, but, come on, it's not nothing."

Agnes says, "So my sister goes to UCLA, and she's like this huge hobag there, right? And she says that sleeping with all these randos is her way of owning her sexuality." Agnes now sits up and faces both Dri and me, her bangs restored. "She even has a file on Evernote where she keeps track of everyone she's slept with."

"You kind of have to admire her commitment," Dri says. "Banging for feminism."

We laugh again, and I think about Scar and how she'd feel

right at home here. I continue to flip through the yearbook, looking but not looking for SN.

"Hey, can I ask you guys a question?" I ask.

"Course," Dri and Agnes say at the exact same time. Scarlett and I used to do that too. We called them our mind meld moments.

"Do you know anyone in our class who had a sister who died?" I know I shouldn't try to figure out who SN is, that finding out might just ruin the best thing to happen to me in forever, but I can't help myself. I have this one nugget of information, and I want to run with it.

"Don't think so. Why?" Dri asks.

"Well, there's this guy . . . ," I say, and wonder how to tell this story without making it all sound weird. SN and me, our constant texting despite his anonymity. How I feel like he's really starting to know me, to *see* me, even though we've never even met.

"So many great stories begin 'There's this guy.'" Agnes giggles.

"Shut up," Dri says. "Let the girl talk."

And so I do. It feels like I'm in a safe room, and not despite Agnes's teasing, but maybe because of it. These are people who, if they aren't already, are well on their way to becoming my real friends. I don't mention the specifics: our new three things game or how he told me to befriend Dri in the first place. The former, at least, belongs only to us. But I confess that I like him, whatever that means when you've only talked online.

"You totally want him to half peen you," Agnes says.

"A girl can dream," I say.

Later, when I get back to Rachel's house, I find Theo lingering outside our parents' bedroom, obviously eavesdropping.

"You are not listening to them, you know, doing the nasty. Please, please, please tell me that's not what's happening here," I demand.

"Ewww. Gross, no. And shush. They're fighting," he says, and pulls me next to him, right near the door, so I can hear them too. Turns out that's unnecessary, because soon they're shouting so loud I'm sure the neighbors have turned off whatever reality show competition they are watching to tune in to this instead. "I think they might be breaking up, and then this long national nightmare can come to an end."

"'Long national nightmare'? Seriously?" I ask.

"What the hell, Rachel? It's just a fucking dinner," my dad says, and that's when I know it's serious. My dad rarely curses, opts instead for the faux cursing favored only by ten-year-old girls and Southern women and Dri: shut the front door, holy sugar, eff off. "I need to study."

"It's an important work dinner, and it's not unreasonable of me to want my husband there. We're married, remember? This is important to me," Rachel says, and I wish I could see through the door. Are they standing or sitting? Is Rachel the type to throw things, to smash the thousand-dollar accessories that litter the house? But who needs a six-foot-tall white porcelain giraffe anyhow? "Forget it. Maybe it's better if you don't come."

"What's that supposed to mean?"

"Nothing. It means nothing." Oh, the passive-aggressive

type. Says things without saying them. Agnes would hate her. "You and I both know this is not about you needing to study. You already told me you can take that test in your sleep."

"Fine. I'll admit it. I wanted one night to myself. One night when I did not have to be judged by all of your friends. Do you think I don't see how they look at me? How you look at me when they're around? I even let you take me shopping so I can dress the part, but come on! Enough," my dad says, and now my cheeks flame. No doubt, I feel out of my element at Wood Valley, but it never occurred to me that my dad would have trouble adjusting to life in LA too, that all this fitting-in stuff doesn't end in high school.

"No one is judging you," Rachel says, and her voice turns coaxing, soothing. "They all like you."

"So sue me that I don't want to watch some indie movie about a Bengali leper who plays the harp with his toes. And you have some nerve correcting my drink order the other night, like I'm a child. I wanted a beer with my steak. Not an over-priced glass of cabernet. Sorry if that offends your high-class sensibilities. That sort of stuff doesn't matter to me."

"I was just trying to keep you from embarrassing your-self," Rachel says, and her voice starts to quaver. Tears are imminent. I don't feel sorry for her. "At a place like that, you don't order beer. You just don't. I was just trying to signal to you—"

"I don't need signals. I'm a grown man, and just because I prefer burgers and beer to organic freshwater fancy-ass fish doesn't make me a barbarian. You knew who you were marry-ing. I've never pretended to be anyone else. Anyhow, I thought it was cool to be different out here. Isn't that why you bought me those ridiculous sneakers? It's like you're training a pet."

"It's one thing to have simple tastes. It's another to be downright antiintellectual. Would it hurt you to read a book once in a while?" Rachel asks. Turns out I was wrong. She's not going to cry. She's doubling down. She's rearing back.

"Seriously? You're insulting my intelligence now? I've never seen *you* read a book. All that's on your night table is *Vogue*. Actually, the only person who reads around here is Jessie. She's the only sane person in this house."

"Jessie's the only sane person in this house? Wake up, Bill! She has no friends. None. I was thrilled to send her to Wood Valley, but aren't you worried about her? Teenagers are supposed to go out and have fun," Rachel says.

Oh, so I'll be the one who will end up in tears. Of course, that's the way it goes these days. I want to yell back, right through the door. *I've made friends! I'm doing my best. I don't need help*. It's not my fault my mother died, that we moved here. I've had to start all over from scratch in every way that matters. My dad chose her, and even more inexplicable, she chose my dad, and I didn't choose either one of them. Sure, my dad's a nobody pharmacist from Chicago, but he's smart, damn it. Brilliant, even. So what if he loves WWF and action movies? My mom loved poetry, and even though my dad never did, they made it work. She let him be himself.

My life is a shit sandwich, with a side of jizz veggie burger. I don't have the strength. My eyes are blurry with tears, and I slide down the wall to the floor. Theo looks at me.

"She talks crap when she's mad. Ignore her," Theo whispers. "She just likes to get her way."

"You're one to talk about parenting." My dad's voice. "My kid is amazing, so don't you dare. Have you looked at your kid lately? The way Theo gallivants all . . ." My dad stops, thank God. *Oh, Dad, please don't say it.*

"All what?" Rachel asks. "My son is gay. So the hell what?"

Rachel is goading him now. It sounds like she wants to fight. For a moment, I think it would be preferable to listen to them have sex. This is somehow even more intimate, more raw. Even worse than witnessing her midnight tears. I don't want to be so close to these grown-up things. It's all so screwed up.

Suddenly, I wonder if this is what happens when people meet on the Internet. A connection without context. A good first impression so much easier to make because it can be manipulated. But they met in an online *bereavement* group, not a place normal people click for a hookup. It's hard picturing someone like Rachel turning to the Internet to help with her grief. She's always so put-together. The opposite of needy.

As much as I'm not a huge fan, I'm starting to see why my dad was attracted to her. Despite being dealt the bad hand of widowhood, Rachel's getting an A-plus at life. She's successful and reasonably attractive and rich. But why did she marry my dad? He's not ugly, as far as middle-aged men go, I guess, and he's kind—my mom used to say she was the luckiest woman in the world to have found him and to have built her life on such a stable foundation—but I'd imagine there are a million men like him in LA who come with fewer complications and more of their own cash. Why did she have to pick *my* dad?

When my parents used to fight, I would slip away to my room and put on headphones. I didn't listen, especially because I knew the fight would last for days—two or three at least—when both of them would use me to talk to each other, one of the downsides of being an only child: *Jessie, tell your father he needs to pick you up from school tomorrow; Jessie, tell your mother that we are out of milk.* They didn't fight often, but when they did, it was explosive and unpleasant.

Everything passes, Jessie. Remember that. What feels huge today will feel small tomorrow, she once said, right after a big fight with my dad. I don't remember what they were arguing about—maybe money—but I do remember that it ended out of nowhere, four whole days after it started, when both of them just looked at each other and started cracking up. I think about that often—not only how that fight broke, but what she said. Because I'm pretty sure she was wrong. Not everything passes.

"Let me just make something clear here." My dad's voice gets low and growly. He's calm, almost too calm, which is what he does when he's really angry. Runs cold. "I'm not some ignorant homophobic hick, so stop talking to me that way."

"Bill!"

"Forget it. I'm going for a walk. I need air and to get far away from you," my dad says, so Theo and I scramble quickly down the hall. Surely my dad knows they've been yelling, but better for him not to know about our front-row seats.

"Good. Go!" Rachel screams. "And don't come back!"

I'm in Theo's room now. I've only been in here once, when I told him about my new job, so I take advantage of the opportunity to look around. He doesn't have anything on his walls, not a single framed picture on his desk. Not much to see. Apparently, he's a minimalist, like his mother.

"You think they're going to get a divorce?" Theo asks, and it surprises me that my heart sinks at the thought. Not because I particularly like living here, but because we have nothing to go back to. Our house is gone. Our Chicago lives. And if we were to stay in LA and move to some sad little apartment, my dad couldn't afford to keep sending me to Wood Valley. I'd have to start again somewhere else. I'd have to say goodbye to my silly crush on Ethan, to my friendship with Dri and Agnes, to my whatever with SN. When Rachel told my dad to not come back, did she expect me to leave too? Are we kicked out?

"I don't know," I say.

"Would make things easier," Theo says.

"For you, maybe. I have nowhere to go."

"Not my problem."

"No, it isn't," I say, and stand to leave. I've had enough of these people.

"Sorry, I didn't mean it. Was your dad going to call me a . . . Never mind."

"He wouldn't have. He's not like that."

"Whatever. Want to smoke up?" Theo reaches for his rolling papers.

"No thanks. And for real, he wouldn't have called you anything bad."

"I'm not so sure."

"I know my dad. He was going to say flamboyant. Which, come on, you kind of are," I say, and wonder if I've overstepped my boundaries. I hold eye contact with Theo, to let him know that I am not trying to be hurtful, just honest.

"I knew in, like, kindergarten that I'm gay, so I figure I should own it, you know? Give the people what they want,"

Theo says, and starts digging through his drawers. "No one should be spared my fabulousness."

"Lucky us," I say, but I smile. I'm starting to have a new appreciation for Theo. He approaches life with manic enthusiasm, an antidote to most of Wood Valley's laconic teenagerness. There's a layer of kindness underneath him too, and he's authentic in his own over-the-top way.

"So who are you texting with all the time?" he asks, and again it occurs to me that he could be SN. Maybe he wanted to help me without having to face our bizarro new family situation. Maybe I've misinterpreted; maybe SN's flirtation was actually just Theo's enthusiasm. I hope not.

"None of your business," I say, which doesn't seem to bother him in the least.

"Since you don't smoke, wanna stress eat instead? I have some emergency Godiva somewhere around here," he says, and finds what he's been looking for: a giant chocolate bar.

"I'm in," I say.

"So you think your dad signed a prenup?" Theo asks, and I hate him all over again.

CHAPTER 16

SN: three things: (1) had waffles this morning in your honor. (2) when I graduate, I really want to disrupt the beverage industry. I mean water, coffee, tea, juice, soda, and a few weird hybrids. WE CAN DO BETTER. (3) I used to dream about my sister all the time, and I'd wake up all shaky and it sucked, but now I don't dream about her at all. turns out that's worse.

Me: (1) I don't dream about my mom anymore either, but sometimes I totally forget that she's gone. I'll think, oh, she'll love this story, I'll tell her when I get home, and then I remember all over again. That's the worst. (2) I didn't have waffles this morning. I had some sort of organic wheatberry granola from Whole Foods that the step-monster loves, and tho it was delicious, I still have no idea wtf a wheatberry is. (3) I've never used the word "disrupt" in relation to any industry. What does that even mean? Are you sure you're 16?

SN: 17, actually. and I now have my billion-dollar idea: wheat-berry juice!

Me: You are so Wood Valley. What? A MILLION-dollar idea wasn't good enough?

I head straight to work after school. I'm not avoiding home. Not really. But what if my stuff has already been packed up again into my duffel bags—Gloria would do it carefully and respectfully, take the time to fold my bras, ziplock my shampoo bottles—and the whole Rachel-Dad experiment is over, just like that? Poof. What will happen to me?

At breakfast, I was the only one sitting at the table, and when Theo stopped in to grab a juice, he just raised an eyebrow and shrugged. Apparently, he's as much in the dark as I am. A few minutes later, Rachel came in, and she did that busy thing she does, where she talks out loud to no one in particular, or maybe to herself, a whirling dervish of nervous energy and rhetorical questions.

"Coffee! Where's the coffee?" she asked, though it was exactly where it always is. In the coffeemaker, brewed by Gloria or an automatic early-morning timer, I'm not sure which, though I put my money on the former. Gloria is amazing at doing things without you seeing her do things, and also doing all the things you didn't even know you needed done in the first place. If we have to leave, I might miss Gloria the most. She calls me Yessie and folds my pajamas under my pillow and insists I eat chocolate calcium chews. "And keys. Where are you, keys? In my bag. Damn it, where's my bag?"

Like all of Rachel's belongings, apparently, my dad was also MIA, and for a second, I panicked that maybe he'd taken off without me and headed back east. When the worst thing you could possibly imagine happens to you, you think maybe other previously inconceivably bad things can happen too. But no way would he ditch me. Of course, I never thought he'd lie about a convention and come back remarried instead of loaded up with samples to give to his middle-age friends like a normal person, but still. Except for the last few months, he's been a good dad.

"Sunglasses?" Rachel asked, which made me realize just how rattled she must have been by last night's fight, because she started patting down the empty white countertops, as if her sunglasses would appear out of thin air. Sunglasses are not usually part of her morning soliloquy.

"On your head," I said.

And then she jumped a little and looked up at me, as if my voice caught her by surprise and she was just noticing I was sitting here. She looked sad for a moment, or disappointed. But then she pulled her glasses off her head and put them on, and just like that, most of her face was covered, and I couldn't read her at all.

• • •

Liam's sitting on the desk when I get to work, playing his guitar and singing to an audience of zero. Turns out I was right: Book Out Below! doesn't get a whole lot of customer action. A few regulars here and there, one guy who thumbs books in the self-help section but never buys, and that's about it.

" 'Imagine,' huh? A classic." I'm surprised by Liam's voice. It's soft, earnest, almost sweet. He looks different with a guitar. Dri's crush makes total sense.

"Sorry. Didn't hear you come in." Liam swings Earl off his shoulder and slides him back into his purple fur-lined case. It's a graceful move, one I'm sure he's done a thousand times.

"You don't have to stop on my account." I wonder if I can somehow slip my phone out and secretly record him for Dri but then realize that's just too weird and invasive. "You're good. I mean, for real."

"Thanks. I wanna go to Berklee College of Music next year, if I get in, but my mom doesn't want me going so far," he says.

"Wow," I say. "That's in Boston, right?"

"Yup. Honestly, what I'd really like to do is skip college and try to hit it big with the Oville guys. But my mom would go postal. I keep telling her that's what Maroon 5 did—they're from Brentwood School, you know—but she's all, 'Maroon what'?"

I laugh, try to think of what to say next.

"So are you coming?" he asks, saving me from my embarrassingly blank brain.

"Excuse me?"

"To my gig. At Gem's party."

"When is it, again?" Of course, I remember when it is. Dri

and Agnes have already convinced me that we should all go, and have even picked out my outfit. They claim Crystal and Gem will be so wasted they won't even notice I'm there.

"Next Saturday night," Liam says. "Okay, so it's not a real gig at a club or anything. But it'll be fun. Promise."

"Cool, I'll definitely try to make it." Liam pats the desk, an invitation for me to sit next to him. I jump up and sit cross-legged but turn so my back rests against the wall. I scan the children's section behind his head, check out the bright covers of the books, which are shelved to face outward. They are not shy at all.

"Are you working today too?" I ask.

I hope not. Working with Liam makes me uncomfortable; it's hard to make conversation for three hours in a row. There are only so many times he can tell me about the food at his Google internship, which apparently was really, really good. I mean, we don't talk the whole time—thank God for my iPhone, which I pull out whenever I feel awkward, but that only gets me so far. Now that I know the basics here, I'm not sure why we would both need to be on duty. It's not like there's anything to really do anyway.

"Yeah, if you don't mind. I need the cash, so . . ."

"Oh, I mean, do you want me to go, then?" I ask, and my heart sinks. Dri and Agnes go to Coffee Bean every day after school. As sad as it sounds, I need Ice Blended money.

And also this: I don't want to go home.

If my dad and I have to move again, will SN and I still write to each other? Will he finally tell me who he is?

"Nah, I figured we could both work. My mom doesn't care." I wonder if he feels sorry for me, looks down on me the same way his girlfriend does, and that's why he's letting me stay. I've noticed the scholarship kids at Wood Valley—you can tell by their clothes and how they stick together in non-designer clumps. No one seems to pay any attention to them. The other day, some girl wore a T-shirt that said GAP across the front. Gem didn't even nudge Crystal. For whatever reason, I seem to be her only target.

"You sure?" I ask. Crap. I sound hopeful, even to my own ears.

"I'm sure." And then Liam picks up Earl again and begins to play.

Dri: SHUT UP. He's serenading you RIGHT NOW? FOR REAL? I'm coming there.

Me: I think he's playing original Oville stuff?

Dri: OMG. Wait, if I come it will be too obvious, right? Right. Shoot! Can you call me and leave the line open?

Me: Really?

Dri: No. That's too stalkerish. Even for me. AHHHHH.

Me: You were right. He's actually really good.

Dri: You're killing me right now.

Me: If it makes you feel any better, I wish it were you here instead of me. I have calc homework. If only I got paid to do that . . .

Dri: Admit it: he's hot.

Me: Not my type, but . . .

Dri: But what?

Me: Let's just say I get it now.

Liam starts playing a new song, one I've never heard before. The lyrics go: *"The girl that no one knows, the one that secretly glows, all right, the girl that no one knows is mine, all mine, all mine. . . ."* It's catchy.

Scarlett: Should I have sex with Adam Kravitz after homecoming?

Me: WHAT?!?!?

Scarlett: Was just thinking it might be nice to lose my v-card to someone who's not intimidating, you know? Then it's done and I can move on.

Me: Is that what you want? Just to be done with it?

Scarlett: Maybe?

Me: I'm not saying sex is such a big deal or anything, but it's not nothing, you know?

I realize I'm quoting Dri here, but I think she's right. It's not nothing. Not to get all parental, but there are diseases and pregnancy, and yeah, I know Scarlett would use a condom—we've all seen *16 and Pregnant,* which is the best form of birth control ever—but still. Adam Kravitz? My old neighbor Adam Kravitz? The only guy who's ever shown any interest in me, if you call interest making out with me once, drunk, at the bowling alley on a Saturday night?

My history with him isn't the issue, though. Scarlett is free to be half peened or full peened by him. I just think she's being a little faux casual about the whole thing. She's more like Dri and me than Agnes's sister, as much as she talks a big game. There's a difference between talking about sex (and even being comfortable about talking about sex) and actually *doing it.* Abstractly, sex is simple—one person's body parts touching another person's, nothing more, nothing less—but for some of us, the reality is something altogether more complex. Equal parts exciting and scary. I can't explain why, but I just know that's how it seems to me.

Scarlett: Don't freak out. Was just a thought.

Me: Not freaking out. If you want to do it, then you should. But just make sure, because the same argument for doing it applies to not doing it. Once it's done, it's done. And I know you don't need me to tell you to be safe.

Scarlett: Adam's face is clearing up. I think he may be on Accutane.

Me: Oooh, I want to see. Send pictures!

Scarlett: I miss you, J.

Me: Me too, S. You have no idea.

Scarlett: ?

Me: Dad and the lady of the manor had a big-ass fight. Was scary.

Scarlett: And?

Me: I dunno. For newlyweds they don't seem so happy.

Scarlett: My parents have been married for 18 years, and they fight ALL THE TIME. Sometimes I think they hate each other. They claim otherwise.

Me: Your parents enjoy fighting. It's their happy place.

Scarlett: I probably won't do it with Adam.

Me: ?

Scarlett: But then again, I might.

There's traffic on Ventura, so I don't get home till after eight. Gloria has left me dinner on the counter: a perfectly serrated leg and thigh of roasted chicken, string beans tossed with almonds, a dainty portion of mashed potato, all showcased under a glass dome. My silverware sits on a cloth napkin. In Chicago, we used paper towels. My mom was an okay cook—a little too prone to experimentation—but I miss her big hearty stews, everything thrown together and unidentifiable. My dad's car is in the driveway, but Rachel's is gone, and I don't hear any noise coming from upstairs, not even the steady bass that usually emits from Theo's room. I eat my chicken alone at the kitchen island, wipe my mouth, and am about to head upstairs, when I notice someone sitting on the deck.

Dad.

I open the glass doors and step outside. Wrap my arms around myself, because there's a sharp breeze and a bite to the air I associate with Chicago.

"Hey," I say, and my dad gives me the same look Rachel gave me this morning. As if my very existence comes as a surprise. *I am here,* I want to scream. *Why am I so easily forgotten?*

"Hi, sweetheart. Didn't hear you. Sit with me."

I flop down into the lounge chair next to him. I want to ask about our status—*Are we evicted?*—but I don't have the courage.

"What are you doing out here?" I ask.

"Just thinking."

"Ouch," I say, and my dad smiles.

"It occurred to me just now that I'm finally, officially, in every single way a person can be, a bona fide grown-up. But honestly, sometimes I forget, and think I'm twenty-two. You know what I mean?" he asks. I hope he knows I do not. How could I? Twenty-two sounds old to me.

"If it helps clarify things any, I'm pretty sure you're forty-four. You've been a grown-up for a long, long time in my book," I say.

"Right. You're almost a woman yourself, and I'm your *father*. But damn, I don't know. I don't know if I'm equipped for adult life. Any of it." His voice suddenly turns raw and shaky. After my mom died, I never saw him cry, not once, but in those first few months, he had perpetually watery and bloodshot eyes, as if he had just finished weeping somewhere unseen.

I don't say anything, because I don't know what to say. My mom is not here to help us.

I'm not equipped for this life either.

"I wish when you were little someone had said to me: These are the good times. Right now. These are the good times. You are young and things are simple. And one day it's all going to blow up in your face or bottom out or whatever metaphor you want to use—your mom would have a good one for us—and so relax and enjoy while you can. When I first started out, I used to have nightmares that I gave out a wrong prescription. That I gave Mrs. Jallorari Valium instead of her heart medication. Or that I dosed out the Zackowitzes' kid's lithium incorrectly. Your mom and I, though . . . that part was always easy." I feel his shoulders start to shake, and so I stare straight ahead. If he's going to cry, if he is going to choose *right now* to fall apart, after everything, after him making all of the decisions—selling our house, getting remarried, moving us here and my having no choice in the matter, *none*—I will not look at him. I'm sorry, but I cannot give him that.

"A wise person in our family used to say what doesn't kill

you makes you stronger," I say, because that is the best I can do. An empty morsel.

I can't say *Mom*.

I can't do that either.

"I know it's not fair that you're the one having to comfort me," he says, eyes on the hills, looking out at the other houses, before glancing back at me. "I do realize that you are the kid here."

"Am I?" I ask. "I hadn't noticed."

He makes his hands into fists and taps his eyes, one-two-three, and then drops them, as if he is done with the self-pity.

"You are just like your mom. An old soul. When you were a baby, you used to lie in your crib and look up at me, and I remember thinking, *Man, this kid already sees right through me*." I look over at him. He is wrong. I don't see right through him. He is deeper and more complex than he likes to admit.

I've seen him order cabernet with steak. Many times. Happily.

"Dad?" The question forms again: *Are we leaving?* But I let it go. "Nothing. Never mind."

"So forty-four is really old?" His face brightens. He's now recovered from whatever gripped him.

"Ancient," I say.

"Better tell Gloria to add Depends to the shopping list, then." A stupid joke, maybe but I laugh anyway because I can. I can give him that much.

CHAPTER 17

SN: three things: (1) my first crush was on Wonder Woman. I'm a sucker for a girl with a lasso. (2) my mom has a whole pharmacy in her medicine cabinet. Xanax. Vicodin. Percocet. all the good stuff. and she takes them. all the time. like it's a problem. (3) you have beautiful hands.

Me: Not in order, but . . . (1) I have my mom's hands. She used to play piano. I quit after 2 lessons but I should have stuck with it. Sometimes I listen to her favorite pieces and pretend she's playing. Oh wow, can't believe I just told you that. (2) I was Wonder Woman for Halloween a few years ago. Except I wore pants instead of blue undies. Chicago = cold. (3) How's this for irony? My dad is actually a pharmacist. For real. So I know about all those drugs. I'm sorry about your mom.

• • •

"Hey, Dried Tubers," Ethan says when I meet him in the library. Same shirt every day, same chair by the Koffee Kart, and now the same table where we met last time. This guy has his routines down.

"Really? That's how it's going to be?" I say, though I smile. I like the familiarity. That he would call me a nickname at all. "I thought you said it made a good insult."

"I decided we should take back the word," he says, and packs up his books. Apparently, we'll be walking again. This makes me happy. It's so much easier to talk when I don't have to see his eyes. Ethan looks different today, borderline peppy. "How about Tub-ee? Tuberoni? No?"

"Did you get some sleep or something?" I ask.

He looks up at me, startled. "Huh?" He runs his hands through his hair, his fingers raking the pieces into a perfect mess. I want to touch his hair, tousle it like Gem did. The color is so dark, it looks like it bleeds.

"I dunno. It's just, you usually seem tired. Today you're more awake."

"That obvious?" He nudges me with his shoulder.

"Honestly? It's like Jekyll and Hyde." I grin at him to show I mean no harm.

"Six hours. In a row." He says it proudly, like he just won an award. "I'm what you'd call sleep challenged. 'I read, much of the night, / and go south in the winter.'"

"What?"

"Sorry. Quoting 'The Waste Land.' I do read much of the night, but I don't go anywhere come winter, except sometimes Tahoe to snowboard. So, have you read it?"

"'The Waste Land'?" Why can't I keep up with him? I'm a smart girl. I get at least seven and a half hours a night. And can he touch my shoulder again, please?

"The Strange Case of Dr. Jekyll and Mr. Hyde."

"Nope."

"You should. It's pretty interesting. It's about a guy with a split personality."

"I'm sure you relate," I say.

"Ha," he says.

"So how about Tubilicious?" I ask. This is all easier than it should be.

"Tubilicious it is, Jessie." He stops, and then I wait for it. "Holmes."

Later, we find ourselves at a Starbucks, though not the one with the weird barista. Ethan buys me a vanilla latte and waves my hand away when I offer some cash. Does that make this a date? Or does everyone know that I'm economically challenged, at least by Wood Valley standards? Then again, it's just a latte, and he seems like the chivalrous type. He memorizes poetry and holds the door, and he hasn't taken his phone out even once to text. Let's be real here: Ethan probably has a girlfriend—someone who has an entire Parisian-like sexual history, open and comfortable and varied. I should ask Dri, but I'm embarrassed. Liking Ethan feels too cliché.

"I assume you aren't going to Gem's party on Saturday night," he says, and blows on his coffee. I'm not sure if I should be insulted by his assumption that I won't be anywhere near the most popular kids in the junior and senior classes on a Saturday night. And why does he always have to bring up the wonder twins? It's embarrassing.

"Actually, I think I am." I shrug, do my best to project a *screw 'em* vibe. So they don't like my laptop and my jeans and anything else about me. That won't keep me home.

"Really?" he asks. "Cool."

"A friend of mine is playing with his band, so . . ." It's reaching to call Liam a friend, but I want Ethan to stop thinking of me as Gem's victim. As a big fat loser.

"You mean Oville?"

"Yeah."

"Who do you know?" he asks. His tone is borderline belligerent, like it's preposterous that someone like me should know someone in the band. What the hell is his problem?

"A guy named Liam. Why?"

"I'm in Oville." Of course. Of course he is. Crap. He and Liam are probably best friends, and now Liam will hear that I dropped his name, like he's a celebrity or like we're besties or something. Thank God I didn't call it Oville. This is mortifying.

"Seriously? I keep forgetting how small this school is. Everyone knows everyone and everything except me."

"Knowing everyone here is overrated," Ethan says.

"What do you play?" I ask.

"Electric guitar, and I sing a little, though Liam really fronts us."

"He's good," I say. "I bet the band is too."

"You've heard him?" That tone again. Is it really that hard to believe that I'm friends with Liam?

"Um, yeah. Just practicing, you know."

"Liam's okay," Ethan says, takes a sip of coffee and then another. Reconsiders. Softens. "No, you're right. He's good."

"And you?" I ask, trying to lighten the mood, which feels heavy. It's two steps forward, one step back with this guy.

"I'm not too shabby myself," Ethan says, and there it is again, his sudden goofy smile. So bright and beautiful, it's like staring straight into the sun.

At home under the food dome: miso cod, a fancy salad with edamame and candied walnuts, sticky coconut rice. Gloria knows how to cook Japanese food? Too bad I'm anti–food porn, because this meal is Instagram-worthy. Again, the house is dark, though Theo sits at the kitchen counter nursing a glass of red wine, like he's forty and has had a tough day at work. It's only been three years since he had braces. I've seen the pictures.

"Upshot? Not talking. Still married," Theo says, and pours me my own glass without my asking. I take a sip, breathe through my nose, like Scarlett taught me. It's not half bad.

"Where are they?" I ask.

"Who knows? Couples therapy? A work dinner? My mom never used to go out this much."

"My dad either."

"They're both idiots."

"Stop it."

"They are. They thought they could just *insert replacement here* and forget that someone they loved actually died. Even I'm more emotionally mature than that."

I drink my wine. Theo's not wrong.

"Now what happens?" I ask. Two sips and my arms start to tingle, that feeling that tells me the alcohol is winding its way into my system.

"No idea. I just didn't need all this shit, you know? Like junior year isn't stressful enough?"

"What are you worried about? You're acing all of your classes, you have PSAT tutors—did you hear the plural there, 'tutors'?—and I'm sure your mom has a friend of a friend on every admissions board. Your life is cake."

"You're describing pretty much every single kid at school. How many people do you think Harvard accepts from Wood Valley? Five."

"Harvard? Seriously?"

"What?"

"Nothing. It's just that I never even considered getting into Harvard. I don't think anyone from my old school has *ever* gotten in there, even our valedictorians." I don't mention that in Chicago I was on track to graduate first or second in my class, and now my rank has dropped just by transferring. Apparently, FDR's classes aren't weighted as heavily. One more way I've been screwed by this move.

"Well, thank you for that little life lesson," Theo says, and for a moment he looks angry—like he's-going-to-have-another-temper-tantrum angry—but then it passes and he just sighs.

"I just mean, Harvard isn't the be-all and end-all," I say, as if I know these sorts of things. "You're going to get into a great school no matter what."

I like wine, I decide. It makes me feel slippery, soft, allowing words to just leak out. It makes it less hard being me.

"My dad went to Harvard." He plays the dead dad card, as if that will get any sympathy from over here. Instead, I laugh. I can't help it. It's funny.

"What? Why are you laughing?"

"Because your dad went to Harvard," I say.

"Why is that so funny?"

"You're a freaking legacy!"

Theo looks at me, starts laughing too. "You're right. And his dad went to Harvard too. My life is pretty much cake. You know, other than being gay and losing my dad. But the rest, fine. You win."

"Here's an idea: You really need to start a YouTube channel where you can whine to the camera. *Boo-hoo, I'm gay. Boo-hoo, my dad died,*" I joke. Theo smiles.

"Already have one. I'll send you the link." Theo clinks his glass with mine. "You know, you can sit in on my PSAT tutoring sessions."

"Really?" I ask.

"Don't get too excited. Mondays only. Not Thursday. Thursday is when the magic happens."

CHAPTER 18

Me: Three things: (1) Not to gross you out, but I have super-long toes. They're kind of creepy. (2) I write very bad poetry when I'm feeling sorry for myself. (3) I hate cartoons, even the ones on Adult Swim.

SN: (1) my favorite day of the week is Wednesday. I admire its in-betweenness. (2) I'd bet you a hundred bucks that your toes are actually cute. (3) I went through a phase in 9th where I painted my fingernails black. yeah: I thought I was SO COOL.

Me: You going to the party tonight?

SN: don't.

Me: Don't what?

SN: don't try to figure out who I am. please. just don't.

Me: I don't get it.

SN: just trust me, okay?

· · ·

Me: HAVE FUN TONIGHT AT HOMECOMING! You look amazing.

Scarlett: Thank you. One of my finer selfies, if I do say so myself.

Me: Don't do anything I wouldn't do. Actually, I take that back. HAVE FUN.

Scarlett: Oh, I intend to. . . .

Scarlett: Did you note the ellipsis there? Because that was intentional.

Me: I noted the ellipsis.

Scarlett: Good. Just making sure.

Agnes applies my makeup with at least fifteen different brushes. When she's done, she sweeps my hair behind my shoulders and makes me face the mirror.

"Voilà!" she says, like we've just finished a makeover scene on a morning show. I look up and smile at the face blinking back.

"Wow," Dri says, and claps in excitement. "You look a-maz-ing."

"Thanks, dah-ling," I say. We gather for a group selfie, since we are all looking pretty damn good, and once we each approve the picture, after only three tries, Agnes Instagrams it and tags us.

Dri has agreed to be our designated driver, since drinking aggravates her IBS. I'm learning that Dri has a lot of what she calls nerd ailments: IBS, asthma, carpal tunnel syndrome, myopia. We all pile into her mom's car and turn up the radio. I feel like a normal teenage girl headed to a normal party on a normal Saturday night. I might have, for at least a little while, taken off my top-secret grief backpack and left it behind.

Gem lives in a mansion. On a hill. Behind a gate. Hidden by ten-foot-high hedges. We hike around the house to get to the backyard, where people are lounging on upholstered couches grouped around the infinity pool. An elaborate bar is set up on a built-in barbecue, and there's an actual stage laid out on the lawn with a professional-grade sound system. I feel relief knowing that Gem and Crystal will likely not even notice that I'm here.

"Drinks?" Agnes asks, and without waiting for my answer grabs my wrist, and I grab Dri's, and we head to the bar, which is filled with bottles, presumably pilfered from everyone's parents' stashes.

"You'll introduce me, right? To Liam?" Dri asks me.

"Course," I say. "I mean, I don't know him that well, but if I see him."

A few minutes later, holding drinks, which are devised by Agnes and are red and potent, we begin our lap around the party. I'm glad I let my new friends pick out my outfit. I'm wearing my short black dress from last year's homecoming paired with Dri's jewelry and strappy sandals.

I feel hands cover my eyes, and I stifle my impulse to scream.

"Guess who?"

"Hey," I say, and twist out of the hands and turn to face . . . Liam. Did I hope it would be Ethan? Okay, maybe a little. Liam gives me a peck on the cheek, which is weird, because we don't kiss hello at the store.

"Hi," I say, greeting him twice.

Hey-hi. Really, Jessie? Best you can do?

"Hi," he says, and his voice is thick and loose. He's drunk, I realize, though I'm not sure how far gone. He's not stumbling, but he rests his hands on my shoulders. He has what Scarlett and I would call penis fingers. Dri would call them manly. "I'm so glad you came. We're going on any minute."

"Cool," I say, and then I notice Dri standing next to me. "Liam, have you ever met my friend Dri? She's the best. You guys have, like, literally the same taste in music."

"Yo," he says, and tips an imaginary hat at her. Yup, very drunk. Liam is not a hat-tipping kind of guy. Dri freezes, because Liam Sandler is talking to her, and though I'm sure she's fantasized about this moment many, many times, it's a very different thing when fantasy meets reality. Agnes elbows her to wake her out of her stupor.

"Hi," Dri says. "Oville is, um . . . You, I mean, you guys, are really very, I mean, good."

"We aim to please," he says, a little cocky. Maybe he's not so different from the other senior guys after all. Someone far away whistles. "That's my cue, ladies. See you later, Jess?"

Liam heads toward the stage, and once he's out of earshot, Dri grabs my hands.

"Did that just happen? Oh my god, oh my god, oh my god," she says.

"He's seriously drunk," I say.

"No shit, Sherlock," Agnes says, and gives me a pointed look over Dri's head, though I'm not sure what she's trying to say.

"Let's get closer to the stage." Dri leads the way, and we all hold hands again and snake through the crowd to get a better view.

"What?" I whisper to Agnes.

"Nothing," she says, but it's the kind of nothing that means something.

We make our way to the front, and then I see the whole band, right there onstage, which also means I see Ethan, and my stomach drops. He has a blue electric guitar strapped across his chest, his hair is even messier than usual, and he looks like an actual rock star, despite the Batman logo emblazoned across his chest. Like he was born to be up there, born to hear pathetic girls like me squeal his name. Our eyes catch—a second, then another, one more—but I look away because: Holy crap. I'm no longer cold.

I want to look back. I want nothing more in this life but to look back and have him look at me, but I know he's now on to more important things, like playing guitar and having eye-sex with other girls, and I just can't take it.

"Aren't they amazing?" Dri asks, even though they haven't started playing yet.

"They look like a real band," I say, which is the greatest understatement of our time. They don't look like a real band. They look like rock gods. "I mean, not like high school kids."

"I know, right? We thought they were going to break up last year after Xander died, but then Liam joined and took his place—" Dri stops talking because the music starts and I don't get a chance to ask more. Who is Xander? Was he the kid who Theo said overdosed on heroin? Have I completely misunderstood Liam and Ethan? Do they live, like, rock-star lives, with needles in their arms and scantily clad girls giving them blow jobs in their tour van? Is that why Ethan always looks exhausted? Too much partying?

Oville starts with a fast one, and the crowd all knows the words and starts dancing with arms thrown in the air. Liam sweats and belts his heart out: *We tried, I cried, you hide, and then we do it all over. Do it all over. We tried, I cried, you hide, and then we do it all over.*

Simple lyrics, maybe, but before I know it, I'm dancing too, transfixed. Maybe it's the alcohol—not maybe, of course it's the alcohol—but I find myself staring at Ethan. I don't care if he notices, thinks I'm a cray-cray stalker; he's onstage asking to be stared at. For a second I feel his eyes on mine—I swear I do, and I shiver—but then he looks back into the crowd and I think I must have imagined it.

"We're Oville, and we'll be back," Liam says, and jumps off the stage to deafening cheers. I turn to Dri, grab her shoulders.

"You were so right about them," I say. "Oh. My. God."

"Right? Right?"

"Not you too," Agnes says, and rolls her eyes, though she was dancing right alongside us.

"Not about Liam," I say. "But—"

"Not about Liam, what?" Liam says, and there he is again, standing next to me, shiny with sweat and elation. Thank God I didn't finish my sentence. I don't need the humiliation of Ethan finding out I have a debilitating crush on him via Liam.

"Nothing. You guys were amazing. Seriously," I say, and nudge Dri to join in the conversation. Before she can say a word, though, Gem runs up and practically jumps into Liam's arms, and wraps herself around his torso. She kisses him and we can all see her tongue.

"Whoa, what was that for?" Liam slowly puts her down. He doesn't sound drunk anymore. Maybe performing burned it all off.

"Baby, you guys, like, totally slayed," Gem says, and then links her arm with his, as if we need another demonstration that she is his girlfriend. *We get it. He bones you.*

"Thanks. Hey, do you know Jessie? Remember I told you about her? She works at Book Out Below!" Liam says.

Gem turns to me and smiles, and it looks so sincere, my first thought, beyond disgust, is that I'm certain that she will one day become famous. This girl can act. Of course Liam likes Gem; he's never actually met her. I wonder what he'd say if he knew she mocks me daily.

"You're new, right? Don't we have English together or something?" she asks. Pure innocence. I shrug, unable to force myself to respond. Agnes thrusts another drink into my hand, and though I don't really need it, I gulp it down.

"Liam, I like the new riff you added to 'Before I Go.' It really works," Dri says, and I so appreciate her jumping in that I want to cry.

"You think? Ethan thought it was a little flashy," Liam says.

"Nah, you needed a break right then. Too much tension or something."

"That's exactly what I said."

"Lee-lee, we need to go. Crystal is calling us," Gem says, and starts to pull Liam away, like he's a yippy dog sniffing something disgusting.

"I'll be there in a sec," Liam says.

"Come on, I want you to make me your special vodka and Red Bull." Gem says it like an invitation, as if she is asking him to lick her, not to prepare a drink. How does she do that? Talk with innuendo? Is that something I will ever learn how to do, or is it a skill she was born with, just a bonus in her overflowing genetic swag bag?

"I do make kick-ass cocktails. Catch you guys later?" Liam asks, and gives us a wide smile, big enough that Dri can now cross *see Liam Sandler smile at me* off her bucket list.

SN: you look beautiful.

Me: are you here? where are you?

I don't acknowledge his compliment because it's too easy to lie. Maybe Agnes has a point: writing is different from speaking after all. My mom used to tell me I was beautiful, but I always felt like she meant it in a general way, from the perch of someone whose own body had betrayed her, and maybe also as a public service message, a way to build up my flagging self-confidence. Scarlett's mother, on the other hand, used to say that Scarlett could be gorgeous if she only lost ten pounds, which was cruel, of course, but also specific, as if her mom thought she was worthy of an honest assessment.

I look around. A tall, good-looking guy in the corner wearing glasses and a gray T-shirt is staring at his phone. It takes me a moment to place him. He was the first person I saw at Wood Valley: Kilimanjaro gray T-shirt boy. The one who spent the summer climbing mountains and building schools in Tanzania. I doubt he's SN—I picture SN as more of a homebody, unlikely to have spent his summer scaling mountains—but it's worth further investigation.

"Who's that?" I ask Dri, motioning to the guy in the corner.

"Caleb. Agnes went to junior prom with him last year as friends. He's cool. Why?"

"Trying to figure out who SN is," I say. Dri jumps up onto one of the lounge chairs to get a better view of the party. I try to pull her down. I don't want him, wherever he is, whoever he is, to see her scoping him out. Dri is many wonderful things, but subtle is not one of them.

"I'd say three-quarters of the guys at this party are texting right now," she reports. "Could be Caleb, though. He's a little weird like that."

"SN is not weird," I say.

"Right," Dri says. "Because anonymously texting someone all day every day is not weird at all."

SN: nice try. i'm good at hiding in plain sight. i rock the camouflage.

Me: Fine. Are you having fun?

SN: a little bored, which is why I'm texting you.

Me: You could just talk to me, you know, IN PERSON instead.

SN: one day. not tonight.

Me: We don't have parties like these back home. Like with a real band.

SN: you liked Oville?

Me: I thought they were amazing.

SN: eh. they used to be better.

Me: I think I may be drunk.

SN: me too.

Me: So let's meet. Come on. What's the worst that can happen? You don't even have to talk to me. . . .

SN: what are you implying?

Me: I don't know. I warned you I was drunk.

SN: the old "I was drunk" excuse.

Me: Not an excuse. An explanation.

SN: I love how you're always so precise with your words.

Me: I don't get this. What's the point?

SN: ?.

Me: Of all this talking. Are you embarrassed to be seen with me? Are you worried I won't like you? I don't get it.

SN: none of the above. I just like this. a lot. this IM'ing thing works. I'm too drunk to explain now.

Me: The old "I was drunk" excuse.

SN: I promise we will meet. soon.

Me: You keep saying that.

SN: you know what I think about sometimes?

Me: What?

SN: you know that piece of hair that always falls into your eyes—the not-quite-a-bang piece? I want to be able to tuck it behind your ear. I want to be able to do that. I want to meet you when I feel comfortable enough with you to do that.

Me: You are so weird.

SN: you are not the first person to say that.

Me: Am I the first to say that I really like that about you?

I look over at Caleb again, try to imagine SN's words coming out of that guy's mouth, try to picture him making as romantic a gesture as tucking my hair behind my ears. Him understanding that touching my hair requires a certain amount of intimacy. No, the image doesn't work. Instead, I picture Caleb as a future frat president, the type to yell at his pledge to chug a beer. SN's probably not Kilimanjaro gray T-shirt boy then. But who the hell is he?

"I'm drunk," I tell Dri and Agnes.

"You've already told us," Dri says. "Like a million times."

"Sorry. Apparently, I'm the type of drunk who likes to let other people know," I say.

"It's charming," Agnes says, in her typical dry way. "I'm a little drunk too. Though not as sloppy as you."

"I'm not sloppy," I say. I look down. Am I sloppy?

Everything seems to still be in place except my mind, which is rolling around in my head. I've gotten drunk before, though usually alone with Scarlett. I guess my tolerance is two Agnes Specials.

"You're both sloppy," Dri says. She throws her arms around our necks, which I'm grateful for because it helps me with my balance.

"Do you think it's possible to have a crush on two people at once?" I ask, which is one of those embarrassing questions I would never ask sober. Maybe I should never drink again.

"Totally. I'm usually into, like, five guys at a time," Agnes says. "I like to keep it varied. Optimize my chances."

"So who do you like? SN, obvi, but who else? Please, please don't say Liam."

I'm about to say it out loud, tell her *Ethan,* and finally get the entire scoop since I know Dri is not the type to withhold details: she'll tell me his life story, what he was like in sixth grade, whether he has a girlfriend, whether he's a d-bag. Maybe she'll even help angle us closer to him so I can say hello. So far, our only contact has been when he passed by me after the show—a "hey" that was neither rude nor friendly nor an invitation to talk more: the same closed-up can of nothing he seems to lob at everyone else. I thought we were getting past that. I guess I thought wrong.

Just as the word is about to come out of my mouth— "Ethan," which is a pretty word, don't you think?—Gem comes barreling toward me.

"You stay away from my boyfriend, you skank," she says, and gets right up into my face, my grill, which is an expression I've never once had an occasion to use until right now.

"Umm . . . ," I say. I wish I could go back in time and not drink those two drinks, because I'm having trouble understanding what's going on. Why is Gem yelling at me? I've grown accustomed to her passive-aggressive under-the-breath taunts, which I can usually pretend I don't hear. I can't do that with her yelling into my mouth. And skank? Really? "What?"

I want to wipe her breath off of my face, a slathering of onion and alcohol. I want be far away from here, maybe tucked in bed. California is exhausting.

"Stay. The. Hell. Away. From. Liam," Gem says, and then flicks her hair, like she's in some mean-girl movie, and struts away. I take it back. She's not a great actress. She lays it on too thick.

I look around to see if anyone saw, but it's just me, Dri, and Agnes in our own little circle in the vast backyard.

"Holy crap, did that just happen?" Agnes asks, and starts to giggle.

"It's not funny," I say, though I wish it were. "What the hell?"

"Gem's been all messed up since her dad got arrested last year. It was, like, all over the tabloids," Agnes says. "I mean, she wasn't that nice before, but since then she's gone full-on raging bitch. I hear he could go to jail."

"What did he get arrested for?" I ask, though I don't really care. I hate her. No Wood Valley sob story is going to get sympathy from me.

"Her dad solicited a prostitute," Dri says. "And there's some sort of tax fraud thing."

"Seriously?" I ask.

"Whatever," Agnes says.

"Just tell me one thing?" Dri asks, and I can hear the plea in her voice. "Before, were you just about to say you liked Liam?"

"No, of course not," I say, but I can't tell if she believes me.

Me: I'm DRUNKY.

Scarlett: Me too.

Me: Having fun?

Scarlett: A BLAST.

Me: Yeah, me too.

Even through my drunken haze, I realize I'm lying. My hands are shaking. My teeth are chattering. I want to go home. No, *home* doesn't really exist anymore. I lower my expectations. I want to go to bed.

I see Ethan only once more before we leave the party, on our way out the door. He is lying down on one of the lounge chairs, alone. I'm pretty sure he's sleeping. *Good,* I think. *He needs it.* It takes all of my willpower not to brush the hair from his forehead.

CHAPTER 19

Me: Three Things: (1) I have a headache. (2) The room is spinning. (3) I'm never drinking again.

SN: (1) I intend to waste most of my day playing Xbox, with occasional breaks to eat pizza, preferably with eggplant, which I get a lot of shit for, but whatever. sue me. I don't like pepperoni. never have, never will. (2) I was up early, so I've been listening to Flume all morning. (3) my mom is still sleeping, like she's the teenager in the house.

Me: You're American, right?

SN: yeah, why?

Me: PEPPERONI! Not liking pepperoni is like not liking apple pie.

SN: will that analogy be on the PSATs?

Me: So you ARE a junior?

SN: relax, Nancy Drew.

Me: I'm doing homework today. Calc is kicking my ass.

SN: and what a fine one it is.

Me: Shut up.

SN: was that objectifying? sorry.

Me: Have I mentioned lately that you're a weirdo?

SN: I seem to recall you saying something like that.

Me: Later I have to work. Do you have a job?

SN: nah. my parents won't let me. rather give me an allowance and have me focus on my schoolwork.

Me: How Wood Valley of them. I'm glad they're supporting your Xbox habit.

SN: I know we're all ridiculous to you, and I couldn't agree more. where do you work?

Me: I'm not sure I want to tell you.

SN: ?

Me: Too stalkerish.

SN: yesterday you were begging to meet me, now telling me where you work is too stalkerish?

Me: I wasn't begging.

SN: sorry. poor word choice. asking.

Me: Guess.

SN: where you work?

Me: Yeah.

SN: ok, but let me ask a few questions first. (1) do you like it? (2) do you come home dirty?

Me: (1) Actually, yeah, I like it a lot. (2) NO!

SN: coffee shop?

Me: Nope.

SN: The Gap.

Me: Are you making fun of me?

SN: no! why?

Me: Never mind.

SN: I got it. I forgot for a minute that you're a book nerd. Barnes and Noble. am I right??? I'm totally right.

Me: Close. Book Out Below! Up on Ventura. You should come visit.

SN: so fickle. now you want me to visit?

Me: Maybe I do. Maybe I don't.

• • •

Me: So . . .

Scarlett: If you must know . . .

Me: I MUST, I MUST.

Scarlett: My hymen is intact.

Me: Surely you could have told me in a less graphic fashion.

Scarlett: I know, but it wouldn't have been as much fun.

Me: I'm hungover.

Scarlett: Me too. And my face is all chafed from Adam's beard.
    I think he must have practiced a lot after smooching you.

Me: What makes you say that?

Scarlett: Dude, THAT BOY CAN KISS.

When I come downstairs, my dad is in the kitchen wearing an apron that says CHEF BITCH, which I assume belongs to Rachel but could just as easily belong to Theo. Music is playing in the background, something country, an overly sentimental ode to pickup trucks and short denim shorts. What Scarlett calls WPM: White People Music.

"Pancakes, sweetheart?" my dad asks, full of annoying morning cheer. He looks all wrong in this kitchen. He's never made pancakes. That was my mom's job. Syrup and flour congeal on the pristine marble countertops. Does he feel at home here, comfortable enough to man the stove and serve up pancakes barefoot? I feel awkward when I use the microwave. I don't want to leave crime-scene splatters on its insides, or any other evidence of my existence.

"Umm . . ." Will I be able to eat breakfast without throwing up? No choice. I've never once turned down a carb, and I don't need my dad getting suspicious about my drinking. "Sure," I say. What I don't say: *What's going on? Are we staying? Are you suddenly really happy or is this an act?* "You made breakfast? This may be a first."

"Gloria's day off."

"Right."

"Listen, we need to talk," he says. My stomach drops out, and vomit pushes its way up. Clearly, this whole kitchen act is a sad departure gift. My dad and Rachel are breaking up, and we are leaving. They are unraveling that which never should have been raveled in the first place. That's what this faux happy performance is about: a way to butter me up before the news. I put my head down on the cold counter. Screw it. Who cares if he knows I've been drinking? He's guilty of much bigger transgressions. In fact, he's lucky I've never had the energy to seriously rebel. I should win a Trouper of the Year award. Should have been given a little brave golden man statue or some sort of plaque to hang on my wall.

This breakfast must be a last hurrah before we have to hit the road. Makes sense that my dad would take advantage of his final chance to use a Viking range and fancy-ass pans and organic pressed coconut oil in a perfectly measured spray. I should run upstairs and wash my hands with that delicate, monogrammed soap that still has a price tag on it. Learn what a hundred dollars gets you in the soap world.

"Here, these will help settle your stomach." My dad places a stack of perfect circles on a plate and puts them in front of me. They smell surprising, not like the thing itself but like a representation of the thing. The fragrant-candle version of a pancake. "Just tell me you didn't drive last night."

"Of course not. Dri did," I say.

"Dri?"

"I have friends, Dad. Don't be so surprised. Did you think

that I wouldn't talk to anyone ever again?" I don't know why I'm being mean, but I can't help it. For once, my words are one step ahead of my mind, not the other way around.

"No, I just . . . I'm happy for you, that's all. I know it hasn't been easy."

I laugh—not a laugh, exactly, more like a nasty neigh. No, no it hasn't. Nothing has been easy for a long, long time. Even last night, my first attempt at fun since we moved, ended with a sociopathic blonde calling me a skank.

"I guess I deserve that," my dad says.

"So what now? Are we leaving?"

"What? No. Why would you say that?" he asks, and his surprise seems genuine. Did he not realize the entire city of Los Angeles heard his fight with Rachel? That the other night he basically admitted that this whole thing has been a huge mistake? Doesn't he know that I've spent the entire week psychologically readying myself for another departure?

"Your fight with her."

"It was just an argument, Jess. Not the end of the world."

"But she said—"

"I sometimes forget that you're just a teenager. But I remember that—how everything feels bigger or, I don't know, somehow just *more* when you're your age."

"Don't you of all people dare be condescending," I say. There's a sharpness to my tone, and of course, I'm a hypocrite, accusing him of talking down to me while acting like a stereotypical teenager. All snark and pouts.

But screw him.

Seriously.

Screw. Him.

My dad sighs, as if I am impossible, as if I'm the one who doesn't make sense.

"She said 'leave and don't come back.' I heard her."

"Stop saying 'she' and 'her.' Rachel. Her name is Rachel. And people say stupid things when they're angry."

"And people do stupid things when they're grieving, like get married and move across the country and not give a shit about their kid."

"Don't."

"Don't what?" I'm yelling now. I don't know when my control slipped. Because here it is. The anger delivered, whole and solid. Hot and unwieldy. Placental.

"Do you want to leave? Is that what you're saying?" he asks.

I think of SN, of Dri and Agnes, of Ethan with his electric-blue guitar and his dismissive "hey." No, I don't want to leave, but I don't want to feel like this either. Like an interloper in someone else's home. If I do throw up today, which is more likely than not at this point, I don't want to have to worry about soiling Rachel's bathroom. I don't want to feel in constant danger of eviction.

No, none of that is important. What do I really want? I want to punch my dad in the face—connect fist to nose, crush, crunch, make him bleed. Kick him hard and watch him bend over and squeal and scream the words "I'm sorry."

This feeling is new. This anger. I've always found a way around the pain, have never burrowed straight through like this.

My dad doesn't look delicate right now, not like the other

night, not like most of the last few years. Why have I been the one wearing kid gloves all this time?

"I'm not saying anything. Forget it, Dad. What did you want to talk about?" My fingers are pulled into actual fists. I can trust myself not to throw an actual punch, right?

"I just wanted to see how you're doing. How school is. Just checking in. I know I've been busy. And the other night, I didn't even ask about your day. I felt bad about that."

"Busy? I can count the number of conversations we've had since we've moved." The rage stays clean and pure and red, like last night's drinks. Does he have any idea what my life has been like? Funny that he checks in only when I've finally started to find my footing.

Too little, too late.

"I just. Wow. I didn't know—"

"Know what, Dad? That moving here has been hard for me? Are you serious right now?"

"Let's—"

"Let's what? Talk about this later? Sure, great idea." I push away the plate, resist the urge to throw it in my father's face, and storm out of the room.

"Trouble in paradise?" Theo asks, because of course he is coming down the stairs as I'm marching up, two at a time. I'm shaking with anger, vibrating with the pulse of it. My mouth tastes bitter, full of bile. I imagine switching targets, connecting my fist to Theo's jaw. Ruining his pretty, pretty face.

"Screw you," I say.

He shrugs, nonplussed.

"Rage is totally your color."

Later, at Book Out Below!, I sip herbal tea and play *Candy Crush* on my phone. Only two purchases so far, and one jerk who took a picture of a book to buy online. By late afternoon, just as evening seeps in and I start to feel bored and lonely, the bell dings: new customer. My head snaps up, full-on reflexive now, and I gasp in surprise.

Caleb.

Kilimanjaro gray-T-shirt boy. Who I saw texting at the party. No one from school, other than Liam, has ever walked into this store while I've been working, not even Dri, though she promises to visit. I told SN just this morning about this place. So it doesn't take great powers of deduction to conclude that this must be him before me, finally, in the flesh. My heart squeezes—so this is the person I've been spilling my guts to for the last two months—and I wait for the disappointment to hit. It doesn't.

Instead, I feel disoriented, the same thing that happens after I ask someone for directions and then forget to listen, realize that I'm still just as lost as before. It's hard to imagine SN's words coming out of this guy's mouth. He's attractive, yes—hot, even—but in a normal, run-of-the-mill way. Generic. A variant of the presumptive prom king type you find in any high school in America. No special sauce. What do I say? Do I introduce myself? Play dumb? Act like I assume this is all just a strange coincidence?

He is wearing the same gray T-shirt as last night and as the first day of school, when I literally applauded him for climbing a mountain. He must have felt bad for me then, must have seen that I needed some help since I couldn't even manage to find the right homeroom. Hopefully, somehow, he didn't notice the grass stuck to my ass.

Mind officially blown. Sploof.

Kilimanjaro gray T-shirt guy.

"Hey, is Liam here?" he asks, and smiles down at me, like he's in on the joke, though this doesn't feel particularly funny. Just uncomfortable. Is this why he hasn't wanted to meet until now? Knew it would feel this awkward and random?

"Um, no, sorry. He doesn't work today." *Jessie, this is SN. Up your game.*

"Oh, I think he has my phone," he says. "I lost it last night at the party. You go to Wood Valley too, right?"

"Yeah, I'm Jessie," I say, and reach out, too formally, I think a moment too late, to shake his hand. His fingers are long and dry, his shake a bit limp. A mismatch to his voice.

"Caleb," he says. "Nice to meet you."

"You too." I smile back, try to say with my eyes what I don't have the nerve to say with my mouth: *I know it's you.* This is a weird game we're playing, but I guess so is IM'ing anonymously.

"So how do you like it so far? School, I mean."

"I guess you could say I'm still adjusting."

"Yeah, cool, cool." Caleb turns to leave—is he as nervous as I am?—and I suddenly feel desperate to make him stay, to reestablish our connection. I feel like I've already screwed things up. All it took was thirty seconds face to face.

Should I ask him about Tanzania? That's where Kilimanjaro is, right?

"Um, would you want to have coffee sometime?" *Did I*

really just say that? Out loud? Take a deep breath. Slow your roll. "I mean, I just, I'm trying to meet new people, that's all."

He seems surprised, tilts his head to the side as if to get a better look. He's checking me out, and he's not subtle about it.

This whole thing is vaguely insulting.

No doubt we should stick to IM'ing.

"Sure. Yeah, why not? What's the worst that can happen?" he asks, with a mysterious grin, an obvious reference to the same question I asked him just last night. I'm about to answer, I have a million things to say, but it turns out he's just being rhetorical, because he has already walked out the door.

SN: how was work?

Me: It was nice of you to stop by.

SN: funny.

Me: not the word I'd use.

SN: ?

Me: ?

SN: okay, then. moving on. spent so much time with my Xbox today that I actually got bored. #neverthoughttheday wouldcome

Me: Sore hands?

SN: rising above obvious joke. aren't you proud of me?

So this is how we're going to play it. Pretend this after-noon never happened. Maybe this is for the best. Maybe SN/ Caleb has been right all along. Writing is better.

Real-life talking? Way overrated.

CHAPTER 20

"This is a long-ass poem," Ethan says. "And it's kind of annoying and complicated. I can't keep all the voices straight."

We're back at Starbucks, what I now think of as *our* Starbucks, which I would never admit to Ethan in a million years. I'm sipping the latte he bought for me after asking if I wanted the same as last week. He even remembered that I like it extra hot. He was so casual about it—ordered, slipped a credit card out of his wallet—I didn't even feel weird about not offering to pay. Next time I'll say something like "I got this one" or "This one is on me." Or maybe not.

"I agree. I mean, I write terrible poetry, but I don't know. I can't help but write in my own voice. I am who I am who I am. Whether I like it or not."

"A rose is a rose is a rose. Jessie is Jessie is Jessie."

"Don't tell me you've read Gertrude Stein?" I ask. My mom was a huge Stein fan, so when she got sick, that's what I read to her out loud. Mostly *The Autobiography of Alice B. Toklas*, but some of her poetry too. "Sacred Emily": a soothing nursery rhyme of a poem and, it turns out, where *rose is a rose is a rose* comes from. Not Shakespeare, which would have been my first guess.

Other things I learned then: Chemo blinds you. Steals your hair and blinds you. My mother couldn't even read at the end.

Rose is a rose is a rose.

"Not much. Just *Toklas*. Talk about writing in someone else's voice." How does he find the time to read everything? Had I not insisted on working on this project, no doubt he *would* have delivered me an A. Come to think of it, I may end up actually bringing our grade down.

"My mom was an English professor at our local college, and she always used to quote Gertrude Stein. Called her G.S., like they were friends or something. Actually, for her fortieth birthday, my dad and I got her a vintage edition of *The World Is Round*. It's this bizarre kids' book. So random that I just thought of that." I stare out the window to regain my equilibrium. I don't talk about my mom to anyone, not even to Scarlett. Certainly not to my dad. Talking about her is like acknowledging that she's gone, a jump into the unfathomable. Rendering true that which cannot be.

But we are talking about Gertrude Stein, which means we are already talking about my mom, and, I don't know, the words just came out.

Ethan looks at me and waits a beat. He's comfortable with silence, I realize. He's comfortable with everything.

Ethan is Ethan is Ethan.

"I just want to say I'm sorry about your mom. People talk around here. Anyhow, it fucking blows," he says. "I know that's a crazy understatement, but it fucking sucks that people have to die and there's nothing you can do about it. And so yeah, I just wanted to man up and say I'm sorry."

"Thanks," I say into my coffee cup, because I can't look at him. I am not brave enough to lift my eyes. I don't know what I'll see there: pity or empathy. But I'm going to add "brave" to my inner Ethan tally, and "honest," and "right," because it does fucking blow and he is the first person to actually say that to me. Everyone back at FDR mumbled "sorrys," probably because their parents told them they had to, and they were so obviously relieved when the words were out, the requisite box checked, that they could move on, even if I couldn't. Not that I blame them. Death makes everything awkward.

"Yeah, we don't have to talk about it, but I hate how when something like that happens, people just like to pretend it didn't because it's uncomfortable and scary and they don't know what to say. Not knowing the right thing to do is not an excuse for not doing anything. So," he says.

"So," I say. I do it. I bring my eyes to his. *"I will show you fear in a handful of dust."*

"And I'm not the only nerd who memorizes 'The Waste Land.' This first section is called 'The Burial of the Dead,' you know."

"I know." I smile, because I like Ethan and how he's not afraid of anything, except maybe sleeping. And a smile is, in some ways, the same thing as saying thank you.

"Of course you know," he says, smiling right back at me.

• • •

An hour later, we're still sitting here. This week's assignment is long done—one page on T. S. Eliot's repeated references to dirt—so now we're just hanging out, chatting. Maybe becoming actual friends, not just study partners.

"You never told me what you thought of Oville," Ethan says after he has refilled his cup for the third time. He takes his coffee black. No fuss. Pure, unadulterated caffeine.

"Seriously? You guys were amazing." If I were Gem or Crystal, I'd probably be smart and play it cool. Not fangirl all over him. But whatever. They indisputably rocked. "You're all really talented."

"I wish we could just play in my guesthouse, no shows at all, but apparently, it's not up to me. That's what we used to do before." He says it like the "before" should be capitalized. Before and After.

"Before what?"

"Nothing. I mean before Liam joined. He's all serious about launching a real music career, and I just want to play some music. Hang out." Ethan stirs his coffee with a stick, a mindless habit since there's nothing in there that needs mixing.

"Do you get stage fright?" I ask.

He pauses, as if I'm asking an important question that deserves a precise answer.

"Nah, not exactly. I just feel, I don't know, more alone when everyone is staring up at me. It's . . . isolating, I guess. And tiring."

"I thought most performers feel the opposite. That it's the only place they don't feel alone," I say. "Everyone wants to be the guy up onstage."

Ethan shrugs.

"When I go to concerts, and it's crowded and no one is bothering me, and it's like, just me and the music . . . *that's* when I don't feel alone. I guess I'm not much of a people person," he says.

"Really? Tell that to everyone at Wood Valley," I say.

"Huh?"

Does he not notice that every girl in school lusts after him? That people actually *line up* to talk to him?

"Come on, it's like you have a harem at lunchtime." Again, I say too much. Seriously, I need lessons on how to flirt.

"Nah. That has nothing to do with me. It's because of . . . Never mind. Long story."

I want to say something like *I have time,* but I see how he is, that things are pretty straightforward: When he wants to talk, he talks. When he doesn't, he doesn't. I don't know him well enough yet to push.

"Who writes your lyrics?" What I really want to know is who wrote "The Girl No One Knows," but I don't want to admit to knowing Oville's entire playlist. Dri sent me all of their songs, but I keep listening to that one on repeat, my tally now so high I'd die of embarrassment if anyone ever saw it. At the store, Liam only sang the chorus, which is simple and catchy and misleading because the rest of the song is something altogether different. Brooding, beautiful, desperate.

A poem, really. An elegy.

"Depends on the song. Me, usually. Some Liam. Oh, and this guy Caleb, who's not actually in the band but hangs around and pitches in." My head shoots up. Caleb? Did he write "The Girl No One Knows"? If so, then it all makes sense. SN is the type to write song lyrics, haunting, melancholy ones, but not the type to get up onstage and sing them out loud. In front of people.

"Caleb's the tall guy, right?"

"Yeah. You know him?"

"Not really. Sort of. Met him the other day at work."

"Yeah, he and Liam are tight." I guess Ethan knows I work at Liam's mom's store. I must have told him last week when I mentioned knowing Liam. Or did Liam mention it? Oh shit. Have they talked about me? My palms start to sweat: I picture Ethan and Liam laughing about how I made it seem like Liam and I are close friends.

Is that why Gem called me a skank? Does everyone think I'm obsessed with Liam? Does Liam? Does Ethan? Does Caleb?

"You think I'll ever figure this school out?" I ask Ethan. It's frustrating how everyone knows each other. My closest friend here is SN—or should I just call him Caleb?—and our relationship consists solely of text messages. I need to hire Dri to give me a full background on everyone so I can stop stepping in it.

"Nope," Ethan says. "I haven't, and I've been here since kindergarten. But you know what I did figure out?"

"What?"

"You don't have to."

"I don't?"

"Nope. Not even a little bit."

"Really?" I now stir my latte, which is finished, which means I'm stirring an empty cup. I need to keep my hands busy. The desire to touch Ethan's hair, even his hands, has become borderline uncontrollable. I want to bite his earlobe, which looks like it once housed an ill-advised earring. I want to ask him how he can run so hot and so cold, how right now he can be so reassuring, almost a real friend, and at the party, I wasn't worth enough of his time to stop and say more than that one syllable, that dismissive "hey."

"Yup. Who cares about all these assholes? A few of them are great people, the vast majority are not, and at the end of the day, you just have to be yourself. If they don't like you, screw 'em."

"Jessie is Jessie is Jessie."

"Right. Jessie is Jessie is Jessie."

Fine, I'll admit it: I'm sad when Ethan stops saying my name.

Home. Or, more accurately, the place I eat and sleep. Under the dome: chicken Marbella or marsala or something with an "M," spears of asparagus, a dollop of wild rice.

SN: your day? go.

Me: great, actually. yours?

SN: memorable.

I only saw Caleb once today. He was leaning against a locker in the hall at school, and when he saw me, he saluted me with his cell phone and then whispered something to the guy standing next to him, a senior who has the feltlike complexion of a Muppet. I assume his cell salute meant something like *Let's keep talking with our phones, not in person,* since there's been no attempt to make my suggestion of a date a reality. But thirty seconds later, my IM dinged.

SN: three things. (1) Hendrix was the most amazing guitarist who ever lived. even better than Jimmy Page. (2) sometimes when I listen to music, I actually feel lighter. (3) and sometimes when I play Xbox, I feel nothing.

Me: Which do you like better? Music or Xbox?

SN: ahh, that's a good question. no doubt my mom's medicine cabinet is like her Xbox, right? so I'm going to say music, because there's nothing scarier to me than becoming my mother.

SN: but truthfully?

SN: Xbox.

I think it's becoming clear Caleb and I will never actually chat over hot beverages, never say out loud that SN is Caleb and Caleb is SN, and maybe it's better that way. Maybe we've said too many scary things online already, and knowing what we've already shared, all that honesty, makes talking in person impossible.

Still, it's sad, because I'm starting to appreciate his particular brand of hotness. Sitting across from him wouldn't be distracting the way it is with Ethan. He's a blanker, simpler, well-balanced canvas. Like Rachel's white-on-white walls.

Me: Your day was memorable? Memorable=good? Or memorable=bad?

SN: good. what was under the dome tonight?

Me: Fancy-pants chicken. And you? Please tell me not Whole Foods sushi again? I'm starting to worry about you getting mercury poisoning.

SN: my mom cooked, actually, which, as you know, is weird. it was good, though. homemade mac 'n' cheese. my favorite when I was a kid. I guess still my favorite.

Me: That's sweet of her.

SN: yeah, it felt like an apology. like she knows she's been . . . absent.

Me: Did she seem, you know, clear?

SN: hard to tell, but yeah. i'm allowing myself to think so. at least for tonight.

Me: Good.

SN: then again, do you know what's the number one sign of mercury poisoning?

Me: What?

SN: optimism.

That night, I dream about Ethan and Caleb, both of them in my room and perched on my day bed, except they've switched T-shirts. Ethan wears gray, and Caleb wears Batman, and neither of them talks to me. Caleb plays with his phone, texting someone else—maybe me, but not the me in this room—and Ethan strums his guitar, lost in some complicated finger work, lost in the way that happens when he looks out the library window. I sit behind them, quiet, just watching and admiring the backs of their very different necks, trying not to be bothered by the fact that they don't even realize I'm right here.

CHAPTER 21

"What do you guys think about me getting a pink stripe? Like just slightly off center?" Dri asks, and runs her fingers through her unruly brown hair. We are sitting outside during our free period, our faces tilted up toward the sun like hungry cartoon flowers. I now have sunglasses—Dri and Agnes helped me pick out a knockoff pair—and I love them. They feel transformative, like I'm somehow a different person with large squares of plastic covering my face.

"Pink?" Agnes asks.

"Pink with an exclamation point instead of an 'i,' pink?" I ask.

"Maybe," Dri says. "Either. Both."

"No." Agnes says it straight out, no attempt to preserve the possibility. Pure veto, which is exactly what Scarlett did when I suggested getting my inner ear flab pierced. Well, after she told me to Google what that part of the body is actually called, because she never wanted to hear the words "my inner ear flab" together in a sentence again. Can't say I blamed her.

Turns out it's called your tragus, which sounds vaguely dirty. No one should have their *tragus* pierced.

"How about all pink?" Dri asks. "Dye my whole head."

"I don't know," I say. "I like your hair the way it is."

"Why? Why would you do that to yourself?" Agnes asks, though neither Dri nor I have the nerve to point out that Agnes's red hair is as artificial as Dri's would be if she were to dye hers pink. Then again, Agnes's red somehow works in a way that I don't think Dri's pink would. Not a fine line between red and pink when we are talking hair.

"I just want a change," she says.

"This is like the ukulele. You just want to be noticed," Agnes says, blunt but not unkind. "I get it."

"I feel . . . I don't know, sort of invisible these days. Like, you know, except for you guys, no one would notice if I didn't even go to this school," Dri says, and leans back so that she's lying down, staring up at the vast blue sky, so open there aren't even clouds to read. I consider telling her that SN told me to befriend her, that he obviously has noticed how cool and funny she is, but for some reason, I'm embarrassed. I want her to think our friendship was totally organic.

"Honestly, I'd kill to be invisible," I say. "Gem and Crystal won't leave me alone."

"Screw them," Agnes says. "They just wish they could be as cool as you."

"I am not cool. I am the opposite of cool," I say.

"You are cool. I mean, now that I know you, I realize you're actually something better than cool. But you somehow give off this badass, above-it-all vibe. And you're hot," Agnes says. "In Gem's world, no one else is allowed to be hot."

"Seriously? Who are you even talking about right now?" I ask.

"They're just jealous because Liam likes you. Honestly? I'm jealous because Liam likes you," Dri says.

"Liam doesn't like me," I say. "I just work at his mom's store."

"Whatever," Dri says.

"No, seriously, we're just coworkers. And for the record, I don't like him. Not in that way, at least." I hope Dri believes me. I need her to believe me.

"Then you're crazy," she says. "Because he's smokin'."

"Please do not get a pink stripe because of Liam Sandler," Agnes says. "He's not worth it."

I spot Ethan crossing the lawn, coffee in hand, heading to the parking lot, even though it's only noon. And just like every other time I've seen him like this, what I think of as *out in the wild,* I feel like I have managed to conjure him up, as if he has appeared only because I'm thinking about him. Which I was, since I pretty much think about him all the time. I can be talking pink hair or Liam Sandler, but what I'm really thinking is *Ethan is Ethan is Ethan.*

I wonder where he's going and whether he'll be back in time for English. I hope so. We don't talk to each other much in school, but I like knowing he's behind me, that I could turn around and smile if I had the nerve. Not that I've ever actually had the nerve.

Crap. He catches me watching him. I hope I'm far enough

away that he can't see the goofy grin. He throws me a fast peace sign before beeping his way into his car.

"Now, Ethan Marks, on the other hand," I say, finally confessing my crush to my friends. I've told Scarlett, of course, but she hasn't gone to school with him since kindergarten, so it didn't really count.

Should I have peace-signed Ethan back? No, I can't pull off a peace sign. It's a lot like "cool beans."

"Really? You like Ethan! We used to be friends back in junior high," Dri squeals, and sits up to grab my hands, all girlie enthusiasm. Or maybe she's just relieved that I don't want Liam. She cocks her head, reconsidering. "Though, let's be honest: he's not the most original choice. And—"

"And he's kind of damaged," Agnes says.

"And he's never dated anyone at school. Never. Ever," Dri says, and my heart sinks a little. Not that I thought I had a chance, but still. Now it feels like a technical impossibility.

"But he's totally a panty dropper," Agnes says. "No doubt about that."

SN: three things. (1) when I read your messages, I hear them in your voice. (2) if I were an animal, I'd be a lemur. okay, that's probably not true, but I felt like using the word "lemur" today. and before you say it . . . yes, I know I'm weird. (3) seriously? I'd like to be a chameleon. change my colors to match my environment.

Me: (1) I've watched *Footloose* (the remake, not the original) an embarrassing number of times. But it's so moving. A

LAW AGAINST DANCING. And they fight and win. Swoon. (2) I could be a better driver. The whole *turn left when the light turns red* thing here freaks me out. (3) Just so you know, I take back coffee.

SN: okay, no sugar for you.

Me: What?

SN: a joke. a *Seinfeld* reference.

Me: It's not funny.

SN: it's just coffee. relax.

Me: Fine.

SN: sorry, forgot how mad you get when I tell you to relax.

Me: I don't get mad.

SN: you're mad right now. I can hear it in your virtual voice.

Me: When you tell someone to relax, it suggests that you think they are overly uptight. I'm not being overly uptight.

SN: wow. that's putting a lot of pressure on my "relax." I just meant chill. or no biggie. you forget I'm from Cali. we say shit like that here.

Me: Namaste.

SN: ah, now you're getting the hang of it. now stop writing me and get to class. you're going to be late.

"Slut," Gem fake-sneezes as I make my way into English. SN is right, I'm late, and now everyone is here, laptops already open, watching me get serenaded with profanity and germs as I walk to my seat.

"Whore," she sneezes again, though not sure why she needs the elaborate cover-up. We can all hear her, even, I'm sure, Mrs. Pollack. "Fat ugly bitch."

Just pretend you're wearing Theo's noise-canceling headphones. That you don't see Crystal or Dri or even Theo watching. No, do not look up, do not see that Ethan is here too, back from wherever he went, his eyes following you, blazing with what looks like pity.

Nothing worse than pity.

Almost there. Just need to pass Gem. I can do this.

But I can't. Because next thing I know, my nose hits the desk with a loud crack, and I'm splayed on the floor: a belly flop on the linoleum. My head now an inch from Ethan's Converse.

"Are you okay?" he asks. I don't answer, because I don't know. I am on the ground, my face aches, so much worse than when Liam hit me with his guitar case, and the whole class is looking at me. Gem and Crystal are openly laughing—cackling like Disney witches—and I'm too afraid to stand up. I can't tell if my nose is bleeding, if right now I am lying in a pool of my own blood at Ethan's feet. I do know that my ass

196

is spread across the floor like a smear of butter, at an angle no one should ever be exposed to, especially someone like Ethan.

Thank God it hurts. It helps keep me from feeling the humiliation.

Gem stuck out her foot. Of course she did. I'm so stupid, I deserve to be here smelling the floor.

Ethan squats down, holds out his hand to help me up. I take a deep breath. The quicker I get up, the quicker this will all be over. I ignore Ethan's hand—I can think of nothing worse than wiping my blood on him, nothing worse than this being the very first time we touch—and so I steady myself with the reliable floor. Slowly make my way to sitting, then to standing, and like the *fatuglybitch* I am, I shift my bulk into my seat. Nothing graceful about it.

"Am I bleeding?" I whisper to Dri. She shakes her head, the shocked look on her face telling me that what just happened is as bad, as embarrassing as I imagine. No. Even worse.

"Do you need to go to the nurse?" Mrs. Pollack asks, almost in a whisper, as if she doesn't want to attract any extra attention to me.

"No," I say, even though I'd give anything for an ice pack and an Advil. I just can't imagine standing up again, walking past Gem and then down the hall. Hearing the laughter at my back as soon as the door to the classroom closes. *No thank you.*

"All right, then, back to *Crime and Punishment*," Mrs. Pollack says, and redirects the class. I feel Ethan behind me, though, and I can't turn, can't even utter a pathetic thank you, because I'm scared of what my face looks like, and I'm scared I'm going to cry.

So I keep my head down. As if by avoiding eye contact I

can render myself invisible. *Nothing to see here.* I think of SN wanting to be a chameleon, blending into the background. I somehow make it to the end of class, my eyes focused only on the desk in front of me. Someone has carved into the wood *Axel loves Fig Newtons.* Really, someone took the time to deface the desk to profess their love for a cookie. Unless, of course, there was a student here actually named Fig Newtons, which, considering the fact that we have three Hannibals, four Romeos, and two Apples, is totally possible. As soon as the bell rings, I grab my bag and run for the door. I don't even wait for Dri.

"Jessie, a word, please," Mrs. Pollack says just before I make my exit.

"Now?" I ask. I want to leave this room, get as far away from these people as I can, find someplace where I can be alone and cry, preferably with an ice pack on my nose. I try to focus on Axel and his love of Fig—I've written their whole tragic love story in my head—but instead, Gem's words play on repeat: *Whore. Slut. Fat ugly bitch.* Like song lyrics earworming my brain. They'd sound good set to Auto-Tune: *Whore. Slut. Fat ugly bitch.* Perhaps I should offer them to Oville.

"Yes. If you don't mind." I do mind. I mind very much, but I can't find the way to say so out loud. Mrs. Pollack motions toward a chair in the front of the room, and I sit and wait for the rest of the class to file out. Theo. Crystal. Gem. Dri. I notice Ethan hovering for a second—deciding whether to say something to me? to Mrs. Pollack?—but then he taps my chair with his book and leaves too, and now it's just me and her concerned face and all I want in the world is to get through the next five minutes without crying. *Please, God,* I beg, though my relationship with God is something I have not yet sorted out, *please let me get out of here without embarrassing myself any more than I already have.*

I can't stare at Axel's declaration of love here, so instead, I stare at a poster of Shakespeare, a man in a ruffled collar, with a quote underneath: *To be or not to be: that is the question.*

No, that's not really the question at all. Being seems to be the only thing not entirely up to us.

"I didn't do anything," I say, which I realize is not the point. She's not mad at me—I'm the obvious victim here—but I'm choosing anger over the tears. Anger is slightly less humiliating. Anger is more consistent with the vibe Agnes claims I give off: badass and above it all.

Mrs. Pollack pulls her desk chair out and straddles it backward. She too wants to seem cool and casual. Like she's a student, not a teacher.

"I just wanted to see how things were going. If there was anything you wanted to talk about," she says.

"Nope." I wipe my nose with the back of my hand. The tears are filling my eyes but have not yet betrayed me by falling. They wait on the verge. If I ever write a memoir, that's what I'll call it: *On the Verge.* "I tripped. It happens."

"Switching schools can be tough."

"I'm fine."

"And I hate to say it, but girls in particular can be really cruel at your age."

"I'm fine."

"I'm not sure what to do here. I mean, I can talk to Principal Hochman. We have a zero-tolerance policy toward bullying."

"I'm fine."

"But I have a feeling that just might make things worse for you. Gem's dad is a big donor here, and—"

"Seriously, I'm fine." She looks at me expectantly. What does she want from me?

Whore. Slut. Fat ugly bitch.

"Did you do something to cause her to say those things? I'm just trying to understand," she says, and leans on the pillow she has made with her arms. As if to say *We're just hanging, no problem.*

"Are you asking me if I did something to deserve Gem tripping me and calling me a whore, a slut, and a fat ugly bitch? Seriously? You are asking me that?" I forget that this woman is responsible for one-sixth of my GPA, that she can keep me from getting a college scholarship. I should play nice, but it turns out anger is not only preferable but easier. Comes naturally.

"I didn't mean . . . I'm sorry, I'm just trying to understand—" She looks hurt now, like she's the one who's about to cry. Like she's the one who just busted her face in front of the entire class.

"The answer is no. I have not touched a single guy in this school or actually pretty much ever, not that that would justify a fellow student calling me a whore or a slut. And as for the 'fat ugly bitch'? I presume that's subjective." If I weren't so upset, I'd take a moment to revel in the fact that I found the right words for once, that I said exactly what I wanted to say. But I don't feel like reveling. I feel like running away. "Do you need my BMI? I'm sure that can be arranged."

"No, you got it all wrong. I didn't mean—"

"Are we done here?" I ask. Screw it. It wasn't like my grades were going to be so stellar at Wood Valley anyway. I'm pretty sure that college scholarship thing was just a pipe dream. And at least one mystery has been solved: Gem can do or say whatever she wants because her dad pays off the administration. I guess that's what a little tax fraud buys you.

"I'm just trying to help," she says. "I don't want to make things worse—" But I don't hear the rest of Mrs. Pollack's sentence, because I've already run out the door.

CHAPTER 22

Head down. Thirty feet until I reach my car. *Jessie, you can do this.* Twenty feet. My hands are shaking, but I keep them in my pockets so no one can see. I keep walking. *No one is looking,* I tell myself. *No one can see you.* Fifteen feet. *Almost there.* I will get into my car, I will put the key in the ignition, I will drive and not stop until the gas light comes on. I will head east, find whatever major highway takes me to Chicago. I will show up at Scarlett's in time for her mom to serve me homemade kimchi.

"Hey. You okay?" I see his shoes before I see his face, the guitar strap across his chest, but that's because I don't want to look all the way up. Liam is the last person I want to see right now, except maybe his horrible girlfriend, but at least if I saw

Gem, I would find a way to draw blood. Scratch her with my nails. Break her surgically crafted, six-figure nose. Crack her porcelain veneers.

"Please. Just. Leave. Me. Alone." Tears are kind of like urine. There is only so long you can hold them in. My car is ten feet away. Ten short feet, and then I can drive and cry without anyone ever knowing. I look forward to crossing state lines.

I picture the sign: YOU ARE EXITING CALIFORNIA.

"Whoa, hold it. What's going on?" Liam asks, and grabs my shoulder to stop me from storming off. I shrug, but his grip is strong. "You need me to call someone or something?"

"No. You know what I need? For you and your girlfriend to leave me the hell alone." I am furious, maybe not at Liam, though that doesn't seem to be relevant right now. Gem and Crystal's attacks used to be mostly subtle and stupid: my clothes or my laptop tattoos. Whatever. Now, after I talked to Liam for two minutes at a party, the bullying has become something altogether different. Sorry, but his chitchat really isn't all that exciting. Definitely not worth this.

For a second, I play that game that sometimes soothes me: *What would I be doing right now if I were in Chicago and we had never moved?* I'd be at a newspaper meeting, or maybe yearbook, cropping pictures and picking fonts. I wouldn't be happy, no. But I wouldn't feel like this.

"What are you talking about?" Liam looks confused. I wonder if he is not so bright. According to Dri, he and Gem have been dating for six months, which is five months and twenty-nine days longer than he should have needed to realize that his girlfriend is a royal bitch.

Liam swings Earl off, rests him on the ground next to a

203

car. A Tesla. Seriously, some kid at Wood Valley drives a freaking Tesla. Who the hell are these people?

"Forget it. Please just leave me alone. You talking to me? The opposite of helping," I say.

"I don't understand."

"You want to know why I'm upset? Just go ask Gem," I say, and finally, finally close those last few steps to my car.

"Wait," he says. "Will you be, you know, working this afternoon?"

Of course I'm not driving or flying to Chicago today. There will be no signs, literal or otherwise. Escaping is mere fantasy. I have to save up first, since I barely have enough cash to fill my gas tank.

My body deflates—there will be no running, no hiding.

This, right here, this is my life.

This.

"Yeah, I'll be there." I get into my car, reverse out of my spot so fast I wonder if I've left skid marks.

I wait until school is far in my rearview mirror before I start weeping.

SN: watched *Footloose* yesterday. both versions. in your honor.

Me: and?

SN: they don't make sense. you can't have a local ordinance against dancing. that's a restriction of our constitutional freedom of expression. not to mention the whole church/state thing.

Me: Groan.

SN: and even if you suspend disbelief on that MAJOR plot point . . . well . . .

Me: WHAT?!?!

SN: they just aren't very good movies.

Me: Tell me how you really feel.

SN: but still, somehow I liked the idea of you liking them. does that make sense?

Me: Not at all, but I'll take it. I'm having a shitty day. Considering hightailing it back to Chicago.

SN: NO!

Me: Ha. Love when your shift key comes out. And your day?

SN: my mom hasn't left the couch once. brought her lunch. she didn't eat it. so far gone she didn't even look up at me.

Me: I'm so sorry. I wish I could help. What about your dad?

SN: he's talking about sending her to rehab, but honestly, drugs aren't really the problem. I mean, they are, but they're more a symptom of the problem.

Me: What do you mean?

SN: she lost a kid. you don't just bounce back from that.

Me: But she still has you.

SN: why was your day so bad?

Me: Nothing important. Just one of those days.

SN: don't leave LA. please. you just can't. promise?

I pause. What does a promise to Caleb mean? We've glided past his rejection of my coffee offer, have just dug in deeper, as if it never happened. Still, I'd be lying if I didn't admit that his complete unwillingness to hang out with me in real life doesn't hurt.

Again today he didn't say hello to me in the hallway. Just another phone salute.

I tell myself it's because he's scared of ruining our never-ending conversation, but I tell myself a lot of things I don't actually believe.

So I lie.

Me: Promise.

When I get to work, Liam's mom is behind the counter. Pure relief that I don't have to face Liam. Instead of saying hello, she hands me a box of books, asks me to shelve them.

"Sure thing," I say, looking through the pile. A lot of financial guides. *Overnight Millionaire. Beat the Market. Money Now.* I head over to the shelf that Liam's mom has labeled GET RICH QUICK! and begin to sort the books alphabetically by author. For a second, I think about picking one up for my dad, but then I remember that (1) we are no longer on speaking terms, and (2) my dad could actually write one of these books, though it would be a bit short: *Marry Up.*

"I like your can-do spirit," Liam's mom says, since I shelve fast. Anything to keep busy. She smiles Liam's smile at me. I've worked here for weeks now and I can't remember her name. I just think of her as Liam's mom, or sometimes, I guess, Mrs. Sandler. I bet if I ran into her somewhere else, un-bookstore-related, I wouldn't recognize her. She looks a lot like the moms back home: no-nonsense hair, everything maximized for efficiency, not necessarily attractiveness. Like a real mom, not an aging actress.

I try to think about Caleb's smile, but I'm not sure I've actually seen it. Which makes sense. SN is not exactly the smiley type. I can easily picture Ethan's smile, though: how it unfolds across his face, from left to right, like a perfect sentence.

Clearly, I need to stop this Ethan obsession. Not healthy.

"You okay? You look a little . . . smeared," Mrs. Sandler says, handing me a tissue. "You want to talk about it?"

Damn it. Forgot that I experimented with mascara this morning. Despite my protests that makeup and I are not friends, Agnes had promised that waving a wand against my eyelashes would change my life. Now it's just unclear what's smudged mascara and what's bruising.

"Not really." I wonder if Mrs. Sandler likes her son's girlfriend, if she has ever met Gem. Does Liam have to keep his bedroom door open when she's over? Somehow, I doubt it. Those are quaint Midwestern rules; they don't apply in LA, where the kids openly smoke pot and drive fresh-from-the-dealership cars and have parents who will donate money to get them out of trouble. Liam's mom probably buys him condoms, jokes over take-out sushi about not wanting him to make any Little Liams.

I think of Caleb's mom, prone on the couch, so out of it she can't be bothered to eat lunch. What did he bring her? I wonder what his mom looks like, if she too is tall and handsome. If she too prefers to wear gray.

"Better?" I ask after I wipe my face, and I turn to face Mrs. Sandler. The Kleenex is black, probably a little salty now too.

"Much. You're a really beautiful girl. Inside and out. Do you know that?"

"Um, thanks?" I say, or ask. How strange, I think, to be called both ugly and beautiful, two words I rarely hear, in the same day. The former because most people are neither that mean nor that truthful, the latter because it has never applied to me. Agnes called me hot today too—another word never before used to describe me—though I think of hot as altogether different from beautiful. Hot seems to be about guys liking you. Beautiful is about liking how you look.

Of course, Liam's mom is old enough to think all sixteen-year-old girls are beautiful. Gem, on the other hand, sees me through clearer eyes.

"You can take the afternoon off if you need to," Liam's mom says, and her kindness almost makes me ache. Reminds me that when I go home, it will be to Rachel's house. My mom will not be there to nurse me back from this. There is no longer a person in the world who is interested in everything I have to say just by virtue of the fact that it comes out of my mouth. Scar tries, but it's not the same.

My mom will not make me a cup of cocoa with mini marshmallows, and we won't share a plate of Chips Ahoy, more than a dozen between us, an indulgence reserved for bad days. My mom wasn't strict about what counted when it came to me: a B on a math test I thought I had aced or losing my favorite charm bracelet. When she needed the boost, though, our ritual was reserved for only the very worst occasions: a cancer diagnosis, or later, a T-cell count being low. The word "spread" being used by a medical professional after looking at a black-and-white photo of her insides.

Eventually, I made the cocoa and drank both of ours. Ate all the cookies.

"Thanks, but I honestly could use the cash." I picture Scarlett's parents' basement. Not home, not even close, but closer than what I have now. A big L-shaped couch and an oversized TV from last century, as thick as it is tall. The slightest hint of mold in the air, almost but never quite covered up by the smell of fresh laundry. It wouldn't be so bad. School would be familiar and easy after Wood Valley. I'd have Scarlett back, maybe even my old job at the Smoothie King. My dad would barely notice I'm gone. He might even be relieved not to have to worry about me. I could do it. I really could.

Me: Your parents' basement couch available, maybe next term?

Scarlett: For reals?

209

Me: For reals.

Scarlett: ABSOFREAKINGLUTELY. Though you might need to wipe it down first.

Me: Why?

Scarlett: Let's just say it's where Adam and I like to, um, play.

"So is all okay? Are you going somewhere?" Liam's mom asks, breaking my intense bout of texting. Clearly, I should put my phone away and finish shelving. Today is not the day to get fired.

"Sorry?" I ask. She points behind me, and it's only then, when I follow her finger, that I notice I've subconsciously migrated over to the travel section.

CHAPTER 23

Dad: Can we talk tonight, honey?

I pause. Since our pancake fight eight days ago, I have successfully avoided my dad. Not so much as passed him in the halls of Rachel's house. This is his first overture toward peace, but screw that. Why should I always operate on his timetable? Be available when it's suddenly convenient for him? Be the good daughter who makes things easy and simple? Be the one who plays along, tries to make him feel better about his bad choices? What about when I need him? Where is he then?

I quit.

He married Rachel. Let that be her job now.
I have nothing to say to him.

Me: Sorry, working late.

Dad: I miss you.

No, I have nothing to say at all.

CHAPTER 24

And so here it is: Wood Valley Giving Day. I take SN at his word and wear my Vans, mostly because I don't have anything resembling work shoes and it's too hot for my winter boots, which are comfy and ugly as hell and which would most certainly make Gem weep with joy at how easily I make myself a target. I wear my mom's old University of Illinois T-shirt, the one that's been laundered so many times the writing is fading, and an old pair of ripped jeans and pull my hair back into a ponytail. Not at all chic, but I figure a day devoted to physical labor/community service does not require chic, even at Wood Valley. I pat some concealer on the bridge of my nose, cover up the bruising. Lesson learned: no mascara.

School is closed today; instead of going to our normal

classes, we're expected to report for work at the Habitat for Humanity site. For once, Theo wanted to drive in together, since he was worried about getting lost and carjacked, though the neighborhood looks not too different from where I grew up. But apparently, this place is in desperate need of two hundred rich kids who have never before touched a power tool.

We are supposed to erect the frame of a house.

Someone has not thought this through.

Gem is here. Because she is everywhere, she and Crystal, and there is nothing I can do about their omnipresence. She wears a tank top with huge armholes thrown over a sequined sports bra, which is one of those things that probably shouldn't exist but for which the one percent are willing to pay large sums of money nonetheless. Her shirt bears the words, I kid you not, THUG LIFE.

And although this place is pretty big—a whole house will be built on this plot of land—Gem is for some reason drawn to that which she hates, and she finds me. Walks right by, so close that I shouldn't be surprised when I feel her shoulder jam into mine. And yet, I am. The pain is sharp and perverse, and I imagine it hurt her just as much as it hurt me.

Maybe more, since she's bony.

"Excuse me," she says, all righteous indignation. Theo and I have just arrived, so I haven't even had a chance to find my friends, to at least surround myself by my wholly ineffective girl team. Not that Dri and Agnes could do anything, necessarily, but still.

What does Gem want from me? A scene? A punch? Tears? Or am I giving her exactly what she's asking for when I stand here and look at her, slack-jawed? No words come, not even the easy ones she likes to slug at me.

"Really?" Theo says, and at first I think he's talking to me, and I feel so alone that I may actually cry, right here, right now. Finally give the people what they want. "Touch Jessie again, and I swear to God, I will ruin you."

Theo is talking to Gem, actually pointing his finger in her face. He looks menacing in his own version of a community service day outfit: lumberjack flannel shirt, designer jeans, spotless, intentionally untied Timberlands. She just stares at him, and I can see her gum sitting stupidly in her mouth.

"Blink once so I know you understand what I'm saying," he says.

"Whatever," Gem says, just as Liam comes over to join us, all cheerful and oblivious, blocking her exit.

"Hey, guys. Happy Wood Valley Giving Day." Liam smiles at us, at me, as if yesterday never happened. And like this is all fun, spending the morning outside among "friends." He already has a hammer in his hand, ready to build. I can almost hear his mom praising his "can-do" attitude. Onstage, he seems like a rock star. Right now, he's more like a Boy Scout with a sprinkling of whiteheads on his chin. I'm not a particular fan of either look, but where's Dri? She'd lap this up.

"Liam, keep your girl on her leash, okay?" Theo says, and walks away, his job done, I guess, and though I appreciate his support, I'm mortified. And left standing here, like an idiot.

"What's he talking about?" Liam asks Gem, but then I notice he's actually looking at me.

"Nothing," I answer, and then spot Caleb on the other side of the lawn, staring into his phone. Screw it. My first instinct was to text SN—he always cheers me up—but I might as well just go talk to him. I'm too beaten down for this anonymity nonsense. It also occurs to me that Caleb may be the only person here who actually knows what he's doing. He built a school, after all. "Later, Liam."

I cross the lawn, vaguely hear Gem and Liam begin to argue.

"Hey there," I say, once I'm in front of Caleb. Instead of his usual uniform, he's sporting a USC sweatshirt and jeans with paint splatters, a baseball cap pulled low, as if he wants to downplay his good looks. Still a Ken doll, just the construction version. "Always on your phone." I smile, the closest I get to flirting, which is its own form of double-talking, I guess. I hope he can't see my bruises.

"Yeah," he says. "Thank God Liam found it at the party. Not sure how I would have lived without it."

"Phew," I say, and exaggeratedly wipe my hand against my brow. I look like a moron.

"About that coffee—" he says.

"Like I said, we don't have to. I just—" I want to say: *I like talking to you every day. I look forward to your three things. I think about you. A lot. Let's make this real.*

But of course, I don't. For whatever reason, he wants to keep up the virtual divide.

"No, I'd really like to. It'll be fun to show a newbie the ropes. Maybe after school on Thursday?"

"Sure," I say.

"Cool," he says, and salutes me with his phone again, that weird *let's IM later* signal. I feel bad about his brush-off—he obviously doesn't want me to stay and chat—but a minute later, my phone buzzes.

SN: saving the world, one nail at a time.

Me: I will sleep well tonight knowing I did my good deed for
   the year.

SN: your sarcasm is endearing.

Me: Is it really?

SN: yes, yes it is.

Dri hugs me as if we didn't just see each other less than twenty-four hours ago, and as if she didn't text me ten times last night to make sure I was okay. Clearly, she feels bad about not helping me yesterday, but what could she have done? I'm the one who let myself be tripped.

"I *love* WVGD. I'd take this over classes any day," she says, and squints up at Liam on a ladder, his shirt now off, advertising an impressive almost-but-not-quite six-pack and a splattering of freckles. "Not a bad view."

"I know. She's one-note," Agnes says, with an apologetic look. "Sorry to hear about all the Gem drama yesterday. You want me to kick her ass?"

"Would be fun to watch, but no thanks." I think about how many people have offered an ass kicking on my behalf since I moved here, and I feel grateful. Although I wish I didn't need defending, it's nice knowing there are people who have my back. "Theo was actually my knight in shining armor today."

"Seriously? Theo?" Dri asks.

"Yup. I'm about as shocked as you are."

"Look at that. Family comes first," Agnes says.

"Maybe it does," I say, looking over at Theo, who has found Ashby—her hair is no longer pink, but a shocking white—and they're laughing on the fringes of the job site totally unconcerned about participating in today's events. In fact, I'm pretty sure he's rolling a big, fat joint.

Lunch is a full buffet, set up in aluminum trays over fire burners. None of that bag-lunch nonsense. It almost looks like Gloria was here, perhaps Rachel's donation to WVGD. But no, it turns out it's Gem's dad who is responsible. There's even a card on the table saying *Thank you to the Carter family for this organic feast!*

Shit. I wonder if that means I can't eat.

"Whatever. Don't let her stop you," Ethan says, and I jump as much from the fact that I didn't realize he was behind me as from the fact that he has read my mind.

"I know it's stupid, but—"

"Nah. Not stupid, but if it's as good as last year, I promise you won't want to miss it. Even out of pride."

"It's not pride. It's not wanting to give her another reason to come near me."

"Seriously? I thought you were tougher than that," Ethan says, and he takes two plates and piles them with food. Hands one to me.

"What made you think that?" I ask. He shrugs, motions for me to follow him, and so of course I do. I've noticed that

Ethan has the ability to find a space and make it his own, and he's even managed to do that here, though we are only spending a single day on this construction site. He sits on the ground behind the half wall of the future kitchen and under the shade of an enormous grapefruit tree. Away from the rest of our class, and though not quite out of view, in a direction no one would think to look.

"So listen. Sorry about yesterday," Ethan says.

"Why? You didn't do anything," I say, and follow his lead and start eating. He's right: the food is delicious. Cheeseburgers, though the cheese is neither yellow nor processed and probably has a French name I can't pronounce and the burger resembles a burger only in form. Kobe beef, according to the tiny flag stuck in its center, as if this designation is one small step for man, one giant leap for mankind.

Thug life, my ass.

It's Gem's world, I think not for the first time. *The rest of us just get to live in it.*

"Exactly. I sit there and listen to those girls say stupid crap and I just pretend I can't hear them because it's all so dumb, it doesn't seem worth it. But I don't know. I should have said something. And I wish I had seen her foot."

"It's not your job to protect me," I say, and reflexively reach up and press the bruise.

"Still. I should have. Does it hurt?" he asks, and his hand goes out as if to touch my face, and then he thinks better of it, brings it back to his side.

"Yeah, a little," I admit.

"You deserve . . . I don't know . . ." Ethan shrugs, and for a moment, I think he may be blushing. I hear Agnes and Dri in my head: *He's damaged. He's never ever dated anyone at Wood Valley.* "Not that . . ."

"You know what I deserve? An A in English," I say, and Gem can suck it, because Ethan and I toast with our gourmet cheeseburgers.

"Thank you," I tell Theo later, on the ride home, as we glide past little houses and minimalls with signs written in Korean and car washes and a vast array of fast-food franchises. A million non-Kobe hamburgers to choose from.

"It was nothing."

"Well, I appreciate it. You didn't have to." I pretend to be deep in concentration as I make a tricky left turn, but really I feel shy. This thank you feels somewhat like an I'm sorry, though I'm not sure why. Recently, my existence feels like everyone else's burden.

"Gem once called me a faggot," he says, so low that at first I'm not sure I heard correctly.

"Seriously?"

"Yup. I mean, it was a million years ago, and it was actually the first time I had ever even heard the word. So I went home and asked my dad. I actually said to him, like, 'Daddy, what's a faggot?'" Theo looks out the window, his hand up against the glass, like a child trapped on a long road trip, desperate for human connection from the other passengers on the road.

There's nothing lonelier than a hand on glass. Maybe because it's so rarely reciprocated.

"What did your dad say?" I'm curious about Theo's father, whether Rachel has some sort of type. I picture him as bigger than my dad and more handsome, dressed in shirts with little polo players and pressed-by-Gloria khakis. There aren't pictures of him around, which would be weird, but then I realize there aren't very many pictures at all. Like Theo has arrived into almost-adulthood in this current form and shape, nothing to prove he was once a dimply baby.

The walls of my old house were covered with pictures of my family. Each of my school photos were framed and mounted in chronological order, even the ones where I was caught with my eyes closed or with a messy ponytail or in that horrible awkward phase when I had both braces and baby fat. My own personal time line leading upstairs.

Who knows? Maybe Rachel thinks family photos, like color, clash with her decor.

"My dad was great about it, actually. Said it's not a nice word, that there are better words for boys who like boys. And he said that it would be okay if one day I decided I liked boys too, and it would be okay if I didn't. That he loved me no matter what—" Theo's voice cracks. I don't look over, keep my eyes on the road. Wait for him. "I was really lucky. I mean, I never even had to really come out to my parents. They always knew, and it was always okay. Or not even okay, better than that. Not something that had to be evaluated at all. It just was. Like having brown hair."

"Your dad sounds like he was really cool."

Theo nods.

"Have you ever wished it was the other way around?" he asks me.

"What do you mean?"

"I mean that it was your dad instead of your mom?"

"Honestly, all the time."

"It would like, literally break my mom's heart if she heard me say that, but he got me, you know? He understood. Just everything."

"My dad knows I would switch if I could, I think. Maybe that's why he never wants to hang out with me anymore. Because he sees it on my face." Even as I'm talking, I realize this is not quite true. I just think he finds Rachel more interesting.

My mom got sick right around the time when I was supposed to stop wanting to hang out with my parents—when the pull was supposed to turn to pushing—and yet that never happened. I didn't just love my mom, I liked her. And though she was only genetically obligated to love me, I'm pretty sure she liked me too.

"Maybe you remind him of your mom, and he's trying to move on," Theo says, which is sweet, him defending my dad.

"Maybe," I say, even though I don't think that's quite true either. My mom and I looked nothing alike, were nothing alike. She was brave and big-mouthed, more like Scarlett than like me. And she used to joke that she wouldn't have believed I was hers—we were physical opposites in all ways—if she hadn't seen me come out herself.

I don't remind my dad of my mom, I know that, but for the first time I wonder if he wouldn't switch us too—me for my mother—given the chance.

"You and Ethan are friends, right?" Theo asks, seemingly apropos of nothing, and yet I'm happy for the change of topic. I don't want to think about my parents. About how little control we have over our own lives.

"Yeah, I guess. Sort of. I don't know," I say.

"I saw you eating lunch together."

"We're partners in English. The 'Waste Land' thingy."

"Right. It's just that—and not to get all big brother on you—"

"I'm pretty sure I'm older," I say.

"Whatever. Just be careful with him. I'm not trying to throw shade or anything, but I get the sense that he's . . . trouble."

"In a Taylor Swift way? Or like, for real?" "Damaged" was the word Dri used, which makes him sound like a defective iPhone.

"I don't know. It could just be rumors. But I think he could be into some heavy shit. Like his brother."

"What do you mean? Like drugs?" Ethan's brother must be older and out of the house. He's never mentioned him. Funny how having no brothers or sisters myself, and no aunts and uncles (both of my parents were only children), I always forget about other people's. It just seems so unnatural to me, the idea of a family being more than three, shaped in a way that is not a triangle, though come to think of it, mine is now 2-D: a line.

"Yep."

"I don't think Ethan's on drugs." Of course, I have no basis for defending him. I don't know what he does or even where he goes. Three times this week alone, I've seen him leaving campus before lunch, coming back just in time for English. He arrives dazed and withdrawn, but then again, he always seems dazed and withdrawn. And onstage, he looked altogether un-familiar, like someone who could easily spend his days and nights shooting up.

"I hope you're right. He always looks pretty rough, though, and his family is just so screwed up. You have no idea."

"I'm so tired of the Wood Valley learning curve," I say, wondering how different it would be—how different *I* would be—if I'd grown up here with these people, had known their families and histories and awkward phases as well as I know my own. It's so inefficient playing catch-up.

"I'm just saying be careful, that's all," Theo says.

I think of Ethan's eyes—the pockets of shiny purple underneath, the swelling of his lids, the bright blue center—and I wonder if I'm capable of being careful. Because I think of those eyes, open and looking at me, closed and asleep at Gem's party; I think of his hands fixing me a plate, almost touching my banged-up face, and all I can think about is how much I want to kiss them: his eyes, his hands too.

All of him.

His damaged parts.

All of him.

CHAPTER 25

Me: French fries or potato chips?

SN: easy. ff any day of the week. ketchup or salsa?

Me: Ketchup. Harry Potter: the movies or the books?

SN: you're not gonna like my answer . . . but honestly? the movies.

Me: Seriously?

SN: I know, I know. you're never supposed to admit to liking the movie better than the book, but come on. two words: Emma Watson. Starbucks or Coffee Bean?

Me: Starbucks.

SN: me too.

Me: *Star Wars* or *Star Trek*?

SN: NEITHER.

Me: ☺ me too.

When I come home to find Rachel in my room, I remember that this is not my room at all. This is Rachel's guest room, and my sleeping here confirms what I already know: I am merely an interloper. I glance around, wondering if I left my laptop open. I don't need her to see my IMs with SN, or, God forbid, my Google history, which has way too many questions that begin with "Is it normal to . . ." Phew, my cover is closed, tattoos visible even from the door. No, nothing for her to see here. Bras and thongs away in the drawers, the dirty ones in the wicker box Gloria has considerately provided. My tampons too are hidden. Even my toothbrush is tucked into the bathroom cabinet, banished, along with all of my makeup, so that Rachel's counters remain empty except for her self-congratulatory soaps.

"Oh, hey," she says, pretending she wasn't just looking at the only thing I have on display: the photo of my mom and me. "I was waiting for you."

"Okay," I say, cool but not impolite. I am mad at my dad, which by extension may now include Rachel, but I don't know how these stepparent things work. My parents were usually a single unit, had very little patience for me playing one off the other. Usually, if I was mad at one, I was mad at both. But Rachel is still a stranger. Her vows to my father have done little to change that.

"Your dad says you're not talking to him," she says, and sits down on my bed, or her bed, or whatever. She is sitting where I sleep, and I would prefer she didn't.

"I'm not sure that's any of your business," I say, and then instantly regret it. Recent circumstances with my dad notwithstanding, I don't do confrontation. When someone bumps into me in the hallway, my reflex is to say sorry.

But maybe I'm not sorry. Who is she to get involved in this? I didn't marry her.

"You're right. That's between your dad and you. I just wanted to give you this. Well, we wanted to give it to you, but your dad thought since it was my idea, I should be the one . . . Just here." Rachel hands me a folded piece of paper.

"What is it?" I ask, wondering if it's an eviction letter or something. A quick glance makes clear it's not a check. Damn. That could have been useful.

"Open it," she says, and so I do. A flight itinerary: LAX to ORD for next weekend. Round trip.

"I don't understand."

"We thought you might want to go home for a visit. See Scarlett, hang out with your old friends for a few days. I heard you were homesick," she says, and she picks up the photo, a conscious decision to look at my mom and me and to let me know she's looking. She examines our details: how I held on to my mom's leg, like an anchor. Or maybe Rachel is not looking at me at all but is trying to get a sense of my mother, of her husband's first wife. I want her to put it down—I don't like how her fingers are leaving tiny smudges.

"Who said that I was homesick?" I ask, which is a stupid question. Of course I'm homesick, the longing sometimes so overwhelming that I've even marveled at how accurate the word is, how the feeling comes over me like the stomach flu. Violent, unforgiving. No cure, just waiting for it to relent.

"Scarlett's parents called your dad," Rachel says, and finally, finally puts down my photo. It takes all my willpower not to move it so it's facing the bed, not the door. To wipe the glass clean with some Windex. Erase her fingerprints. Reclaim it as mine. "But how could you not be? This has been a huge adjustment. For all of us."

Is that regret flickering across her face? Does she wish she never married my father, that there was an easy way to undo their joint mistake?

"Wait, what?" Scarlett's parents called my dad? Did they tell him about my plans for their basement? What did Scarlett tell them? I'm not sure if I should be angry or thrilled, because right now, I have in my hand a plane ticket, an actual plane ticket that will take me from here to home, to Scarlett and to a life that's familiar, in under six hours door to door. We didn't fly out here when we moved. Instead, Dad and I caravanned our two cars through too many states. The world flat and devoid of life: miles upon miles of nothing but dust. The occasional stop at McDonald's to eat and pee, a gas station to refill, a cheap motel to sleep. My mind as blank and empty as the roads. As numb as SN feels playing Xbox.

We barely talked, my dad and I, on the trip. He might

have tried, I don't know. Only once did Rachel come up, over lunch at an Arby's, as if he were answering a question I hadn't even asked.

"Rachel's an extraordinary woman. You'll see. Don't worry, you'll see," he said, though I hadn't said I was worried. I hadn't said anything at all.

"Apparently, Scarlett's mom said she was concerned about you. And frankly, so am I," Rachel says now. "Go. Enjoy. And then come back to us refreshed. Your dad has . . . well, he saved my life. He's totally real and normal and understands what I've been through, and I couldn't be more grateful for that. We're so different, but together we're stronger. Whole. But I don't want you to think that I don't realize that this—all of this—has come at a cost to you."

She's matter-of-fact. Her voice a normal decibel for once.

"Everyone in this house understands how hard it can be to start over," she says.

I look at my ticket. I leave Friday morning, get back Sunday night.

"What about school?"

"Theo will email you notes and stuff, and we'll let your teachers know it's an excused absence. You deserve this." Rachel pats the bed next to her, invites me to sit. I've been pacing, I realize now, midstep, on my second lap around the room.

I sit, stare at the ticket. Coffee with SN/Caleb on Thursday, his mask unveiled, I hope, and then I'm off. I'll miss my weekly "Waste Land" meeting with Ethan, but he'll understand. Scarlett and I will watch bad television and pop microwave popcorn and eat real pizza, not this whole-wheat-crust crap they have in California. I will talk and she will listen, and there will be no need to explain everything or have anything explained; we've known each other too long for all of that. I even want to drink that green tea her mom always brews, the one I used to think tasted like pee but that now makes me think of home.

"Thank you," I say, and force myself to look Rachel in the eye. My dad didn't do this, I realize. Big gestures are not his style, or at least, they weren't before he married Rachel. And a plane ticket was never something that could be so casually purchased. "I . . ."

My eyes water, and I stare straight ahead to get the tears under control. Not here, not now. The tears only seem to come when they are least wanted, almost never in the quiet depths of night, when the emptiness is so real, it feels like a phantom limb. When tears would actually feel something like relief.

"No problem," Rachel says, and stands up. "But just so you know, there is one condition."

I wait for it. What could she possibly want from me? Rent money? For me to make up with my dad?

"You have to come back."

Me: OMG! OMG! OMG! 2 sleeps!

Scarlett: Woot! Woot!

Me: What did you tell your parents? Obvi they freaked.

Scarlett: They were talking about turning the basement into a gym. I said maybe they should wait to see if you were moving back, and they were all like: WHA?

Me: Whatever. I'm coming home! I'm coming home!

Scarlett: Cannot wait. BTW, you don't mind if we hang with Adam while you're here, do you? I had plans with him on Saturday, and . . .

Me: Um, sure. Yeah, course.

Scarlett: Maybe I should host a welcome home party.

Me: You know I'm not much of a party person.

Scarlett: Not a party-party. More like a get-together.

Me: SQUEE. I'm coming home!

Me: Guess what?

SN: chicken butt.

Me: ?

SN: sorry. what?

Me: I'M GOING HOME. For only three days, but still.

SN: !!!! so happy for you. but?

Me: But what?

SN: YOU ARE COMING BACK, RIGHT?

Me: ☺

SN: smiley faces are cryptic. say: "I am coming back."

Me: I am coming back. FWIW, I'm not sure why you care so much. It's not like we couldn't IM from Chicago.

SN: not the same. and I like seeing you every day.

Me: You see me every day?

SN: you give good face, ms. holmes.

Me: Hey. Need to reschedule Friday. Going home for the weekend.

Ethan: "Yet when we came back, late, from the Hyacinth garden / Your arms full, and your hair wet, I could not / Speak, and my eyes failed, I was neither / Living nor dead, and I knew nothing, / Looking into the heart of light, the silence."

Me: That's my favorite part. I get that. Not being able to speak. Not feeling alive or dead.

Ethan: Me too.

Me: Maybe if you slept more . . .

Ethan: Ha! You must be so psyched to go.

Me: I am. Beyond.

Ethan: Good. Eat a slice of deep dish pizza for me.

Me: Will do. Can we meet next week to make up the assignment?

Ethan: Course. Monday after school?

Me: Sure. You'll probably have the whole thing memorized by then.

Ethan: Already do.

Would a drug addict take the time to memorize poetry? Theo has to be wrong. Ethan is not on drugs. Ethan is an insomniac and maybe damaged, whatever that means. Except I do know what that means, because who's kidding who? I am damaged too.

CHAPTER 26

I can't eat lunch. Too nervous. In just a few hours I'm meeting Caleb for our first date, though it's not really a date, and I'm not sure it can even be called a first, since we talk online all the time. Last night, we IM'd so late, I fell asleep with my computer on my lap and woke to his words dinging on my screen. *Three things,* he said: *(1) good morning. (2) I have keyboard marks on my face. slept on the "sdfgh." (3) you leave in 24 hours, and I'm going to miss you.*

"I'm not buying that Caleb is SN," says Agnes, when I refuse her fries for the fifth time on grounds that I'm worried I might throw up. "I mean, Dri is right, he's weird like that, but I dunno. He's not, you know, shy. He's like the most direct guy I've ever met."

"But I told him where I worked and then he showed up there. I totally saw him texting at Gem's party at the exact same time we were writing. And whenever I talk to him, he does this weird phone shake thing, to say like, 'I'll write you,' and then a second later he always does. And he quoted me back to me. It has to be him," I say.

"It's definitely him," Dri says. "And I'm impressed that you made the first move. Ballsy." Dri is not looking at us. She's staring at Liam, who is sitting on the other side of the cafeteria, nowhere near Gem. "You think they broke up?"

"No idea," I say, and shrug. "Nor do I care."

"You may have actually brought down Gemiam."

"Gemiam?"

"Gem and Liam. Gemiam."

I roll my eyes at Dri.

"I want to talk about Jessaleb. I just feel like I would have heard if his sister had died," Agnes says, and my stomach clenches.

"You said he never really talked about her." Dri multitasks: she talks to us and watches the Liam show at the same time. I'd worry about her being too obvious, except Liam is clueless. I just hope Gem won't notice. "And there were rumors."

"I mean, yeah, I had heard she was a total cutter, and she had a major eating disorder, so who knows. But I thought her parents sent her off to some mental hospital on the East Coast, not that she, you know, offed herself or anything like that," Agnes says. Her tone is so casual, as if we're talking about a character in a book, and not someone's actual life. Whether a real person, in the real world, is alive or dead. It strikes me how callous we all are, how comfortable we are belittling other people's problems: *Total cutter. Major eating disorder.* So easy for us to say.

I wish I had never mentioned his sister. Now I feel like I've betrayed Caleb, spilled secrets that weren't mine to spill. I'm glad I've never said anything about his mom.

"Maybe he meant it metaphorically? Like it *felt* like his sister died," Dri offers, but I shake my head. Caleb wasn't at all vague. "Or maybe he just said it to connect with you, you know, about your mom?"

I take Agnes's french fry, nibble it slowly and deliberately. I will ask Caleb later, if I have the nerve. I've never really wished anyone dead before, but it would be so not cool if he made the whole thing up. No, Caleb has lost someone close to him. We are a select crew, the dead family club, and I think I can tell who is for real. He counts the days, you know, *since*, just like me.

No one could make up counting days.

In English, Gem takes her seat without looking at me. I just see her straight back, her ponytail swishing its disapproval, the side of her arched brow. Her beauty is so classic, so generally agreed upon, that it's almost impossible not to stare. I hate myself for it, but I long to look like her, to cast spells without even having to open my mouth. To have a body like hers, assembled from lean, proportionate parts, as if dreamed up and arranged by the fantasies of all the men.

I wonder if Ethan is staring at her too. If he can help it.

If, at night, Ethan thinks about Gem the way I think about him.

I try not to. Think about him, I mean. I've tried to do a bait and switch, put Caleb where Ethan's face appears, but it never works. I may spend my evenings IMing with Caleb, but I spend my dreams with Ethan. In them, he's awake, his hands eager, his eyes on mine. In them, I'm not scared of sex, of intimacy, of anything at all. In them, I don't feel ugly or compare my body to Gem's. I feel beautiful and strong and brave.

In the morning, I wake up flushed, sad, when the feeling gets wiped away by the reality of day. When I wash my face in the mirror, see whiteheads, red splotches, round baby cheeks.

"Ms. Holmes?" Mrs. Pollack asks, and I wonder how long she's been calling on me.

"Um, yeah?"

"Care to answer the question?" I remember suddenly that she's been going around the room. I had ample warning, knew I was next up, but still I somehow got lost in thought. I look up at Mrs. Pollack; she's attractive, might have looked a lot like Gem when she was in high school. I bet she's never had a pimple.

"I'm sorry, I—" The whole class looks over, Gem and Crystal snicker in duet, and my face flashes hot. A bead of sweat threatens to streak down my right temple. I flick it away, try to calm my beating heart. Back in Chicago, English was my strongest subject. "I mean, I wasn't paying—"

"That scene with Raskolnikov at his house with his mother and sister. How he's able to act like everything is normal, even though he's actually going crazy inside," Ethan breaks in, and though I have no idea what he's talking about, his comment satisfies Mrs. Pollack, who moves toward the front of the room to write something on the blackboard.

"Exactly," she says, giving me one last look, which catches me by surprise. Because it's not mean. It's not even pity. It's something else entirely. Empathy.

• • •

"Thanks," I say to Ethan after class, once we are safely in the hallway. "You saved me."

"My pleasure, Tuberlicious."

"I hope I don't ruin your grade with our project." I fiddle with my bag, which feels too heavy on my shoulder. "Especially after I kind of made you work with me."

"I'm not worried." He smiles, so I force myself to look him straight in the eye, to bathe in the blue. No, not like a serial killer's, like I first thought. More complex than that. Like a gathering. I hear Theo's warning in my head and check for dilated pupils, but they look normal-sized to me.

"Good," I say. Not clever. Not flirtatious. Not anything. Maybe in an hour, I'll come up with a better line. Something funny and light to punctuate my exit.

But now: nothing.

Ethan rubs his head, as if trying to wake up his hair. Smiles again.

"Have a safe trip tomorrow."

"Thanks."

"Don't forget about us," he says, and before I can even articulate a question—What does he mean by us? Wood Valley? LA? Him and me?—Ethan is gone, out the front door and halfway to his car.

I wait for Caleb near the school's entrance, stand idly by the stairs. He said we should meet at three o'clock, and now it's three-fifteen, and I pretend not to be nervous that he won't show. I stare at the screen of my phone as if I'm deep in thought, as if my life depends on this text I'm typing. But I'm not really texting anyone, because the person I normally write to at times like this is Caleb. So I'm just thumbing over and over with my fingers: *Please don't stand me up. Please don't stand me up. Please don't stand me up.* I wonder how long I'm supposed to wait and at what point it will become obvious to me that I'm an idiot.

Gem walks by, because of course if there must be a bystander to witness my humiliation it will be her. For a moment, my stomach drops with the thought that SN may be Gem, that he has been a joke all along at my expense, but then I catch myself and let the thought go. No, Gem has better things to do than to text me late into the night as part of an elaborate practical joke. My friendship with SN is real, even if Caleb is not yet ready to face me.

"I wish you'd just go back to where you came from," Gem says as she skips down the stairs, words thrown over her shoulder as sharp as darts.

"Me too." I say it low enough that she can't hear.

"Me too, what?" Caleb says, and now he's next to me, and I can't help but grin from ear to ear. He didn't stand me up. He's here, car keys dangling from his long fingers, ready to go. We will have coffee and finally talk and it will be as easy as it is with my fast-moving thumbs. As strange as it is to trust him, I do. *Three things,* I start writing in my head: *(1) You understand me. (2) Tell me about Kilimanjaro. (3) Were you scared up there?*

"Nothing," I say. "Just talking to myself."

"Do that often?"

"It's been known to happen," I say. Caleb is so tall that I need to look up to talk to him, my neck arched back at an unfortunate angle. Maybe later I'll take a selfie to see what I look like to him from way up there, the entire plane and slope of my face. All chin and eyebrows. It can't be pretty. I'm not Barbie to his human Ken doll.

"Listen, about coffee," he says, and the disappointment hits me full force, even before he says the words. *This is what you get for being ballsy.* Ridiculous of me to be so optimistic and open, to assume this was going to happen. I keep letting myself be lifted and dropped, like a stuffed animal in an old-fashioned claw machine. I'll never actually be chosen, especially by someone who looks like him. "I think we shouldn't."

"Have coffee? Okay." I want to pick up my phone again. IM SN. Write what is too hard to say: *Why not? Why aren't I good enough for you in person?*

I think of the whitehead on my chin, which I covered with makeup in the bathroom just a half hour ago. I think of my arms, flabby and pasty, not browned and toned like Gem's. My eyebrows, which, no matter how long I spend in front of the mirror, always come out just slightly mismatched. My clothes, which are almost as nondescript as Caleb's, but girls, I guess, are not supposed to aim for nondescript. The width of my nose—which has never bothered me until right now—my chipped fingernail polish; even my earlobes, too loose, like long hanging fruit. And of course my forever-disappointing chest, which somehow manages to be both small and floppy at the same time: stupid, sad, flat funnels.

Caleb will not see my disappointment. I mirror his

240

casualness. Shrug, like it's no problem. Keep the smile from dripping down. Act like I don't feel the small, hard knot in my intestines, as if someone has reached into me and plucked them into a hideous bow. I grin through the pain—an actual, literal, visceral pain.

"You know, because of Liam," Caleb says, and now he's gone fuzzy and I don't understand at all. He's speaking a foreign language I've never heard before. One overly punctuated and aggressive, nasty simply because of the sounds of its hard, cruel letters.

"Liam? I mean . . . Wait, what?"

"I just think he'll get the wrong idea. And he's my best friend, so, you know," he says. But I don't know. What does Liam have to do with my getting coffee with Caleb?

"I still . . . I mean, I'm confused. What wrong idea? What does Liam have to do with anything?" Again, my brain is stalling. Maybe Caleb is right after all: let's keep everything in words on a screen, where they are so much easier to let out. Where they are clear and can be saved so they can be returned to later in case of a misunderstanding.

"You know he broke up with Gem, right? Because of you." Caleb's tone is so matter-of-fact, as if this is basic Wood Valley knowledge. And also as if it has little to do with him.

"Um, no. I didn't know they broke up, and if they did, I had nothing to do with it." I swallow, start again, hear that I sound defensive, though I don't know what about. "I mean, she's a huge bitch, and maybe he saw that she's been, you know, so mean, so indirectly, I guess it could tangentially have to do with me. But wait, what?" I'm rambling because I'm nervous. I stop, let my brain play catch-up. He's not saying what I think he's saying, is he? No. Liam couldn't have broken up with Gem because he likes me?

No, that's not possible.

Oh God. I finger the paper in my pocket. My ticket back to Chicago. Tomorrow cannot come soon enough. I need to get far, far away from this place. I think of Dri hearing this somehow, through that weird Wood Valley network I'm not at all clued into, and her thinking I've betrayed our new friendship. She knows I have no interest in Liam, right?

None of this makes sense. Gem is the kind of girl who makes *men*, not just boys but *men*, do double-takes. There is no universe in which someone would break up with her for me. Unless . . . Is Liam somehow SN? Do we have some sort of intellectual connection that would make him want to bridge that impossible gap between Gem and me?

No. Liam's an only child. No dead sisters—real or otherwise. And it's not like we really connect when we talk in person. At least, I don't think so.

Liam did tell me the other day at the store that I was "easy to talk to" and a "really good listener." They seemed like throwaway words, the right thing to say to someone who is a little shy. Honestly, I am not that good a listener. I am just good at letting other people talk.

No, Caleb must have the story wrong.

"All right, whatever. But I can't get involved," he says, and starts to walk away.

"Wait," I say, wanting to ask a million questions but realizing I should probably just IM him instead. More direct and efficient.

"What?" Caleb looks back. He's shaking his stupid phone

again, like that alone should satisfy me: the promise of a future message.

"Nothing," I say. "Just talking to myself."

SN: excited for your trip?

Me: CANNOT WAIT TO GET OUT OF HERE.

SN: day was that bad?

Me: I just. You know what? Never mind.

SN: anything I can do?

Me: No, not really.

So I was wrong. It's not easier to write the words, to spell it out: *You hurt my feelings today. I don't like Liam. My fingers are tired of this. It was just coffee.*

Or this: *How can you like me so much in words and care so little for me in person?*

Or maybe even this, just to be one hundred percent sure: *You are Caleb, right?*

I lie back on my bed. It shouldn't be surprising that SN doesn't want to hang out in real life. Even before I stopped talking to him, my own dad barely wanted to speak to me.

The self-pity creeps in, slow, stealthy, hungry, the monster under my bed. I try not to think of my mom, so handy in these moments as a cheap, easy trigger. A way to justify feeling sorry for myself: the loser with the dead mom. A shortcut that is as demeaning to her as it is to me.

Dri: OMG! OMG! OMG!

Me: ?

Dri: I was right! Gemiam is SO OVER.

Me: Wow. Cool.

Dri: Methinks this occasion deserves more enthusiasm. And get this: HE BROKE UP WITH HER.

Me: Huh. Guess he figured out who she really is.

She hasn't heard the second part yet. Maybe Caleb is wrong. Maybe I have nothing to do with anything. Maybe I misunderstood what he was saying. That would make a hell of a lot more sense. Either way, I'm not going to be the bearer of this ridiculous gossip, especially because I'm hoping it isn't true.

A mere two months ago, when I was eating lunch by myself on that lonely bench, the idea of a senior, any senior, asking me out would have been not only inconceivable but thrilling. More than just flattering: the stuff of my dork-girl fantasies. He's the lead singer of the coolest band in school, after all. But now Liam could screw up everything: my friendship with Dri, my job, maybe even things with Ethan, who always gets weird when Liam comes up in conversation. And, of course, Caleb, who now has found a convenient excuse to keep our relationship online only.

This new Jessie, the California Jessie, lives on unstable ground. I need Dri and SN and even Book Out Below! Dri worries about being invisible. My worry is its distant cousin: that without those three things that add up to my life out here, I might just disappear.

Dri: HOW WAS COFFEE? Sorry took me so long to ask. Was freakin' over L and G.

Me: Didn't happen. He canceled.

Dri: So sorry. You okay?

Me: It is what it is.

Dri: How very Zen of you.

Me: I am one with the universe and the universe is one with me.

Dri: Screw him.

Me: That too.

CHAPTER 27

My phone is turned off, tucked into the zippered pocket of my duffel bag. And though it's been only a few minutes, I miss it. Have to fight the reflex to reach for the screen. Instead, I look out the window, watch as LA gets smaller and smaller, a collection of buildings and houses and cars on the freeway that from up here look harmless and neutral, like any other place in the world that isn't home. My PSAT prep book sits open on my lap, but I can't bring myself to read it. In T minus four hours, Scarlett will pick me up from the airport and drive us straight to DeLucci's and we will order two slices of pizza each and Diet Cokes in big frosted glasses, and all of our shared history, our lifetime of inside jokes, will come alive again across their dingy folding tables. My two months away erased. I will tell her about the mess I've made of things, how my new life feels on the verge of unraveling, and she will tell me how to fix it. How to keep my friendship with Dri, how to make Caleb want to, you know, *actually be with me in person,* how not to lose my job. How to rid myself of my ridiculous unrequited crush on Ethan, who by all accounts is damaged and possibly dangerous, and also unattainable.

And she'll remind me that everything that is new always feels tenuous, that a lot of this, maybe even most of this, is in my head.

In T minus four hours, I will be home again. Even though my mom won't be there, at least, finally, I will be someplace I recognize.

I'm so relieved that I let the tears fall now that there's no one here to see. I even let them blur the words on my vocab list, let them bleed their fat, wet stains onto the page.

Later, in the car, I sideways glance at Scar. She looks different, older somehow, like her features have set. Her hair is short now, a messy, asymmetrical bob. She never mentioned she'd cut it. I wonder if she made a Pinterest board of options first, like we used to, or if it was a spur-of-the-moment decision. Either way, she rocks it. Scar taps the wheel of her parents' battered old Honda to the beat of some song I don't recognize. Both the music and the heat are blasting. My coat and scarf are necessary outside, but in the car, dressed for Chicago and with my seat belt on, I'm overheating. I should have taken them off before I got in.

I think of the weather back in California, how I never need

to check the forecast. Blue skies, short sleeves, every day. A breeze so slight, it tickles.

"I feel like I just got out of prison," I say, and crack open my window and lower the radio so we can talk. I smell the familiar smell of Scarlett: coconut and mango from her lotion and something unidentified and peppery. "For reals."

"I guess if you define prison as living in a huge freakin' mansion in Beverly Hills and having a maid and a personal chef, then sure. You're totally out of prison," Scarlett says, and I can't decide if I hear a hint of something new in her voice. A lack of patience with me.

"First of all, I don't live in Beverly Hills. You know it's not like that."

"Relax, I'm joking," she says, and fiddles with the radio. Not as loud as before, but still annoying. "So what do you want to do while you're here?"

"Honestly? Just hang out with you. Eat pizza. Talk. Laugh. I've missed, you know, us."

"Yeah. It's funny I didn't realize how much of our time we used to spend together until you left." She keeps her eyes trained on the road, and again I can't tell if I'm being paranoid. Is Scar mad at me for something? Of course we used to spend all of our time together. That's what best friends do.

"I love your hair. It looks really cool."

"I needed a change," she says, and turns the radio way up again.

Over pizza at DeLucci's, which at least is one thing that is as good as I remember it, I catch her up on everything in LA. Tell her the whole story, from beginning to end. My figuring out SN is Caleb. Liam and Dri. Even what Theo said about Ethan being a drug addict, which at first I'm scared to tell her because I want her to like him, even if they will never meet. But I tell her anyway because I've never been able to censor with Scar. I ramble a bit, am nervous. The caffeine, probably. Had a cup of coffee on the plane. Black, a pathetic tribute to Ethan.

"So what should I do?" I ask, because Scar always knows what to do. She's one of those wise old people trapped in a young person's body. Her middle name is actually, I kid you not, Sage.

"What do you mean?" she asks, and sucks on the lemon from her Diet Coke. "Some guy broke up with his girlfriend and wants to ask you out? Sounds like a high-class problem."

"Well, I just . . . I don't want—"

"I think you're kind of overthinking it all, J." She takes a moment to look me up and down, to see the ways in which I look different from two months ago, weighing and measuring the changes. My hair is longer, because I haven't bothered to get it cut, and I'm a few pounds thinner, mostly because Rachel is not fond of carbs. Other than that, I look exactly the same.

"Maybe. It's just—"

"By the way, Adam is coming over later. And so is Deena." Scar interrupts me midsentence.

"You're friends with Deena now?"

"She's not so bad."

"Okay." I bite my pizza, avoid her eyes. Scar knows I've always hated Deena. She tried to sabotage my friendship with Scar back when we were freshmen. Told her I was talking shit about her behind her back, when of course I wasn't. And she'd always make these comments to me that were jabs disguised as jokes. Not elevating bullying to the art form that Gem has, but still on the mean-girl spectrum.

"You know, you're not the only one this has been hard on." Scar puts down her Diet Coke, and it splashes onto her plate. She hasn't taken a single bite of pizza. "I mean, I had to make all new friends too."

For a moment, I switch things around: think about what it would have been like if Scar had been the one who took off and I'd been the one left behind. What it would have been like to start all over with the people we have known forever. All of those people we had already chosen, for one reason or another, *not* to be friends with. Until now, it has never once occurred to me that my leaving happened to anyone but me.

"I'm sorry. I didn't really think about it."

"Yeah, no shit."

"Scar!" I look into her eyes, try to gauge what's going on. Are we fighting? Scar and I have never fought. Our friendship isn't like that: we don't do that teenage-girl moodiness or jockeying for positions. We've always just been each other's favorites. This is new, and the shock of it, Scar being angry with me, maybe even having moved on from our friendship, makes me ache with loneliness. "What's going on?"

Her eyes fill, and so do mine. I wanted so badly to come home, to sit in this booth that we've sat in hundreds of times, to just relax for maybe the first time in months. And instead, now, suddenly, I want to be anywhere but here.

No, the truth is I don't want to be anywhere at all, because wherever I go, I still come with me. I'm stuck in this brain, in this body, in this ugly swamp of humanness.

How do I manage to screw everything up?

My first instinct is to IM SN, to unload and tell him how badly it's all going here, how everything is flipped, how home doesn't even feel like home, but then I remember yesterday and how he wouldn't even drink a cup of coffee with me.

"Nothing. Forget about it." Scar busies herself with the pizza—scatters powdered cheese, red pepper, salt.

Still doesn't take a bite.

"Scar." There is pleading in my voice: *Let's start over.* I don't have the energy to fight this one out. No, energy is not the problem. Courage is. I can't bear the thought of us yelling at each other, dissecting each other's weaknesses, saying out loud the things those who love you the most are never supposed to say. Things like what she just implied: *You only think about yourself.* I can't bear the thought that we might not be friends in the aftermath of those kinds of words.

"Let's just not talk about it, okay?" Scarlett bites into her lemon again, and a drop of bitter juice slides down her chin. I hand her a napkin.

"Okay." I finish off my two slices, but Scar just picks hers up, dressed and uneaten, and dumps them in the trash.

Scarlett sits next to Adam on the couch, her legs dangled over his lap. Deena's brother, Joe, who is a freshman at the local community college and as annoying as his sister, has brought a case of beer, perhaps the new price of admission to Scar's parents' basement, and Deena passes cans around even though they're warm. Adam's best friend, Toby, is here too, and though we've known each other since preschool, I'm not sure we've ever had an actual conversation.

Everyone looks different but the same. Adam's face is clearer—Scar was right—and he seems less gangly and boyish, like it's not as ridiculous a proposition that he could be somebody's boyfriend. That Scar would choose to hook up with him. I picture Adam lifting weights he ordered from the Internet in his basement, which is exactly like the one in my old house—linoleum-covered and low-ceilinged and the perfect locale for that sort of self-conscious project. Deena seems older too, but maybe it's just that she's standing straighter, her scoliosis less pronounced, and she keeps whispering things into Scar's ear and then laughing. *Okay, I get it,* I want to say. *You guys are besties now.*

"What's LA like?" Adam asks, and then the room turns its collective attention to me, and though just a minute ago I felt stuck on the outside, I suddenly feel too much like the center of attention. Talking about LA might make Scar even angrier at me, especially when the questions come from her— boyfriend? friend with benefits?

"You know," I say, and swig my beer. "Sunny."

"Scar says that you, like, live in a palace and shit," Toby says, and clinks his beer against mine, as if my moving to LA was some sort of personal coup, like getting into my first-choice college.

"Yeah, not really. I mean, it's a nice house, but it's not mine. I miss it here." I try to catch Scar's eye. She's not looking at me because she's too busy snuggling with Adam. I think about Rachel's house—the walls of windows that beg you to look outward—and then I look around this basement. Remember that we are underground.

"She said that you go to, like, some fancy-ass private

school, where all the kids are super-rich and are followed by paparazzi." Toby's voice surprises me; it's deeper than I imagined. I can hear his Chicago accent, which I've never thought of as an accent at all until right now. Is this what I sound like to everyone at Wood Valley? All low, growly "da's" instead of "the's"?

"I don't know. The kids are definitely different." All this time, did Scar think I was humblebragging whenever I described my plush new world? She and I have always spoken the same language. Surely she must have understood that I'd so much rather be here, in this basement, maybe not drinking warm beer with Deena and Adam and this strange crew, but eating popcorn and watching Netflix with her. That the stuff that makes Wood Valley sound interesting and cool is exactly what makes it so lonely. I'm not impressed by tall hedges and Kobe beef.

I picture my new friends hanging in Chicago, wonder whether they could slip into my old life the way I've tried to slip into theirs. Despite their excessive coffee-spending money and their after-school SAT tutors and the fact that they've never set foot in a Goodwill, Dri and Agnes would happily help themselves to a can of Schlitz and chat about whether Scar should let her hair grow out again. Caleb could hang here too, because he blends. Sort of. They'd all adapt.

Ethan is the only one who I can't superimpose on this image, but maybe that's because I have trouble picturing Ethan anywhere but in his hideouts. He's more like me, I think: burdened with the realization that what goes on in his mind is somehow different from what goes on in everyone else's. Even those closest to us.

And how you can't think about that for too long, because that thought—the truth of our own isolation—is too much to bear.

I'm drunk, and the warm beer sloshes sour in my stomach. Scar and Adam are in the laundry room, door closed, and it occurs to me, based on the sounds emitting from that general vicinity, that they are likely having sex, and probably not for the first time. Maybe she has told Deena all the details, and her new best friend was able to give her lots of tips, the pertinent information that seems incredibly complicated in the little Internet porn I've seen. Not just the condom-on-the-banana talk we got in sex ed, but the hows and the whys and the what-feels-goods that I don't yet know. Perhaps this is why Scarlett no longer wants to be my friend, because I can't provide that kind of useful counsel. And because I use expressions like "useful counsel" when I'm drunk.

Come to think of it, I don't want to be my friend either.

Deena and Toby are kissing in the corner, in the L part of the Schwartzes' couch, the exact location I fantasized about just a week ago, when moving back and sleeping down here seemed like the answer to all of my problems. Joe, who since I've left has had a tattoo of headphones inked around his neck, the stupidest tattoo ever, since technology will progress and pretty soon that will be the equivalent of getting a tat of a rotary phone, keeps trying to talk to me, inching closer with each question. Of course, he asks dumb ones like *Have you seen Brad and Angelina? And can you sit on the letters of the Holly-wood sign?* I guess he assumes that we should get together by process of elimination, that I pick who I make out with via an uncomplicated algorithm of who happens to be left in a room.

I take out my phone, and I can't help it. I message SN.

Me: You awake?

SN: I'm always at your service. how's Chicago?

Me: Honestly? Effed up.

SN: ?

Me: I just. First of all, I'm drunk, and there's this stupid guy who won't leave me alone.

SN: for real? are you okay? should I call the police?

Me: NO! I didn't mean. No. He's fine, just annoying. And Scar is mad at me, but I don't know why. Deena is her new best friend or something. And I just feel so—

SN: alone.

Me: Alone.

SN: I'm here.

Me: But you're not. Not really.

SN: I am.

Me: You're not even there when I'm there.

SN: do you always get so existential when you're drunk?

Me: You didn't even want to have coffee with me. It was just coffee.

I am crying now, and it's this—my tears, not my IM'ing, or my pushing his hand off my leg, that finally gets Joe to give up and move away. Second choice to hooking up with me is, apparently, playing games on his phone. I hear intermittent beeps. At least my tears are quiet. Everyone else is way too busy to notice.

SN: what are you talking about?

Me: YOU KNOW WHAT I'M TALKING ABOUT.

SN: I really don't.

Me: STOP PRETENDING I DON'T KNOW WHO YOU ARE.

SN: wait, Jessie, for real, I'm confused. you know who I am? I mean, I thought maybe you did the other day, but then I thought no way. and I was going to tell you, but—

Me: It was only coffee. Am I that, I don't know, horrible, that . . . Never mind.

SN: I don't know what you're talking about. seriously. should we wait till you're sober to have this conversation? this is not going the way I wanted it to—

Me: Yeah. Me neither.

I turn off my phone. Run up the stairs to the small bathroom. Throw up my DeLucci's pizza and six cans of beer and don't even feel the tiniest bit of nostalgic relief when I see Scar's map of the world shower curtain or even the Cat in the Hat soap dispenser that has been there for as long as I can remember. I sit on her old fluffy blue bath mat and try to hold still as the world continues to spin.

CHAPTER 28

"Wake up, sleepyhead," Scar says. I open one eye. She's wearing flannel pajamas, her hair is back in a mini ponytail, and she doesn't look even the slightest bit hungover. There's an obvious hickey on her neck that I hope she will cover before seeing her parents. She sits cross-legged at the end of her bed, which I apparently slept in, though I don't really remember how I got here. She hands me a glass of water. "Please tell me you did not hook up with Joe."

"Eww. No. Course not." My head throbs, a pain radiating from the inside out, like my brain is rotting. I sit up and then lie right back down. Too fast. All too fast. "So, I was thinking about going back early."

The words come out before I think them through. I just

can't stand to be near Scarlett and for us not to be us. I imagine this is what breaking up with someone feels like.

"Don't. J. Seriously. Not like this."

"I don't know why you hate me so much." My eyes are closed, so the words are easier to say, to slip them right into the darkness. I must have spent all of my tears last night, because none come now. Just an overwhelming feeling of loss.

"I don't hate you." Scar scoots up the bed, so she is sitting next to me now, and her arm is around my shoulder. "God, you stink."

I laugh. "Thanks a lot. I threw up."

"No shit."

"Scar—"

"I don't hate you." She pauses. Gathers the words. "But you left. Not me. You are the one who left."

I look out the window, behind Scar's head, and see that the trees are almost bare already, even though it's still autumn. Their leaves have been shed, one by one, leaving the branches naked and unprotected in the cold. I shiver, pull the blanket up.

"That's not fair. I didn't want to go. You know that."

"But you barely even ask about how I am. You didn't just leave, you, you know, left."

"I just, I guess I just assumed you were the same. There's been so much going on with me, I wanted to tell you all about my life. That's what we do," I say, and now my bottom lip begins its familiar quiver. Maybe she's right and I'm wrong, and everything is all my fault. Scarlett, my dad, SN, soon Dri. Maybe my mom, in some strange cosmic way. Maybe self-centered narcissists like me don't deserve mothers.

"You know how hard it's been for me? You think I wanted to hang out with Deena? When you left I had nobody. Nobody," Scar says. "You never even ask, like, I don't know. Anything."

"I'm sorry. You're right. I've had my head really far up my own ass."

"And I feel bad even being mad at you, because it's like, your mom died, and then you had to move and live with the evil steppeople. They don't seem so bad, by the way. But I still need my best friend, you know? Not everything is about you." Scar folds into herself and then starts to cry so hard, her body shakes. I put my arms around her from behind, my stomach to her back, though I have no idea what's going on.

"Scar, it's okay. It will be okay. Talk to me," I say, but she's in no condition to talk. Too many tears and too much snot. So I wait. I can do that. I can wait and then I can listen.

"Adam is going to break up with me," she says, after I've gotten out of bed and handed her a wad of toilet paper to clean off her face. The floor undulates, but I can power through this hangover for Scar.

"Why? I mean, what makes you think that? He seems so into you," I say, because he does. Before they made their not-so-subtle escape to the laundry room, he kept glancing at her, checking to see her reaction each time he made a joke. Wanting not only to see her laugh, but reveling in being the one to make that happen.

"I just, I don't know. Partially it's the sex thing."

"Which sex thing?" Does she not even realize that she hasn't yet told me they've slept together? Have we drifted that far apart without my even noticing?

"You know, that we're not having it yet. Like, Deena had

260

this big pregnancy scare last year, and I'm just, I'm not ready. It's embarrassing, but I'm scared. I don't know what I'm doing."

"No one knows what they're doing the first time, right?"

"And I'm just so—" She stops, pulls the blanket over her head. This new Scar is unrecognizable. The Scar I know is fearless, certainly not like me, afraid of the inconsequential things in life, like guys and their silly, dangling parts.

I pull the blanket off her, force her to face me.

"Tell me."

"I'm so into him, I can't even take it. I didn't expect to even like him a little bit, and now, holy crap. I don't know what to do with myself. All I think about is him," she says, and I know exactly what she means. That's how I think about Ethan—damaged, impossible-to-date Ethan. All the time, even when I don't want to. Even when he is completely irrelevant to whatever I'm doing, like drinking with annoying Joe and wondering how Ethan would fit in. He'll never come to Chicago. Never see Scar's basement. But he was there anyway, in my mind.

And as stupid as it is, I admit I think about SN that way too. Not Caleb, not the real-life version of SN, but the one on my screen. The one who is always there for me.

He's not real, of course. We're all better versions of ourselves when we get that extra time to craft the perfect message. The SN I know and obsess about can't translate into real life. He's a virtual soul mate, not a real one. I do realize that.

"Scar, that's amazing."

"No, it's horrible. I feel like an idiot. It's Adam, for God's sake. Your-old-neighbor-the-worst-kisser-in-the-world Adam. Though he's a great kisser now." She pulls the blanket over her head again, and I rip it off.

"Look at me. He's into you too. Seriously, he's been working out. I can tell. Why else would he suddenly start working out? And he can't stop touching you and looks at you all the time. I mean. All. The. Time." I throw my arms around her, because I'm so happy. She deserves a good boyfriend and everything else she could possibly want. Certainly, she deserves the happy ending of the romantic comedy about the boy next door, even if, technically, he was my neighbor, not hers. Close enough.

And she's right: I did leave, and I didn't for a second worry about what my moving would mean for her. I haven't asked enough about Adam, about her new life, have only been focused on complaining about mine.

"I'm so sorry for not being here for you. I was an asshole. But I'm here now, okay?"

"Okay," she says, and snuffles into my shoulder.

"So tell me everything," I say, and she does.

Later, we eat Scar's mom's tofu noodle soup with hot sauce, which Scar promises is an ancient cure for hangovers. The food is staying down, so I consider it a win.

"Adam wants me to make him some tattoo stickers for his computer," she says, and I smile at her. She really has it bad. No matter what we're talking about, she finds a way to work him into the conversation.

"They're awesome. You should totally sell them on Etsy."

"Yeah, he's already picked out what he wants if he ever gets real ones, but I want to make one that means something. That symbolizes him, or us. But I don't know. It's probably too soon."

We slurp our soup, stare into our murky bowls. I don't know if it is too soon. This is not my area of expertise, and I don't want to screw things up for her.

"Is that your phone that keeps beeping?" Scar asks me. Since we sat down, I've clocked at least ten messages, but it could be more.

"Yeah," I say.

"And you don't want to check it?" I have purposely left my phone in my bag. An intentional, not an FAA-mandated, untethering. When I powered it on this morning, I already had a bunch of messages that I was too afraid to read. A few from Agnes and Dri, but I figure if they want to drop me as a friend, it can wait till Monday. Perhaps most terrifying of all: one from SN. I can't believe I was stupid enough to IM drunk. I need to get a phone-locking Breathalyzer. Does that exist? If not, I'm going to invent it, *disrupt* the industry, and make a bajillion dollars.

"Not really."

"It could be an emergency," she says.

"What emergency? If my dad needs to reach me, he has your landline. I'm all yours right now. No Wood Valley crap."

"I like to hear about the Wood Valley crap. Seriously," Scar says, and stands up, stretches in a way that makes me wonder if she's taken up yoga. "I just want to talk about me too, sometimes."

"I'm sorry." My new mantra. Hope my repetition of those words—I've said them maybe a hundred times this morning—doesn't cheapen them. When my mom died, that was the expression I hated the most because it seemed like an easy way for people to deal with me and move on, the words a beautifully wrapped gift box with nothing inside. No recognition that her having died meant that she was now dead, every day, forever.

"I'm getting your phone."

"No. Please don't."

"It must be done." She grabs my phone from my bag, swipes the screen. "What's your code?"

My tongue burns and my eyes water from the hot sauce. Still, I take another sip of soup. Avoid her eyes. Stir noodle and seaweed into a tangled knot.

"Fine. I know it anyway."

"You do not," I say, though of course she does.

"One-two-three-four. Yup, right in. How many times have I told you that you need to change that?"

I laugh, but I'm scared. What's in my phone? What does SN have to say for himself? Why are both Dri and Agnes texting when they know I'm away? I pray that they're writing to tell me that Liam came to his senses and he and Gem are back together, not because they're mad. It's strange that Wood Valley has seeped all the way here, halfway across the country.

"No way!" Scar squeals and claps. "I was so hoping it wouldn't be him!"

"What are you talking about?" I ask.

"Look!" Scar hands me the phone, which is open to a three-way message between me, Agnes, and Dri.

Agnes: BIG NEWS. Just saw Caleb at Barney's.

Dri: So?

Agnes: HE WAS WITH HIS SISTER!

Dri: She's not dead?

Agnes: Nope. Alive and well, and buying a thousand-dollar handbag.

Dri: JESSIE!!!! OMG!!! OMG!!!

Agnes: Told you Caleb wasn't SN.

"Wait, what?" I look at Scarlett. I'm confused. Of course SN is Caleb. I mean, he has to be. The way he dresses like someone who wants to remain anonymous. The fact that he had his phone out at the party. And the way he showed up at Book Out Below! after I told him I work there. The way he always texts minutes after we talk in person. That whole phone-shake code thingy. Did he make up his dead sister?

And didn't SN and I talk about my coffee offer once, that time when I took it back?

I search for the message. And there it is:

Me: (3) Just so you know, I take back coffee.

SN: okay, no sugar for you.

Me: What?

SN: a joke. Seinfeld reference.

Me: It's not funny.

SN: it's just coffee. relax.

I give my phone back to Scar, like it's something toxic. Did I have it all wrong? Did SN think it was a typo? That I was saying that I take my coffee black? I thought he meant it was just coffee, that meeting in person was no big deal.

"Yeah! I was so not rooting for Caleb. He seems like kind of a dick—no offense. Kilimanjaro notwithstanding. Like, if he was going to spend all this time messaging you, he should want to hang out."

"Wait, so you think it's not him. For real?" My head is spinning again. Scar was wrong. This soup is no hangover cure. I feel the hot sauce make its way up the back of my throat, burn, burn, burn.

"Of course not. Who makes up a dead sister?"

"Weirdos who anonymously text their classmates."

"No way. It's official. SN is not Caleb."

"Then who the hell is he?" I ask.

"Look," Scar says, and hands my phone right back.

SN: I'm worried. are you okay? you can be mad, but just tell me you are okay?

SN: hello?

SN: okay, trying to calm down, even though it's the middle of the night and impossible to think clearly. i'm just going to tell myself that your phone died or you turned it off because you didn't want to talk to me, which is fine, though i don't get it, but you're not in some ditch somewhere drunk with that stupid jerk who wouldn't leave you alone.

SN: morning now. you're okay, right? right. RIGHT?

SN: three things: (1) I've only told you one lie. the rest, everything else, has been the truth. and though it was a big one, I think you'll understand why. god, I hope so. (2) THIS is more important than anything else. this is real. even if everything else feels like it's not most of the time. (3) I've been thinking about it all night, have reread your messages a million times, and I'm pretty sure I know who you think I am and you're wrong.

SN: just for today, I'm doing a number 4. Let's meet.

"So it *is* Caleb. Because he says he lied. So it has to be Caleb," I say. "He lied about his sister and everything else is the truth."

"No way. He lied about something else. Or maybe he lied about his sister, but it wasn't Caleb who did the lying. It's just not him. I know it," Scar says, and for some reason, though she has never met any of these people, I believe her. Caleb has been so dismissive of me—not interested in even the smallest of small talk. SN is the opposite—always wants to hear more, all of the details that add up to the entirety of my day. "I think he's Liam."

"No way," I say.

"It explains why he would dump Gem for you."

I smile at Scar but not because any part of me hopes SN is Liam. That would suck for so many reasons, not least, because of Dri.

"You've been listening," I say, and feel so grateful she's still my friend, that she will be, hopefully forever. She knew my mother. And the me of before. That's no small thing.

"Of course I've been listening."

Me: Sorry about last night. Wasn't myself. Long story. But yes . . . let's meet. I think it's time.

SN: it's definitely, unequivocally time.

CHAPTER 29

"You know what's weird? There are a ton of randos at school. SN could be anyone. I mean, he could be that guy Ken Abernathy, who, like, has a real farting issue. I mean, it's sad. He could even be Mr. Shackleman!" Scar and I are driving around. No destination in mind. Just looping the streets because they're familiar. Unlike my former classmates, the surroundings here look the same as before: the trees may be naked, but they're naked in the same way they were last fall and the one before that. Even my house looks almost exactly the way I remember it, even though it's been overtaken by a new family. Only difference is there's now a tricycle with tasseled handlebars on the front lawn and a football wedged in a bush. When we drive by, I squint so these new additions get erased from the image.

Home but not home.

Mom, where are you? Silly of me to think you'd be more here than there.

"Who's Mr. Shackleman?" Scar asks.

"My gym teacher. He's a total perv."

"Oh my God. How funny would that be if SN turned out to be some old dude with, like, a neck beard?"

"Yuck. He's balding and has a beer gut."

"I think you're going to have to get up on the Liam train, because he's totally SN." Scar pulls into the 7-Eleven, and we sit and just stare at the storefront and its big windows, into the fluorescent lights and shelves of processed food and the gleaming hot dogs on spits. I like it here in the car. A cocoon of plastic and metal.

Mom, I miss you. I love you.

"I just don't, I don't know," I say, and focus. "I don't see Liam in *that* way. He's cute and all, but . . . it's just kind of awkward with him. Fine. I know I sound weird and crazy picky. I should be happy anyone likes me—"

"Come on, that's ridiculous. If you aren't into him, you aren't into him. I'm not saying you should be *desperate*. I'm just saying you might not see what's right in front of you. Like Adam and me." I laugh, I can't help it. Adam and Scar. Scar and Adam. The whole thing is kind of adorable. "Okay, fine. Laugh. Get it out now. Because I'm far from done."

"Scar and Adam sitting in a tree. *K-I-S-S-I-N-G.* First comes love, then comes marriage. Then comes baby in the baby carriage."

"God forbid."

Here is what I want to say, but it sounds weird, even in my

own head: *Liam sometimes makes me feel noticed but never actually seen. I want to be seen.* And maybe that's another reason why I don't think Liam is SN. Because SN really sees me. I believe that. He gets what I've been through. We connect.

"So the sex thing. Want to talk about it?" I ask. Sex—the *to have or not to have* question—is the only part of her relationship with Adam we haven't dissected in minute detail yet.

"I want to do it. I mean, my girlie parts definitely do. But what if I'm bad at it, or I gross him out, or, you know, I get pregnant?"

"Remember Health last year? With the condoms? Banana. Penis. Same difference, right? And you are so not going to gross him out."

"Even if I manage to figure it all out—how to get the condom on him—they, like, can break, or just not work, or whatever. I could go on the pill, but I don't see how I can do that without talking to my mom, and she'd totally freak." Scar stares straight ahead. This conversation is best had with our heads parallel. No eye contact.

"Is Adam pushing it? Have you talked to him about it?" I ask.

"Not really. I mean, I know he totally would—do it, I mean, not talk about it. Though I guess he'd do that too."

"Why not wait and see how it goes? He's probably a virgin too. And if your mom sees you guys hanging around all the time, maybe she'll bring it up."

"You have met my mother, right?"

"I don't know. You don't have to figure it all out now."

"You don't think I should do it?" she asks. It's strange seeing her this way. So vulnerable, in doubt. In love. I think

271

about what my mom would say, since I imagine us being close enough to talk about this kind of stuff if she were still alive. Most likely, we wouldn't have been, though. Something happens when you turn sixteen, I think. Your parents become less your allies, more your biggest obstacles. I'm the only teenager I know who would want nothing more than to be grounded by my mother. The opposite of a punishment.

"It doesn't matter what I think. You should do what you feel comfortable with."

"Cop-out answer, Jess." I laugh, elbow her ribs. It occurs to me that what Scar needs right now is a friend like Scar: someone to break it down and tell it like it is.

"Honestly, and I know this is funny coming from me, but you're overthinking it. Relax. Do what you want to do when you want to do it. If you're ready, go forth and prosper. If you're not yet, that's totally okay too. It feels like this huge deal now, but maybe it's not." I sound wise and sure, words I've never before applied to myself, especially in this context. "You just need to figure out whether you're scared because it's your first time—I mean, the first time is supposed to be a little scary, right?—or because you aren't ready. There's really no right answer here."

"You sound like me," Scar says, and finally turns her head. There are tears in her eyes, which makes me sad, because she should be happy. She's getting what she always wanted, to love and to be loved, even if it's not exactly how she pictured it all.

"I learned from the best," I say, and smile. Then, in unison, without talking about it, like the old Scar and J, we open our car doors, stride into the 7-Eleven. And just as we used to, long before everything got so complicated, we head straight to the back, to the always-reliable Slurpee machine.

Dri: Did Liam ask you out?

Me: No!

Wait, is that a lie? If he's SN and we're going to meet, does that count? And assuming Caleb has his facts straight and I'm the reason for the demise of Gem and Liam—I can't bring myself to call them Gemiam—do I have an obligation to tell Dri?

"Don't tell her!" Scar says, reading my mind at the same time as she reads my texts over my shoulder. We're back in the basement, and beautiful vampire men are saving helpless teenage girls from other, murderous vampires on television. We're eating popcorn. I couldn't be happier. "Seriously, it will just hurt her feelings. And it's not a lie. Liam hasn't asked you out."

Dri: I think he will. He likes you.

Me: I'm not interested.

Dri: What if he's SN?

Me: He's not SN.

Dri: But what if he is?

Me: Dri!

"She wants you to say you won't go out with him. You can't say that. If he's SN, you need to give him a chance. You just do," Scar says, her confidence back. This is the best friend I recognize: the one who tells the truth, no sugarcoating. "And if she's really your friend, she'll understand that."

"She *is* my friend, but we're new. It's different. We haven't built up trust, you know?"

"Still."

"Liam is not SN."

"Whatever. He totally is." I smile at Scar, because it's funny how she talks about my friends from Wood Valley like they're characters from a TV show, like she's betting on the next plot twist. In some ways, I do that too. Wood Valley sometimes feels like my pretend life.

Dri: Liam doesn't have a sister.

Me: See.

Dri: I don't know. I still think Liam is SN. And yes, I'll admit it. I'm totally jealous.

Me: Please. Don't. Be.

Dri: Fine. Love you anyway. Going to go listen to "The Girl No One Knows" on repeat and feel sorry for myself.

Theo: WHAT THE WHAT? Liam broke up with Gem to be with you?

Me: Who told you that?

Theo: EVERYONE. Liam's H-O-T. How'd you pull that one off?

Me: I didn't pull anything off.

Theo: Girl, you are full of surprises.

Me: Not really.

Theo: He's telling everyone you're "like a breath of fresh air."

Me: That's sweet of him, but it kind of makes me sound like a deodorant.

Theo: By the way, your dad is making me pick you up from the airport, so you better not check any bags. Don't keep me waiting.

• • •

Me: Three things. (1) I don't know who you are. I wish I did, and Scar has her theories, but I just don't know. I thought you were someone else, but now I know I was wrong. (2) I've never lied to you, I don't think. Well, except that first day, when I said I have a black belt in karate. I've never done karate. I'm a crappy liar. I think it's easy for me to talk to you, because I don't know who you are. I guess it's different for you? (3) I don't know where home is anymore.

SN: Maybe home doesn't have to be a place.

Me: Maybe not.

CHAPTER 30

Back in the air. This time it's Chicago that slips away, gets smaller and smaller, until I can't see the city at all, my home vanished just like that, and now there are only big swaths of green and brown, a patchwork quilt of earth. Again, my PSAT book sits on my lap, opened but not read, and I stare out the window, trying to decide which way I'd rather be flying: east, back to Scar, who has her own life now and less room for me, or west, back to Rachel's house and my distracted dad, where scary things await. Facing Liam, and, if he doesn't back out, SN. As for my father, I've ignored his calls and texts for the past week. Our silence is getting too loud, my sulk having crossed over into something tangible and hard and malignant.

I wait until the fasten seat belt light goes off to take out the envelope Scar slipped to me just as I was leaving. *A parting gift,* she said. I flip it around in my hand, nervous to open it. I hope there are words of wisdom here, the sort of prescient advice Scar has always been able to freely share. When my mom died, Scar and I sat on my bed, and before she started the full-time job of distracting me from the pain—which she performed admirably and with such skill I never even noticed how much work she must have put into it—she said the only thing that made sense at the time, maybe the only thing that has made any sense since: *Just so you know, I realize that what happened is not in any way okay, but I think we're going to have to pretend like it is.*

Because it wasn't okay and never will be. We will power through it; I will continue to power through it—all the stagnant, soul-crushing grief—but it will never be okay that my mom is not here. That she will not be at my high school graduation; that she will never give me *the* lecture, and I won't be able to play along and pretend to be embarrassed and say, *Come on, Mom;* that she will not be there when I open my college acceptance letters (or rejections); that she will never see who I grow up to be—that great mystery of who I am and who I am meant to be—finally asked and answered. I will march forth into the great unknown alone.

I open the envelope and out slips a new laptop tattoo, bigger than the other ones Scar's made for me. This image in black-and-white. A ninja wielding a samurai sword, his eyes wide and blank and fierce. Attached is a small note: *I wanted you to see yourself the way I see you: as a fighter. Strong and stealthy. Totally kick-ass. Completely and utterly your mother's daughter. Love you, Scar.*

I hug the sticker to my chest, take it as an omen, the only way forward. I will stop being afraid of everything. Of hurt and rejection. Of my father's ambivalence about me. Of hurting Dri's feelings. Of facing Liam and Gem too. Of meeting SN in person, face to face. Of venturing forth, day by day, naked and unprotected into the bright, bright sun.

CHAPTER 31

Theo is wearing a charcoal-gray pin-striped blazer with matching shorts and a chauffeur's cap, and is holding up a handwritten sign with my name on it. Not for the first time, I wonder how he has a costume for every occasion. Was he able to pull this together from the vast selection in his closet, or did he shop for the perfect pick-Jessie-up-from-the-airport outfit? Either way, I love the effort, even if he didn't do it for my benefit.

"Hello, my lady. Your chariot awaits," Theo says, and grabs my duffel bag and throws it over his shoulder. "This is all you brought? What about shoes?"

I point to the Vans on my feet.

"You're a lost cause," he says, and leads me out of the air-conditioned terminal into the soft, warm Los Angeles evening.

"So I only offered to do this because I thought you were going to spill. So . . . spill it."

"Ah, so you offered? I thought you said my dad made you."

"Whatever. Sometimes I'm nice. Don't tell anyone. Now spill."

"Spill what? I've got nothing," I say, and avoid his eyes, even though it's the truth. Liam breaking up with Gem to be with me is just rumor. Liam has not called or texted or asked me out. I have never given him any reason to think we should be together, and I intend to keep it that way. The whys of their breakup are as much a mystery to me as whatever brought them together in the first place. And it's not like Liam and I even have a relationship outside of work. Unless he's SN. Which he's not, regardless of Scar's big theory.

"Okay, then I'll tell you what I know. Apparently, Mr. Liam has it bad for you. Like a serious case of the hots. Apparently, he thinks you are 'a very good listener,'" Theo says, using air quotes, and leads me across the congested median into the parking lot, even putting his arm out to protect me from the traffic. I'll give him this: Theo is gallant.

"That makes no sense," I say. "I mean, he had the most attractive girl in school. Literally. I saw the sophomore super-latives. She won most attractive in last year's yearbook. There's a picture."

"The world is a wondrous and mysterious place. And there's no accounting for taste." He takes another pointed look at my Vans. I scratch my chin with my middle finger.

"I don't want Liam to ask me out." Theo leads me to his car and even opens his passenger-side door for me with a little

281

bow. Sees his performance all the way through, except he doesn't make me sit in the back. The interior of his car is pristine, so different from Scar's parents' Honda, which is filled with candy wrappers and gas receipts. "Even if I should be, you know, flattered."

"Why not? He's a cool guy. Maybe not the brightest, but still—" Theo swings out of the parking spot and navigates easily out of the lot and onto the freeway. He's a more comfortable driver than I am, moving in and out of lanes as if he owns the road and he's just being kind by letting the other cars share it. "Oh shit, don't tell me it's because of Ethan."

"It's not because of Ethan. And he's not who you think he is," I say, hating the obvious defensiveness in my voice.

"You totally have a girlie boner for him."

"He's my friend."

"You weren't here." Theo's face turns dark, and at first, I think he's just acting. Trying out a new role: troubled. "Trust me when I say you don't want to go there."

"What do you mean I wasn't here?"

"When Xander died. I mean, we all knew he was using, but heroin? That stuff is crazy dangerous. And he was like a god at school, before. Because of Oville." Theo cuts off a mom in a minivan, ignores her honks. "They were going to start playing real gigs, like on Sunset. We were all shocked when he OD'd. But not really, you know what I mean?"

"What does that have to do with Ethan? I mean, yeah, so they were in a band together, but that doesn't mean Ethan's an addict too." I wonder what that must have been like for Ethan, watching one of his bandmates slowly kill himself. Whether he felt as helpless as I did when I watched my mom fight against an invisible army of spreading cancer cells.

"Xander was Ethan's older brother."

"What?" I ask, even though of course I heard him the first time. It's just that I never put a name to what I recognized of myself in Ethan's eyes—that look on his face when he stares out the window, the shell shock, the insomnia. Grief. "Ethan's brother died? From a heroin overdose?"

I say it out loud, just so it seeps in and starts to make sense. Because a thought is forming in my mind, and if I'm right, it will change everything. I am a ninja, and I'll be stealthy and slow and deliberate. Fight for what I want. But I am not a ninja, and I am confused and spinning. It's starting to come together too fast, and my heart is barely beating, too slow, and I whip out my phone because I want to ask SN outright, not wait until our big meeting.

Three simple words: "Are you Ethan?"

Ethan, Ethan, Ethan.

The new mantra in my head, happily replacing *whoreslut-fatuglybitch.*

Was the lie that simple? A sister substituted for a brother? And how could I have not even considered it? How blind I have been to everyone and everything around me.

Ethan, Ethan, Ethan.

I didn't even dare to hope. I barely dare to hope now.

I put my phone away. Shake my head to redirect my thoughts. I've been wrong once. I shouldn't jump to conclusions. Wait. See.

But. Ethan.

"Are you okay?" Theo asks me. "You look a little green."

"Yeah," I say. "Fine."

SN: did you know that there isn't a Waffle House in the entire state of California? we have to go to Arizona.

Me: Why do we have to do that?

SN: WAFFLES. your favorite word. my favorite food. kismet. thought it would have a certain amount of poetic charm for us to meet in one.

Me: Yeah, appreciate the sentiment, but not going to Arizona with you.

SN: fine. then let's meet at IHOP. what are pancakes if not waffles in another form?

Me: Are you this weird in person?

SN: just you wait.

Me: I've been waiting. I have my theories about you, by the way. New theories.

Are you Ethan? Please. Be. Ethan. But I don't say this. When I really think about it, we've grown so good at talking around things, never drilling straight to the point. I think about studying with Ethan, our chats at Starbucks, wondering if he's dropped a single clue. No, nothing that I can think of, even with twenty-twenty hindsight.

I click back to some of Ethan's old messages. Crap. He

uses proper punctuation. Capitalizes the beginning of each sentence.

I lie on my bed, close my eyes. Send out a wish to the universe. Not to God, because if he exists, he's ignored me too many times before.

SN: you do? hope I'm not a disappointment.

Me: Ha. Hope you're not too.

SN: you've always said this arrangement is unfair—me knowing who you are but not vice versa—but when we meet, I don't know. I think everything will suddenly flip.

Me: So when are we doing this flipping? And don't you dare waffle.

SN: Tomorrow after school?

My heart sinks. I already have plans with Ethan tomorrow after school to work on "The Waste Land." Is this some sort of trick? To see which version of him I'll pick? No, maybe I have it all wrong. Maybe Ethan is not SN after all. The disappointment begins its slow bloom.

Me: Can't. Have plans already for a school thing. Have to work Tuesday. Wednesday?

SN: you are a busy woman, but I know you're worth the wait.

Me: I am. Are you?

Again, there it is. That weird flirty tone I used to use when we first started writing but have largely dropped since. The voice that isn't mine, that creeps in only when I'm trying too hard. Have we lost it already, our comfortable rapport, because I'm too nervous to be normal around a guy I could actually care about? No. I rub my finger along the ninja that is now stuck to the back of my laptop. I will not be afraid. This is SN. This, whatever this is, whoever this is—Ethan-or-not-probably-not—is worth fighting for.

CHAPTER 32

"What?" Ethan asks after he hands me my latte and I haven't offered to pay, like I practiced in my head. We are sitting on the stuffed chairs at Starbucks, Ethan directly across from me. I'm having trouble forming words, because I'm too busy trying to sort this all out. I feel stupid for assuming SN was Caleb. I don't want to make the same mistake twice.

"What-what? I didn't say anything."

"You're looking at me funny. Do I have something on my face?" Ethan begins to swat at his lips, which do have a tiny crumb stuck to them from his blueberry muffin, but that's not why I'm staring.

"Sorry. Just a little out of it today." I hold on tight to my cup, both hands cradling it like it's something fragile: an injured baby bird. "I guess I'm tired from the weekend."

"How was it?" Ethan asks, and smiles, as if he really wants to know. Which makes me think he's SN, because SN always wants to know everything. And which, of course, also makes me think he's definitely not SN, because SN already knows how my weekend was.

But most of all, I think he can't be SN because I want him to be SN, and that's the quickest way for it to not happen: for me to *want it* badly.

"Great. I mean, a little rocky at first. Long story. But then it was great. It was hard to leave," I say, which is true and untrue. It was hard to leave and it would have been hard to stay. Not feeling like I belong anywhere has made me crave constant motion; standing still feels risky, like asking to be a target. Maybe that's why Ethan doesn't sleep, come to think of it. Eight hours in one place is dangerous.

"Yeah, I bet. Is that sticker new?" Ethan points to my ninja, and I realize that though I've had it on my computer all day at school, he's the first to notice. Even Gem didn't see it, because her only jab today was to call me "sweaty." Not that creative, considering it's ninety degrees in November.

"Yeah. My best friend from home, Scarlett, made it for me. They're supposed to be like tattoos. I'm kind of in love with them."

"They're all really cool. She should sell them, like on Etsy or something."

"That's what I said!" I look up, and then, when I catch his eye, I look down again. This is all too much. I just need to fast-forward to Wednesday, meet SN, move on. If he's not Ethan, I will let go of this silly crush. Theo is right and wrong: this is playing with fire. I like being around him too much.

He too is cradling his coffee cup now. I've read somewhere that when someone mirrors your body language, it means they like you. Then again, if that were true, I'd be sitting cross-legged, and I'd have long ago caught Ethan's nervous habit of rubbing his hair. Instead of mirroring him, I want to crawl into his lap. Rest my head on his chest.

"Great minds, man."

"Great minds."

Are you SN?

Why do you wear a Batman T-shirt every day?

Why don't you sleep?

"Why don't you sleep?" I ask, because it seems the easiest of my questions. The least invasive, although maybe we're past all that now. I wish conversations came with traffic lights: a clear signal whether you need to stop or go or proceed with caution.

"I don't know. I've never been particularly good at it, but this past year it's like sleep is this fast-moving train and it only comes by, like, twice a night or something, and if I don't run really fast to catch it, I miss it altogether. I know. I'm a weirdo." He looks out the window, that "weirdo" dropped so casually it could be a reference to our messages, or it could just be that he uses the word "weirdo" too. It's a common noun. It means nothing.

"That's very poetic. A train metaphor. Maybe you should take something. I mean, to sleep."

Ethan looks at me, a question in his eyes, or an answer. Maybe both. "Nah. I don't like to take anything."

"Did you really memorize the whole poem?"

"The first section, yeah. I like how it speaks in so many

different voices. It's sort of loud, you know?" I picture Ethan practicing with Oville, strumming his guitar and singing his heart out. Noise as balm. I listen to them on repeat on my headphones after school every day. Try to parse out Ethan's voice, like a middle schooler obsessed with a boy band. He sounds stronger, rougher than Liam. Gravelly. Equal parts angry and resigned.

"I'm sorry about your brother." I blurt it out, and he looks as surprised as I am that I have taken the leap and mentioned it. "I mean, I know 'I'm sorry' is pretty useless, but I just heard—I'm like a year and a half behind on all things Wood Valley—and like you said a few weeks ago, I didn't want to be one of those people who didn't say something just because it's uncomfortable. Anyhow, it sucks, and nothing I can say will make it better. But yeah, I'm so sorry."

I stop talking, even though I have more to say. I want to tell him that he will sleep again, that it gets easier, sort of, despite the fact that it will never be okay. That those cards, *time heals all wounds,* start to feel a bit more true and still not true at all. I want to tell him I understand. But I'm pretty sure he already knows.

"Thanks," he says, again drawn to the window. He's so far away now, I feel like even if I were to indulge my need to touch him—my hand on his arm, my fingers in his hair, my palm on his cheek—he wouldn't feel it. "You're the only person who didn't know me before. Everyone else assumes I'm just like him or wonders why I can't just go back to being how I used to be. But I'm not him and I'm not the same me either, you know?"

"Ethan is Ethan is Ethan. Whoever that may be now," I say.

Ethan's head snaps back, as if he has again come to, the window forgotten. He looks at me instead; his eyes bore into mine, almost pleading, though I don't know for what. God, I want to touch him, but I wouldn't even know where to begin. What if he doesn't want me to? What if he just needs to occasionally have coffee with a person who didn't know him before? Maybe that's all I am.

I can understand that. The idea of leaving Chicago—of not being surrounded every day by the people who had always known me, who expected me to keep on being the same Jessie they had always known—once seemed like the answer, until it turned out it wasn't.

"Exactly. You get it. I am who I am, whoever that may be now."

"I wish I could recite 'The Waste Land,' because I feel like that would be so appropriate right now." I smile, which is almost the same as feeling his skin against mine, but no, not the same thing at all.

"Liam's going to ask you out. I thought you should know that."

"What?" I heard him, of course I heard him, but I don't know what to say. Liam has nothing to do with whatever is going on here. I'm still not sure whether Ethan is SN, but I'm also not sure how much that matters. Because Ethan is real and right in front of me, not just carefully written words on a screen.

I was wrong. I will not just let go of this silly crush, because this is not silly. Not even a little bit. Maybe it's my crush on SN that's ridiculous. He could be anyone. Typing is easy. But talking like this? This is hard.

Ethan shrugs. He knows I heard him.

"I . . . I don't want him to," I say. Now my eyes are pleading, though again I don't know for what. For him to touch me? *Please touch me. Your hand is right there.*

Ethan's coffee cup is interesting to him again; he stirs the black. He doesn't touch me. "Then I think you should say no."

Later, I lie on my bed and replay the conversation over and over again. *I think you should say no.* I measure the literal space that was between us—no more than a foot, probably less—and wonder how, if, we'll ever cross it.

SN: t minus forty-eight hours. i'm nervous.

Me: Me too. But I think if it's a disaster, we can just go back to this. Being friends here.

SN: you think? I don't know.

Scarlett: Did you know you can order the pill online?

Me: Do NOT order drugs online. If you want the pill, GO TO THE GYNO.

Scarlett: Yuck. I hate stirrups. The whole thing is so humiliating. So many personal questions . . .

Me: Come on, put on your big girl panties. YOU CAN DO THIS. Maybe I need to start making you empowering computer tattoos, because I've suddenly become the you in this relationship.

Scarlett: So I've been listening to Oville.

Me: AND?

Scarlett: YUM.

Ethan: I think we need to start writing our paper. Not just discussing.

Me: You do?

Ethan: Yup. I know it's not due until spring. But it's a long poem, and we need to get started. Maybe meet more than once a week.

Am I dancing around my room right now, rocking out, my whole body smiling? Maybe. Maybe I am.

Me: Yeah. Totally.

Ethan: Cool.

Me: Cool beans.

SN: interesting fact of the day: in the days of the telegraph, people used to write in code too. how we do now with abbreviations. like ttyl. that sort of thing.

Me: I didn't know that.

SN: I don't know why, but I thought you'd appreciate the randomness of that.

Me: It's cool that there are so many different ways to talk.

SN: EXACTLY.

CHAPTER 33

"So you need to talk to your dad," Theo says as he throws me a green juice from the fridge before school. I have developed a taste for these potions, though not for juicing as a verb or, come to think of it, as a lifestyle. Unlike Theo, I still require food. Which is why this is not my breakfast; this is my appetizer.

"Why?" We are the only two in the vast kitchen, the only people home. Rachel and my dad both left hours ago. Rachel does prework Pilates. My dad has the early-morning shift. Soon he'll take his exam, graduate to the position he had in Chicago.

"Because he's your dad."

"So?"

"How old are you?"

"Seriously, this coming from Mr. Temper Tantrum?" Turns out Theo did leave a soy sauce stain on the dining chair when he threw his fork. No matter: it is currently being reupholstered.

"One time, dude. I don't do well with change."

"Why do you care about me and my dad?" I sip my juice, imagine it cleaning up my insides, like a Clarisonic for my intestines. Yeah, drinking liquefied kale totally makes me smug.

"You're bringing negative energy into this house. We have enough bad juju as it is."

"Come on."

"You don't know what's going to happen tomorrow. How long they'll last. You only get two parents, and we're each down to one. Better to be good to them while you can." Theo grabs a wooden spoon, drums the counter. He can keep time. I wonder if there is anything he isn't good at.

"Whatever."

"Seriously. You're starting to sound like one of us Wood Valley brats."

"Fine." Of course, Theo is right. Just like Scar was. I need to be better, stronger, more courageous. A ninja, but not really, since we need to talk, not fight.

"Fine, what?"

"Fine, I'll talk to him."

"Good. Glad we had this chat." He chucks me under the chin, like this is the 1950s and I'm his son who hit a homer in a Little League game.

"You are a ridiculous human being. Do you know that?" I ask.

"I've been called worse."

. . .

Me: Fine. Let's talk. Nice move deploying Theo.

Dad: Didn't deploy Theo, but happy you want to talk. This has been TORTURE. I MISS YOU.

Me: Now you're the one being a little melodramatic.

Dad: I read a parenting book, hoping it could help. It was total crap.

Me: What did it say?

Dad: To give you some space.

Me: Hmm. Probably didn't factor in the size of the house.

Dad: When can we talk? Where?

And it has come to this: my dad and I need to schedule our make-up. I remember how normal things used to be between us. Not only normal, but natural. Before, you know, *before,* my mom would cook us dinner each night and we'd all sit around the table and chat. We had a game where we'd each share one thing that had happened since the night before, and I remember I used to save up anecdotes—that Mr. Goodman called on me in chem and I didn't know the answer, that the Smoothie Bandit had come back to the King and nicked some kid's drink, that Scar and I were partners for the science fair and we wanted to build a volcano because it's fun to occasionally be cliché. I remember I would sift through my day, like picking a filter for a photo, and choose the story I wanted to present to my parents like an offering. Not unlike SN and our three things, come to think of it.

What would my mom want to know about the last twenty-four hours? Maybe I'd have told her about the kale juice. Or SN's message this morning, counting the number of minutes till we're going to meet. Or best of all, Ethan's *I think you should say no*, which I haven't stopped replaying on a loop in my head. Six perfect words.

Then again, maybe not. Maybe I'd have kept that nugget just for myself.

Me: I dunno. Later?

Dad: Deal.

"Jessie, you mind staying for a minute?" Mrs. Pollack asks me after English, and my stomach drops. What did I do this time? According to Crystal, Gem's out with a stomach flu and is "like, you know, puking her guts out, hashtag jealous," so the day has been uneventful, which is a relief, since I'm in a striped cotton dress that I'm sure would have made me a perfect target. A little girlier than I normally wear, but damn, it's hot here.

And so I stay in my seat while the rest of the class files out. Ethan gives me a curious glance, and I shrug, and he smiles and mouths *Good luck* on his way out, and I want to pocket that smile and his words, carry them around with me like a talisman. My own goofy smile lingers on my face too long after he has left. Ethan's fault.

"I just wanted to talk to you about last week. I owe you an apology," Mrs. Pollack says, and this time she doesn't sit backward in her chair. She stays behind her desk, like a proper teacher. She has given up the whole buddy-buddy thing, which actually wasn't the problem. Her blame was. "I spent the whole weekend thinking about our conversation, and I realized I handled it all wrong."

I stare at her, thinking of the right words to say. "Thank you"? "No problem"? "No big deal"?

"It's okay. It's not your fault Gem is a total bitch," I say, and then look up in horror. I didn't mean to say that second part out loud. Mrs. Pollack smiles, which is a relief, because I wouldn't know how to explain to Ethan that we got an F on our "Waste Land" project just because I have a big mouth. Until last week, Mrs. Pollack was my favorite teacher, and not just because I was grateful to her for not making me stand up in front of the class on the first day of school.

"When I was in high school, I wasn't particularly cool. Actually, that's a lie," she says, and shrugs. "I was tortured. Really bullied. And when I saw what happened with Gem, I didn't know what to say. I just wanted to help."

Mrs. Pollack looks a little teary. Maybe no one ever gets over high school. She is shiny-haired and beautiful now, a grown-up Gem. It's hard to believe she ever looked any different.

"I just . . . anyhow, I just wanted to say sorry. I've been

watching you, and you so know who you are already. Most girls your age don't have that comfort-in-their-own-skin thing, and that's probably what makes you threatening to Gem," she says, and I wonder what the hell she's talking about. I don't know anything about anything. "Anyhow, high school is just . . . The. Worst."

"Funny that you became a high school teacher, then," I say, and she laughs again.

"Something I should talk to my therapist about. Speaking of which, you could speak to the school counselor if you want. We have a psychiatrist on staff. A life coach too."

"Seriously?"

"I know, right? Finding ways to justify the tuition. Anyhow, if not them, feel free to come talk to me anytime. Students like you are the reason I chose to teach."

"Thanks."

"By the way, I look forward to your and Ethan's 'Waste Land' paper. You're two of my brightest students. I have great expectations." Dickens is next on the syllabus. A literary pun. No wonder Mrs. Pollack was destroyed in high school.

"We intend to reach wuthering heights," I say, and as I walk by, she reaches her hand up, and I can't help it—dorks unite! nerd power!—I give her a high five on my way out.

Later, at Book Out Below!, which is customer-free, I sit behind the counter, message SN. So far, I've successfully avoided Liam since I've been back from Chicago, and I am relieved that he's not working today. If he is really planning to ask me out, I have no idea how I'll say no.

Me: Are you sure we should meet?

SN: yeah, I think so. why? you getting cold feet?

Me: No. It's just, you could be anybody. It's different for you. You know who's going to show up.

SN: well, I promise I'm not a serial killer or anything like that.

Me: Serial killers don't usually confess to being serial killers. In fact, isn't that the first thing a serial killer would do? Say "I'm not a serial killer. Nope, not me."

SN: true. don't take my word for it. let's meet in a public place. I won't bring my scary white van or candy.

Me: And where should we meet, Dexter Morgan? IHOP, really?

SN: yup. love IHOP. they have pancakes that look like happy faces. I have a thing at 3, so how about 3:45?

Me: Okay. How will I know who you are?

SN: I know who you are, remember?

Me: And?

SN: I'll come introduce myself, Ms. Holmes.

Me: Brave man.

SN: or woman.

Me: !!!

SN: kidding.

The bell rings; my head lifts up. It's become Pavlovian. *Please don't be Liam*, I think.

Fortunately, it's not.

Unfortunately, it's my dad.

"So this is where you work," he says, and looks around, his fingers brushing spines, just like mine do. He isn't the reader my mom was, but he still appreciates the magic of books. When I was little, he would read to me all the time. He was the one who introduced me to Narnia. "It couldn't be more perfect. I'm so happy for you."

"I like it," I say, and wonder if that's how we are going to do this. Pretend that we never fought in the first place. That we haven't gone something like fourteen days without speaking.

"Beats making smoothies, I hope?" My dad's wearing his plastic tag, his name printed under the words *How may I help you?* The way it dangles on a steel clip makes me feel tender toward him, as if he came in here with a milk mustache.

"Yeah. Though the Smoothie King has Scar. I miss her." He nods. We haven't even talked about my trip home. He hasn't asked—well, that's not quite true; he texted and I ignored him, and I still haven't said thank you. Maybe Theo is right: I'm turning more Wood Valley than I realize. I wonder if Scar's mom called him afterward and reported back. I don't think she heard me throwing up or knew we were drinking in the basement. The few times I saw her, she gave me big hugs and said, "I missed my other daughter," which was sweet, so it doesn't really matter if it was only a tiny bit true.

"I know." He quickly looks around, sees that we are alone. Nods as if to say *Then we can talk.* "I miss everything."

"Everything" means my mom. Funny that we can't just say those words out loud. But we can't. Some things are harder to say than others, no matter how much truer.

"Can you believe it's ninety degrees in November here? That's just not natural," my dad says, and settles on the floor with his back against the *Get Rich Quick* shelf, his knees bent in front of him. "Never thought I'd miss the cold, and I don't, really. But this weather is . . . unsettling. And the pizza sucks. Pizza should not be gluten-free. That's just wrong."

"Lots to get used to," I say. Should I give him more? Should I get this party started? Say: *Dad, you moved us without even asking me. Just plopped me into a new school, a new life, said "Ta-da!" and then abandoned me to the wolves.*

I stay quiet. Let him make the first move.

"Listen, I know it's been hard. And I was so wrapped up in trying to adjust myself, make this work for us, I didn't do my job as your dad. I thought it would be easier. Everything. I was naive. Or desperate. Yeah, that's it. Not naive but desperate." He delivers this to the bookshelf in front of him, the children's section—which has always seemed a weird arrangement to me and yet so LA, money directly across from the kids. My dad is staring at the cover of a book about crayons going on strike, the primary colors annoyed at being overworked by their owner.

I shrug. I wish we could have this conversation on paper, or better yet, on a screen, in back-and-forth messages like I do with SN. It would be so much easier and cleaner. I'd say exactly what I want to say, and if the words didn't come out right, I could just edit them until they did.

"Do you want to move back to Chicago? If that's what you want, we can do it. I wouldn't want you living at Scar's. We'd rent a place or something, and you could finish out school, and then I'd move back here when you go to college. If you were okay with that, of course. Rachel and I would figure it out. You're the most important thing in the world to me. If you're not happy, then I'm not happy. I know it hasn't seemed like that the last few months, but it's true." I think about last weekend. Scar and Adam, her new life without me. How we've all moved on—forward—and how in some ways, moving back would just be moving backward. It's not like my mom is there, and I guess memories, as much as they can be held on to, are portable. Granted, Chicago would mean never having to feel bullied, a huge bonus, but Gem's not quite scary enough to make me flee the state.

I think about the life I've built here. SN and Ethan, or maybe SN/Ethan, Dri and Agnes, even Theo. Liam too, I guess. How my new English teacher said I'm one of her brightest students, which is a huge compliment, considering I go to a school that sends *five* kids to Harvard each year. How Wood Valley may be filled with rich brats, but it also has a beautiful library, and I get to work in a bookstore, and I'm reading college-level poetry with a boy who can recite it back to me. In a strange way, thanks to Rachel, LA has turned out to be nerd heaven.

I think about Ethan's smile, how I want to see it every day. No, I don't want to move back.

"Nah. I mean, I think about Chicago all the time, and for a minute there, all I wanted was to go home, but that's not what I'm mad about. It's not like it would even really feel like home, anyway. I just feel, you know—" My eyes fill, and I look at the cash register. The 9 button is wearing thin. I hate that I don't know how to say what I want to say.

"You know you can talk to me about anything, right? I don't want you to ever feel alone." And there, he said it for me, so I can say it out loud now.

"Dad, you kind of orphaned me. Like I lost both of you guys, and Scar too. You left me to figure it all out on my own."

I did figure it out.

Most of it, at least. Maybe Scar is right: I am more kick-ass than I give myself credit for.

"Can you imagine how lonely it's been for me? Not now. I mean, now I'm okay. But not so long ago, I felt like I didn't have anyone in the world. And you were out every night with Rachel or holed up with your laptop. It's not like I hate her or anything. I mean, I don't know her, actually. I guess . . . thank her for my ticket, please." I pause, take a breath. Of course I should do that myself, and I will.

"It's just, I moved into this house, and have like, this weird room with these big paintings on the wall, like a third grader did them. What's up with that? Anyhow, it's not the art or even the soap with those strange letters, which make my hands smell nice, really, unfamiliar but nice, but it's just not mine, you know? And I just . . . It sucked, Dad. I mean, it really sucked," I say. Nope, the tears have not retreated; they're back, spilling down my cheeks, and I'm at work, and I just hope the bell doesn't ring anytime soon. I think I have said more to my dad in the last thirty seconds than I have in the last three months. Sometimes when I start, when the words finally find themselves, I can't hold back the momentum.

"Oh, sweetheart." My dad stands up, and I think he's coming to give me a hug, so I wave him off. I don't want to cry on his shoulder. Not right now. I'm not ready yet. "I'm so sorry," he says.

"I don't want an apology. I don't want anything. I'm mad at you, and I have a right to be mad at you. And I'll stop soon. You're my dad, and of course I'll stop. I get it. Our world exploded. And you just didn't have enough left over. I kind of did the same thing to Scar. And I wish I were stronger or better or something and I didn't need anything from you. But I'm not. And I do. It would have been nice if we could have done this together. But we didn't. And it's done. We're here now, and we're making it work. But it's really sucked."

"I think 'really sucked' is too much of an understatement. It's 'fucking sucked,'" my dad says, and he half smiles, and I can't help it, I smile back. He hates foul language; if this had been two years ago, there's no way he would have used the F-word. "Okay, you can still be mad at me. Fair enough. But you can't stop talking to me again. I can't take that. I miss telling you something that happened each day. I've been writing things down so I could tell you when you started talking to me again. And we need to start spending time together."

"Eww, no. I'm sixteen. I can't hang out with my father." I smile as I say it. I miss my dad, probably even more than he misses me. "That's, like, so uncool."

"Let me give you one bit of parental advice, if I may. Cool is way overrated."

"Says the guy wearing the plastic name tag."

"Touché."

"You love her, don't you?" I ask, apropos of nothing, but it's not, not really.

"Rachel? Yeah, I do. I mean, I leapt in a little fast, and we're figuring out the kinks, but yeah, I love her. But that doesn't mean—" I smile at him, bat away his words. He doesn't need to finish his sentence. I'm not a child anymore. I know that how he feels about her has nothing to do with me. Or my mom, for that matter.

I know that love is not finite.

And also this: I'll be leaving for college in less than two years. A part of me will be relieved to know he's not alone.

"I get it."

My dad looks around again, breathes in the paper smell.

"Mom would have loved this place. Even its silly name. Though probably not the exclamation point."

"I know."

"I love you, sweet potato."

"I know."

My phone bleeps. Text from Scarlett.

Scarlett: Holy shit. We did it.

Me: Seriously? It-it?

Scarlett: Yup.

Me: And?

Scarlett: I give us a 7, maybe an 8, which isn't bad for the first time. Hurt a little. And the whole condom thing was tricky, trickier than with a banana, and it was awkward, you know? But still. Good. I think we'll do it again in a minute.

Me: WHERE ARE YOU?

Scarlett: In the bathroom. Had to tell you right away, and had to pee, so I'm multitasking.

Me: So ADAM IS STILL IN YOUR BED?!?!

Scarlett: Yup. ☺

Me: Did you just emoji me?

Scarlett: What can I say? I have it bad. Starting the pill next week to be totally covered.

Me: So happy for you, you little slut!

Scarlett: Love you.

Me: Love you too. xoxo. Tell Adam congrats from me.

"What are you smiling at?" my dad asks, since I am, apparently, grinning goofily at my phone. *Scar lost her V-card!* I want to say it out loud because it's so exciting and I'm so happy for her, but no, no I won't.

"Nothing. Just something funny from Scar."

"Her mom says she has a boyfriend," my dad says, and I laugh, picturing Mrs. Schwartz and my dad gossiping about Scar and Adam.

"Yeah."

"She's really dating Adam Kravitz? He was always a little shrimpy."

"He's been working out."

"Good for them."

"They're happy."

"Any guys in your life?"

"Dad," I say, and blush. Realize that even if I wanted to tell my dad about Ethan, about SN, about all of it, it would be too confusing and complicated.

"Right," he says. "Remember when you were little we used to ask you how you got so big so fast, and you used to say 'I growed!'?"

My dad looks at his hands, which are not holding a phone like mine are, and have nothing to work out the nervous energy. My parents used to talk about my childhood all the time—start stories with "Remember?" and then tell me about something I used to do, and then they would smile at each other, like it had nothing to do with me, as if to say *Look what we pulled off.*

I shake my head. I don't remember.

"Well, sweetheart. You've really growed. I'm sorry I haven't been here. But I'm so proud of you. And your mom would be too. You know that, right?"

Do I know that? I know she wouldn't be not proud, which

is not the same thing as proud. I'm not sure I'm ready to think about her that way yet, to wrap my head around the "would be" part.

"Yeah," I say, mostly because of his empty hands and his name tag and the look on his face. It could be that this adjustment has actually been harder for him than for me. "Of course I know that."

SN: what was under the glass tonight?

Me: Some sort of delicious fish and the big couscous. What's that called?

SN: Israeli.

Me: Ha, I know. Just wanted to make you use your shift key. I want to get you a T-shirt that says "No proper noun left uncapitalized."

SN: and I'm the weirdo.

Rachel is waiting in my room when I get upstairs, sitting on my desk chair, again staring at the picture of my mom.

"She was so beautiful," Rachel says, by way of hello. She looks sad tonight, subdued, and is nursing a big glass of red wine. Again, her volume has been turned down.

"Yeah," I say, but I am not ready to talk about my mom with Rachel. Not sure that is something I'll ever be strong enough to do. "Hey, you took the pictures off the walls."

I look around. The elementary school paintings—which I realize now are probably the work of some famous artist I should know about—are stacked in the corner, and it's just white in here, with a few nails left like punctuation marks.

"I'm sorry. I hadn't even noticed them. My husband—um, Theo's dad—was in charge of decorating the house, and he picked them out. They're probably not the best choice for a teenage bedroom." Rachel sips from her glass, rubs her arms, which are covered in a delicious cashmere. "You should put your own stuff up on the walls. Posters or whatever. Make it yours."

"Thanks for my ticket home. To Chicago, I mean," I say. "That was really nice of you."

Rachel waves her hands, like it's no big deal. And maybe it's not to her, but it is to me.

"And we'll get you a new bed. A queen, maybe? I didn't realize until tonight how ridiculous this one is. Oh and I've told both of Theo's SAT tutors that you'll be joining in. Don't know how I didn't think of it earlier. Sorry about that." Her face falls, and I see she is near tears herself. What happened? I'm not sure I am equipped to deal with this.

"Thanks. The bed's actually more comfortable than it looks. I mean, are you okay?" I can't just let her cry and not ask. That would be wrong.

"Bad days. Good days. You know how it is. Just because I've found your father, who is wonderful—I mean, really, the best—doesn't mean this isn't all hard or complicated or that I don't miss—" She takes a deep breath, the kind that starts down in the belly, the kind you would only learn in a yoga class in California. "And I know Theo misses him, and I'm not enough. I'm just not. So it's hard sometimes. Sorry again for all the balls I've dropped. I shouldn't be in here."

"It's okay," I say, though I'm completely at a loss. This is a house full of pain, of bad juju, as Theo said, but it's also a house of starting over. Maybe we need to light a few candles. Better yet, start putting things on all of the white walls. "You know, I mean, this place is beautiful, but maybe you should put out some pictures too. Of your husband—I mean your, uh, other husband, Theo's dad, and of Theo as a kid. So he can remember."

Rachel looks at me, wipes her tears with her sleeve, and I try not to wince, because she's wearing mascara and her sweater must be dry-clean only.

"That's a great idea," she says, and looks straight at me. Almost smiles. "This is tricky, isn't it? You and I."

"I guess."

"I've been trying hard not to try too hard with you, and then I worry I'm not trying hard enough, you know?" She stands up, walks toward the door. Turns around to face me once more.

"Yeah," she says. "We'll get there."

CHAPTER 34

I'm early, so I sit in the first booth, a cowardly move that ensures I will see SN before he sees me. My back is to the rest of IHOP and their mountains of pancakes, and I watch the parking lot through the glass double doors. In just fifteen minutes, I will meet SN. He will sit down across from me and introduce himself, and our entire virtual relationship will become something real. Will be brought into the light and into the here and now. Based on something both more and less tangible: spoken words.

Of course, this could be a disaster. Maybe we'll have nothing to say to each other in person. He's probably not Ethan. I realize that now as I sit here with sweaty palms and wet armpits. Some things are too much to ask for.

My hair was down and now it's up, and I think I should put it down again. I spent much of the night debating what to wear.

Dri said: *Be casual.*

Agnes said: *Be fabulous.*

I decided in the early hours of the morning that it would be weird to wear anything but my normal clothes, that I don't want to look like I'm trying too hard.

Scar said: *Be yourself.*

But now my stupid jeans and T-shirt feel too normal. I should have put on more makeup, done something—anything—to make me feel prettier. What if SN has only seen me from afar and is disappointed when he's sitting across from me? Am I one of those girls who misleads at a distance?

I sit here, cataloging my flaws, hurting my own feelings. My chin is broken out. My nose is dotted with blackheads. My thighs expand on this plastic seat. No, this is not helping my nerves.

The waitress brings me a cup of coffee and I rip the lids off all the creamers in the bowl, make a pile of wrappers that I knock over and restack. I consider getting up and walking out. I don't need to meet SN. Let us continue as we are. Keep him as my phantom best friend, albeit one I like to flirt with.

Dri: GOOD LUCK! And if it turns out SN is Liam, then . . . go for it.

Me: Seriously?

Dri: Yeah. I just have a crush. Whatever you and SN have is real.

Me: I'm scared. I don't think he's Liam, though.

Dri: Me neither.

Me: You're a true friend.

Dri: Don't you forget that when you and SN are madly in love and don't have time for anyone else, okay?

Me: Ha!

Dri: Is he there yet?

Me: No.

Dri: Is he there yet?

Me: No.

Dri: Is he there yet?

I'm about to type back *No* again—I like this game, it's distracting and kind of funny—but then he is here and my stomach is in my feet. I feel my throat get tight, and tears wet my eyes, and I feel bad that I feel this way. I don't want to feel this way, but I do. How could I have been so wrong?

It's Liam.

Okay.

SN is Liam.

I try to recover, make sense of this. At least he's not Mr. Shackleman or Ken Abernathy. Liam is a good guy, coveted by the most beautiful girl in school. Surely this is a good thing.

He doesn't see me yet. He's at the cash register, grabbing one of those free loose mints, the ones that supposedly have high concentrations of fecal matter on them, but I recognize him from behind. Liam.

Liam is Liam is Liam.

He turns around, and his face transforms when he sees me. He smiles, so bright that I wonder what I've done to earn his good cheer.

All this time: Liam.

"Fancy seeing you here, stranger," he says. "Mind if I sit down?"

I am mute. I want to take out my phone and type to SN: *Sure. Go ahead.* And this: *I don't understand.* I resort to a nod. At least I know Dri won't be mad at me. At least there's that.

I want to type *You are not Ethan. I wanted you to be Ethan.*

But I know that's cruel. Like if he said to me *I wanted you to be prettier.*

"It's nice to see you," Liam says, and folds himself into the booth across from me. He's graceful today, the way he is on-stage: confident and fluid. Human origami.

"Yeah. You too," I say, and try to smile back. It doesn't quite reach my eyes.

"This is totally awkward and maybe not the right time for this, but I've been meaning to ask if you want to, you know, have dinner with me sometime?" And there it is: Liam is asking me out. For real. In real life. Not SN on the page, but SN in the flesh.

But all I can hear is Ethan's voice, *his* words, which were also spoken out loud: *I think you should say no.*

Still, that was before SN was Liam and Liam was SN. That was before the last ten seconds, when everything changed. And what if this is what's real—me and Liam, not me and Ethan? Maybe, again, I've had it all wrong. So what that it's sometimes awkward at the store, that I don't feel like Liam and I have much to say to each other? So what that he dated someone like Gem? People make bad decisions all the time.

"I—" I take a sip of my coffee, look deep into the cup, push down the terror that is rising inside me, the desire to flee this booth. I need the extra time that my phone affords me. Even just a few seconds to organize my thoughts. I try to picture what I would type right now. Typing would make this easier. Using thumbs instead of my mouth. *Yes,* I'd write. Or maybe *Sure.* Or *Cool.* Or . . .

But before I can figure out what to say, I feel a shadow fall over our table. My first instinct is that Gem is here and she's going to punch me, and that's how all this will end. Me knocked out on the floor. Which is ridiculous, because it's not Gem. And punching is not her style. She's subtler than that.

It's Ethan.

Ethan is Ethan is Ethan.

Ethan's here too, and now I'm confused and I don't know what to do. He sees Liam sitting across from me, and his face darkens and then goes blank. I want to see his smile, hear him say those six words one more time: *I think you should say no.*

Surely that will help me make sense of all of this. That will give me a good reason to walk away from SN, walk away

317

from "three things" and delicious midnight conversations and everything that has kept me going for the last few months.

SN is Liam. Liam is SN. A simple equation. Remedial math. Time to accept it.

"Hey," Ethan says, and there is pleading in his eyes. He's saying those six words without saying those six words. And so I don't answer Liam—not yet, anyway—and I turn to Ethan. Buy time another way.

"Hey," I say. Then I'm sure I have this all wrong, that I'm actually dreaming, because all of a sudden Caleb is here too, right behind Ethan, and of course all three of them would be here for the great SN unveiling. This is a dream. It has to be, because the three of them can't be SN, and I've had dreams like this before, when they're all there—Liam, Ethan, Caleb—morphing into each other, swapping shirts.

But no, Caleb is in gray. Ethan is the Batman. And Liam is wearing a button-down, because unlike his friends, he rotates his wardrobe. One point for Liam there.

If this is a dream, next they will break out into song. Serenade me with "The Girl No One Knows."

No one is singing.

This is not a dream.

I dig my fingernails into my palms, just to be sure. It hurts.

"Howdy," Caleb says, and looks from Liam to me and back to Liam and smiles, as if to say *Go for it, dude.* Do he and Ethan both know that SN is Liam, and they're here to see what happens? Or maybe they're all in on it, have shared the SN password and taken turns writing to me. Has this whole thing been one big joke? Is that the lie? There are three of them?

I flash back to my dad's offer to take us home to Chicago,

wonder if that's where this is all headed. Me, on a plane, humiliated and heartbroken.

"Wait," Ethan says, and takes a step forward and then one backward. It's an awkward dance, and his face reddens. "You're early."

"Dude, we're in the middle of something here," Liam says, and looks at me again, as if to re-ask his question. *Right. Dinner.* If I weren't so disappointed, it would be cute, SN starting our first conversation by asking me out on a proper date.

"Liam," Ethan says, and puts his hand on Liam's shoulder. Liam shakes it off angrily. I am so stupid. It's obvious these two have a problem with each other. *There was drama there for a while,* Dri said once. Liam replaced Ethan's brother in the band.

I think you should say no.

I've taken it all the wrong way: those six words had nothing to do with Ethan wanting me. He just hates Liam. The realization is crushing.

"Why are you always throwing shade?" Liam stands up to face Ethan. Months, perhaps years, of pent-up aggression are spewing forth, and I'm unfortunate enough to get caught in the middle.

Liam's hands are curled into fists, as if he is ready to throw punches right in the middle of IHOP, which is of course a dumb place to fight. There are children here, and polyester booths and smiley-face pancakes. Multiple kinds of syrup. Some of the drinks even come with maraschino cherries.

Caleb steps between Liam and Ethan, and Ethan puts his hands in the air. He has no interest in swinging or being swung at. Maybe he has no interest in me.

"You've got it all wrong, man. It's not like that," Ethan says, puts his hands down and into his pocket. He pulls out his phone. "Just give me one second."

Ethan's eyes are on me, not on Liam, and he's talking to me without talking to me. I don't know what he's saying. I just know I want to keep staring at him. Again, everything is too fast for me to understand, and also too slow, because I can hear the thump of my heart and the blood rushing in my ears, can feel the warmth of the coffee cup in my trembling hands.

My phone beeps. I have a message. I look down. I pick it up.

SN: it's me.

I look up again. Ethan is smiling nervously at me. He's typing without looking.

SN: me. not him. me.

SN: let me say this in caps: ME.

"You?" I ask, out loud, without hands, the words right where I need them. Finally, finally, realization dawning. My eyes are locked with Ethan's. I can't help it; I'm grinning. "For real. It's you?"

"Me," Ethan says, and holds up his phone. "You were early.

We had an Oville meeting in the back that ran too long, and then he got to you first."

I look at Liam, who is rocking on his heels, confused and still angry. Watching our conversation but not getting it at all. How could he? I barely understand.

Ethan is Ethan is Ethan.

Ethan is SN.

"Liam, I'm sorry. I can't. I mean, it's Ethan. It's him," I say, which makes no sense at all, but it doesn't seem to matter, because now Ethan is sitting down across from me in the booth. And we are smiling at each other, goofy and giddy, and it's easy, so much easier than it should be.

Liam looks more confused than upset. Caleb shrugs and then rolls his eyes toward the door, as if to say *Give it up, man. She's not worth it.*

"Whatever," Liam says, taking Caleb's cue, the words casually thrown over his shoulder as he walks out the door. Caleb shakes his phone at me and Ethan, apparently his generic goodbye, as he runs to catch up with Liam.

"You?" I ask Ethan again, because I need it to be said one last time. To be sure that I'm not just jumping to conclusions and that I'm not dreaming.

"It's nice to meet you again, Jessie, Jessie Holmes. I'm the weirdo who has been messaging you." Ethan looks nervous, a question in his eyes. "Today so didn't go the way I meant it to."

I laugh, because what I'm feeling is something so much bigger than relief.

"What? You didn't expect to almost get into a fistfight?"

"No, no, I did not."

"I can't believe it's you," I say, letting out the breath I didn't even realize I was holding. My phone beeps.

SN: are you disappointed?

Me: NO!!!

SN: can I come sit next to you?

Me: YES!!!

Ethan switches sides of the booth, and now his thigh is up against mine. I can smell his Ethan smell. I bet he tastes like coffee.

"Hello," he says, and reaches up and tucks my hair behind my ears.

"Hello," I say.

After we've talked for a while, it's like all those other times I've hung out with Ethan but also totally different, because we're not working on a project, we're just together because we want to be, and I now know him, like really know him, because we've spent the last two months talking with our fingertips.

"Why?" I ask. He closes the gap, puts his hand in mine. We are holding hands. Ethan and I are holding hands. I am not sure I ever want to give his back.

"Why what?"

"Why did you email me that first day?"

"Since my brother . . . I feel like I've forgotten how to, like, how to talk to people. My dad made me go to this therapist, and she said that it might help to start writing instead. And when I saw you on the first day of school, there was just something about you that made me really want to meet you. You seemed lost in a way that I totally get. I decided to email. It felt safer to be undercover." He shakes his head, as if to say *Yes, I'm strange.*

"Have you written to anyone else?" I ask.

"I mean, a few times here and there. I like to watch people. I've told some kids stuff in the nicest way possible. I told Ken Abernathy that Gem was cheating off him in calculus. With you, it was different. Ours was a two-month-long conversation."

"So what you're saying is you're kind of like Wood Valley's Batman."

He grins. Looks down.

"Not really. This is my brother's shirt. It's silly, but whatever."

"I like being able to ask you questions and you answering them."

"I like you asking me questions."

"Tell me three things," I say, because I love our three things. I don't want them to stop even though we can now say them out loud.

"One: contrary to popular belief, I do not do drugs. Terrified of them. Won't even take Tylenol. Two: I memorized the first part of 'The Waste Land' just to impress you. Normally, I play Xbox in the middle of the night or read when I can't sleep, but I thought it would make me seem, I don't know, cooler or something."

"It worked. It was totally dreamy." My voice is smiling. I didn't even know it could do that.

"Three: my mom's in rehab as of yesterday. I am not naive enough to be optimistic—we've been to this rodeo a few times—but at least it's something."

"I—I don't know what to say. If we were writing, I'd probably emoticon you." I squeeze his hand, another way to talk. No wonder Ethan can't sleep; his family life is even more screwed up than mine.

"Your turn. Three things . . ."

"Okay. One: I was really hoping it was you. I was sure it was, and then I was sure it wasn't, and for that second, I thought you were Liam and I wanted to cry."

"Liam's not so bad. I need to be nicer to him. Especially now. Oh man, he's going to break my legs." Ethan smiles. He's not scared of Liam at all.

"No he won't. He'll go back to Gem, and they can be prom king and queen or whatever, assuming you even do that here, and it will be fine. It's too bad, though, because I so want to set him up with Dri."

"By the way, how right was I that you and Dri would be friends?"

"You were right. You were right about a lot of things."

"Two . . ."

"Two . . ." I stall. What do I want to say? That for the first time in as long as I can remember, I feel like I'm exactly where I want to be. That I'm happy to sit still. Right here. With him.

"Two, thank you for being my first friend here at a time when I had no one. It really . . . made a difference."

Now it's his turn to squeeze my hand, and it feels so good, I almost close my eyes.

"Three? I don't have a three. My head is still spinning."

"I have one."

"Go for it."

"Three: I want to kiss you, like, very much, please."

"You do?" I ask.

"I do," he says, and so I turn toward him, and he turns toward me, and even though we are in this random IHOP and our table is full of the bizarre array of uneaten foods Ethan has ordered to allow us to keep our table for the past three hours—pancakes, of course, but also pickles and apple pie—everything falls away.

It is just him and me, Ethan is Ethan is Ethan and Jessie is Jessie is Jessie, and his lips touch mine.

But sometimes a kiss is not a kiss is not a kiss. Sometimes it's poetry.

Dear Reader,

In *Tell Me Three Things*, Jessie, my main character, keeps constant count of the number of days it has been since her mother died. Like Jessie, I also lost my mother at fourteen, and of course I'm not going to be coy and pretend that's a coincidence. It's not. And I used to do that too: the counting. I still do it, in fact, but now I count in years instead of days. I'm at twenty-four. Twenty-four?!? How is that even possible? With *Tell Me Three Things*, I was finally brave enough to take a look at a period in my life that I long ago boxed up, put away, and marked with a big red label that read "Too Painful." I wasn't interested in exploring my specifics, necessarily, but I very much wanted to delve into those feelings of first loss and their immediate aftermath. To look back at what it was like to be teenager and to have the worst thing you can imagine happening *actually* happen.

But at the same time, I very much did not want to write a dead mom book. Instead, I decided to combine the loneliness of first loss with something much more magical and universal: the beauty of first love. Jessie is not me—she's so much cooler and more together than I ever was at sixteen, or even am now, for that matter. But she's a version of me, an alterna-me, in the way that all of the characters I create somehow are. *Tell Me Three Things* was an opportunity to

327

gift that me-but-not-me, to gift Jessie, with the one thing I most wanted at sixteen: To feel truly *seen*. To feel *known*. Enter Somebody Nobody.

One of the most amazing things about young adulthood is that it's a time that's chock-full of firsts. Some wonderful and some . . . not so wonderful. At one point, Jessie says of her mother, "She will never see who I grow up to be—that great mystery of who I am and who I am meant to be—finally asked and answered." Now, twenty-four whole years after my mother's death, a lot of my own questions have been asked and answered, even if my mom wasn't here to see it all unfold. Writing *Tell Me Three Things* reminded me of what it felt like when my world was forever widening.

I can't thank you enough for reading. Though this may look just like an ordinary book to you, for me it's one more magical first: my very *first* novel for young adults. Only took twenty-four years to get the courage.

Julie Buxbaum

ACKNOWLEDGMENTS

It is with a heart full of gratitude, as embarrassingly earnest as that sounds, that I thank the following people, without whom this book would just be a big tangle of words on an antiquated hard drive: Jenn Joel, for being a brilliant and kick-ass agent and champion. Beverly Horowitz, for her sharp insights and for pushing me to make *Tell Me Three Things* better with each and every iteration. The wonderful and incomparable Elaine Koster, who is terribly missed. Susan Kamil, who rocks like no other. The Fiction Writers Co-op, for the support and laughs and for making the writing life a whole lot less solitary. John Foley, for naming Book Out Below! Karen Zubieta, for helping me to keep all the balls in the air. The Flore clan, for letting me into your club and allowing me to share your name. Mammaji, who has given up so much so that I get to do what I love; I am eternally grateful. Josh, who keeps me honest and laughing; I won the big brother lottery. My dad because he's awesome. My mom, Elizabeth, who is loved and remembered every day, but whose name doesn't get said out loud enough. And, of course, my husband, Indy, and our two little snugglebugs, Elili and Luca—"love" is too small a word. I am so honored that I get to call you guys mine.

Jessie and SN knew what to tell each other.

Kit and David don't.

♥ ♥ ♥

Turn the page to discover how their story begins. . . .

"Heartfelt, charming, deep, and real.
I love it with all my heart."

—Jennifer Niven, *New York Times* bestselling author
of ALL THE BRIGHT PLACES

KIT

I don't really know why I decide not to sit with Annie and Violet at lunch. I can feel their eyes on me when I pass right by our usual table, which is at the front of the caf, the perfect table because you can see *everyone* from there. I always sit with them. Always. We are best friends—a three person squad since middle school—and so I realize I'm making some sort of grand statement by not even waving hello. I just knew as soon as I came in and saw them huddled together talking and laughing and just being so normal, like nothing had changed at all—and yes, I realize that nothing *has* changed for them, that their families are no more or less screwed-up as they were before my life imploded—that I couldn't do it. Couldn't sit down, take out my turkey sandwich, and act like I was the same old reliable Kit. The one who would make a self-deprecating joke about my shirt, which I'm wearing in some weird tribute to my dad, a silly attempt to feel closer to hi even though it makes me feel like even more of an outcast and more confused about the whole thing than I was before I put it on. Just the kind of reminder I don't need. Like I could actually forget, for even a single minute.

I feel stupid. Could that be what grief does to you? It's like I'm walking around school with an astronaut's helmet on my head. A dome of dullness as impenetrable as glass. No one here understands what I'm going through. How could they? I don't even understand it.

It seemed safer somehow to sit over here, in the back, away from my friends, who have clearly already moved on to other important things, like whether Violet's thighs look fat in her new high-waisted jeans, and away from all the other people who have stopped me in the hall over the past couple of weeks with that faux-concerned look on their faces and said: "Kit, I'm like so, so, so sorry about your daaaad." Everyone seems to draw out the word *dad* like they are scared to get beyond that one sentence, to experience the conversational free fall of what to say next that inevitably follows. My mom claims that it's not our job to make other people feel comfortable—this is about us, not them, she told me just before the funeral—but her way, which is to weep and to throw her arms around sympathetic strangers, is not mine. I have not yet figured out my way.

Actually I'm starting to realize there is no way.

Certainly I'm not going to cry, which seems too easy, too dismissive. I've cried over bad grades and being grounded and once, embarrassingly, over a bad haircut. (In my defense, those bangs ended up taking three very long awkward years to grow out.) This? This is too big for woe-is-me silly girl tears. This is too big for everything.

Tears would be a privilege.

I figure sitting next to David Drucker is my best bet, since he's so quiet you forget he's even there. He's weird—he sits with his sketchbook and draws elaborate pictures of fish—and when he does talk, he stares at your mouth, like you might have something in your teeth. Don't get me wrong: I feel awkward and uncomfortable most of the time, but I've learned how to fake it. David, on the other hand, seems to have completely opted out of even trying to act like everyone else.

I've never seen him at a party or at a football game or even at one of the nerdy after-school activities he might enjoy, like Math Club or coding. For the record, I'm a huge fan of nerdy after-school activities since they'll be good for my college applications, though I tend toward the more literary and therefore ever-so-slightly cooler variety. The truth is I'm kind of a big nerd myself.

Who knows? Maybe he's onto something by tuning the rest of us out. Not a bad high school survival strategy. Showing up every day and doing his homework and rocking those giant noise-canceling headphones—and basically just waiting for high school to be over with.

I may be a little awkward, sometimes a bit too desperate to be liked—but until everything with my dad, I've never been quiet. It feels strange to sit at a table with just one other person, for the noise of the caf to be something that I want to block out. This is the opposite of my own previous survival strategy, which was to jump headfirst into the fray.

Oddly enough, David has an older sister, Lauren, who, until she graduated last year, was the most popular girl in school. His opposite in every way. President of her class and homecoming queen. (Somehow she managed to make something that clichéd seem cool again in her hipster ironic way.) Dated Peter Malvern, who every girl, including me, used to worship from afar because he played bass guitar and had the kind of facial hair that most guys our age are incapable of growing. Lauren Drucker is a living legend—smart and cool and beautiful—and if I could reincarnate as anyone else, just start this whole show over again and get to be someone different, I would choose to be her even though we've never actually met. No doubt she'd look awesome with bangs.

I'm pretty sure that if it hadn't been for Lauren, and the implicit threat that she would personally destroy anyone who made fun of her younger brother, David would have been eaten alive at Mapleview. Instead he's been left alone. And I mean that literally. He is *always* alone.

I hope I'm not rude when I tell him I don't feel like talking; fortunately he doesn't seem offended. He might be strange, but the world is shitty enough without people being shitty to each other, and he has a point about the whole heaven thing. Not that I have any desire to talk to David Drucker about what happened to my father—I can think of nothing I'd rather discuss less, except for maybe the size of Violet's thighs, because *who cares about her freaking jeans*—but I happen to agree. Heaven is like Santa Claus, a story to trick naive little kids. At the funeral, four different people had the nerve to tell me my father was in a *better place,* as if being buried six feet under is like taking a Caribbean vacation. Even worse were my dad's colleagues, who dared to say that *he was too good for this world.* Which, if you take even a second to think about it, doesn't even make sense. Are only bad people allowed to live, then? Is that why I'm still here?

My dad was the best person I knew, but no, he wasn't *too good* for this world. He isn't in *a better place.* And I sure as hell don't believe *everything happens for a reason,* that this is *God's plan*, that *it was just his time to go,* like he had an appointment that couldn't be missed.

Nope. I'm not buying any of it. We all know the truth. My dad got screwed.

Eventually David slips his headphones on and takes out a large hardcover book that has the words *Diagnostic and Statistical Manual of Mental Disorders IV* written on the spine. We have almost all our classes together—we are both doing the junior-year AP overload thing—so I know this isn't school reading. If he wants to spend his free time studying "mental disorders," good for him, but I consider suggesting he get an iPad or something so no one else can see. Clearly his survival strategy should include Mapleview's number-one rule: Don't fly your freak flag too high here. Better to keep the freak buried, inconspicuous, maybe under a metaphorical astronaut's helmet if necessary. That may be the only way to get out alive.

I spend the rest of the lunch mindlessly chewing my sad sandwich. My phone beeps every once in a while with text messages from my friends, but I try not to look over to their table.

Violet: Did we do something to hurt your feelings? Why are you sitting over there?

Annie: WTF!!?!?!?

Violet: At least write back. Tell us what's going on.

Annie: K! Earth to K!

Violet: Just tell me the truth: yay or nay on these jeans?

When you have two best friends, someone is always mad at someone else. Today, by not texting back, I'm basically volunteering to be the one on the outs. I just don't know how to explain that I can't sit with them today. That sitting at their table, right there in the front of the caf, and chatting about nonsense feel like a betrayal. I consider giving my verdict on Violet's pants, but my dad's dying has had the unfortunate side effect of taking away my filter. No need to tell her that though her thighs look fine, the high waist makes her look a little constipated.

My mom said no when I begged her to let me stay home from school today. I didn't want to have to walk back into this cafeteria, didn't want to go from class to class steeling myself for yet another succession of uncomfortable conversations. The truth is people have been genuinely nice. Even borderline sincere, which almost never happens in this place. It's not their fault that everything—*high school*—suddenly feels incredibly stupid and pointless.

When I woke up this morning, I didn't have the blissful thirty-second amnesia that has carried me through lately, that beautiful half minute when my mind is blank, empty, and untortured. Instead I awoke with pure, full-throttled rage. It's been one whole month since the accident. Thirty impossible days. To be fair, I'm aware my friends can't win: If they had mentioned this to me, if they had said something sympathetic like "Kit, I know it's been a month since your dad died, and so today must be especially hard for you," I still would have been annoyed, because I probably would have fallen apart, and school is not where I want to be when that inevitably happens. On the other hand, I'm pretty sure Annie and Violet didn't mention it because they had forgotten altogether. They were all chatty, sipping their matching Starbucks lattes, talking about what guy they were hoping was going to ask them to junior prom, assuming I just had a bad case of the Mondays. I was expected to chime in.

I am somehow supposed to have bounced back.

I am not supposed to be moping around in my dad's old shirt.

One month ago today.

So strange that David Drucker of all people was the only one who said the exact right thing: *Your dad shouldn't have died. That's really unfair.*

What to Say Next excerpt text copyright © 2017 by Julie R. Buxbaum, Inc.
Cover illustration copyright © 2017 by Thomas Slater.
Published by Delacorte Press, an imprint of Random House Children's Books,
a division of Penguin Random House LLC, New York.

CAN A SINGLE KISS
CHANGE EVERYTHING?

New York Times bestselling author of *Tell Me Three Things*

JULIE BUXBAUM

YEAR
ON
FIRE

Turn the page to find out. . . .

Immie

A single kiss had blown up Immie Gibson's life. How strange that two people's lips touching—not even Immie's lips, mind you, but *two other people's lips* and for no more than thirty seconds—could be the reason why, on this first day of junior year, Immie sat sweating in her linen shirt. That's how long Arch had said the kiss with Jackson had lasted: *thirty seconds, tops.*

On reflection, maybe it wasn't that strange. After all, Immie had never been kissed, not properly, not in the way you see in movies, with eyes closed and a sudden, lurching passion.

Maybe everyone else knew that kissing bent the space-time continuum and validated chaos theory and also could indirectly make your best friend low-key hate you.

Maybe this kind of thing happened every day.

"Bad idea," Paige said, pointing to Immie's shirt. "Linen always wrinkles." Her button-down had somehow, during the ride to school, turned from crisp and optimistic to defeated. Crumpled, like her mood.

"Do I have sweat stains? I feel like I have sweat stains," Immie said, pretending she didn't notice the new way Paige liked to throw tiny darts in her direction, how it was not yet eight-thirty a.m. and her torso was made up of a million microscopic seeping wounds.

"Say that a little louder. I think the boys in the back didn't hear you," Paige said.

"You do not have sweat stains," Arch said. "Relax, Im."

Paige had been Immie's best friend since seventh grade, when Immie arrived at Wood Valley Middle School feeling nervous and overwhelmed, a donkey in a field of ponies. Middle school was supposed to be filled with awkward kids—braces and acne, an inability to move smoothly through the world, like you hadn't yet been given the map. Wood Valley, on the other hand, was packed with the well-mannered, the well-groomed, the already slick. The girls even carried cute pouches—canvas and pink polka-dotted and monogrammed—to hold their new menstrual products, like puberty was adorable and fun.

Even at the horrific age of thirteen, Immie knew: these people were *born* with maps. The rules didn't apply.

Also, her period was horrifying.

At their very first assembly in the auditorium, the headmaster stood on the stage and told the gathered mid-pubescents that their admittance to Wood Valley and this important first year of seventh grade were the start of an "illustrious career."

Paige, who was sitting to Immie's right, as she would many times after that by choice, but whose appearance that first day seemed like nothing short of a miracle, sneezed into her hand the word: *bullshit*. Immie thrilled at the transgression. Archer, Immie's twin brother who always sat to her left, who had sat there since pre-K, probably since the womb, wrote down the words *illustrious career* in his shiny, new composition notebook in neat block letters, and then underlined it twice. Arch was born first, by four minutes, so they were always Arch and Immie, a single unit. Or Archer and Imogen, if their dad was angry. They had never been Immie and Arch (or, worse, the matchy-matchy Immie and Archie), which sounded like a crime-fighting duo in a kids' chapter book.

Sometimes things are set in the beginning.

That's what it felt like when Immie found herself sitting in between her brother and Paige on that first day of seventh grade, like the ground was firming beneath her feet, right there at the *start of their illustrious careers* or this *bullshit*, depending on your perspective. They would be Arch and Immie and Paige from then on.

Immie's premonition had been right, or maybe it wasn't a premonition. Perhaps she'd willed it. Either way, they soon became a threesome. Paige had rolled up like seventh grade was just seventh grade. No big deal. Later, Immie would learn Paige could do pretty much anything she wanted and not get in trouble, that sneeze-cursing was the least of her transgressions. Overconfidence and a sly sense of humor were Paige's superpowers, and once Immie understood that about her best friend, she wondered if maybe she hadn't been the one to will their connection—Paige probably had.

But that beginning was a long time ago. Middle school angst had given way to high school comfort—or at least, if not comfort, routine—and so today wasn't supposed to feel like seventh grade all over again. And yet, Immie felt the familiar flutter of panic, the rush of wetness under her arms. If there weren't sweat stains a moment ago, there were now. Paige claimed to have forgiven her, but this was, to sneeze-quote Paige herself, *bullshit*. If Immie had been in her position, if she had thought Paige had kissed her boyfriend, though of course Immie had never had a boyfriend for Paige to kiss because she was a normal living on a planet full of mermaids, she would have been livid. Immie believed in clear lines.

Now, though, if Immie somehow miraculously found a boyfriend, she'd pass him right over to Paige and make them even.

Here, kiss him and hurt me. I miss us.

Of course, neither life nor boyfriends actually worked that way. And Immie hadn't kissed Paige's boyfriend (well, ex-boyfriend now), Jackson, in the first place. But Paige would never know that, *could never know that*, and so Immie was stuck permanently in the aftermath of this ridiculous, self-destructive lie. She was also stuck in this wrinkled linen shirt that gave off a cardboard smell, in this school where she didn't fit in, in this life that made her long desperately for college, as if she had to wait two whole years to pull the emergency exit lever.

That was what she was thinking about—the kiss and her earlier inexplicable optimism and her tiny wounds and their invisible droplets of blood—when the new boy walked in. Later that night, she would tell Arch that the new boy had smelled of smoke, that when she saw him she immediately thought of campfires and s'mores, and so he might be the arsonist. Arch, like a runner throwing a baton, would pass this information to Paige and plant a tiny seed of suspicion. They all felt badly about that later.

But Immie was wrong. The new boy did not smell like smoke. Fires can be a lot like kisses: they can confuse your chronology and leave no reliable witnesses.

Before the alarm went off and they were evacuated to the fields, Immie looked up and saw the new boy, took in his British accent and his sweet brown eyes, and felt an entirely different kind of wound, this one larger, more pointed, possibly fatal. Like someone had put out a cigarette on her heart. (Is that why she thought she smelled smoke? Had her subconscious transformed the image in her mind into something literal?)

Paige, who Immie had thought had gone to the bathroom, but was now sitting next to her again, a tiny bit breathless, tapped her on the arm.

"Dibs," she whispered.

The new boy seemed conjured from her imagination, like that morning Immie had handed God a list not unlike the one she was putting together about herself for those future college applications, and God had handed her this person right back. This feeling was altogether new, and not, if she was honest, entirely pleasant.

"Apologies for my tardiness. Got a bit turned around on the motorway. Total chockablock," he said to Ms. Lee, and handed her the slip of paper in his hand. "Also, you drive on the wrong side of the road here. Bloody confusing, it is." He had tousled hair and brown skin and the sort of accent that conjured up the image of a monarchy. He turned to the class, sad-eyed and wry-smiled, and cocked his head to the side, puppy-like, as if waiting for someone to point to an empty seat and invite him to sit down.

Immie sucked in that *bloody confusing, it is* as if through a straw. She wondered if the new boy was intentionally using as many Britishisms as he could. Like he had decided on the plane ride over the Atlantic that this would be his bit—all Britishisms all the time. Maybe someone had told him that American girls liked that sort of thing.

We do, Immie thought. *We do.*

"It's a freeway, not a motorway," Jackson called out from the back of the room, reminding Immie again of Jackson's existence, which is something she generally tried to forget. Immie had claimed the kiss with Jackson as her own, had reached out and grabbed it, like catching an air kiss blown across the room at someone else. There was no denying she had protected her brother at the expense of her best friend, which, even now, ten days after it all went down, while she was still stewing in the aftermath, felt like the right call.

What surprised her most about the scandal was not the lie itself and how easily she told it; it was how easily Paige believed Immie, as if she had been waiting to be betrayed by her this entire time.

Arch, Immie's twin brother and her better half, her favorite person since birth, had betrayed Paige and kissed Paige's boyfriend, Jackson. Sometimes Immie repeated it to herself—*Arch kissed Jackson and I said I did it*—because it still seemed like a bizarre dream.

Arch liked to joke that he was the first out of the womb because Immie had pushed him. That might have been true. Immie's mom often told the story that when they were babies, Arch wouldn't settle unless Immie was placed beside him in the bassinet. That might have been true too. The point is: Arch and Immie predated Arch and Immie and Paige.

The two of them had never discussed the myriad other possibilities: Arch coming out and claiming that stupid kiss himself. Or maybe separating this particular kiss from some bigger statement about Arch. They didn't even discuss the possibility of him trying what Jackson had managed through the years—cultivating an ambiguous sexual identity. No one would have been surprised to hear that Jackson sometimes kissed boys; he had long ago hinted at his bisexuality or maybe pansexuality, seeming to be above any concerns about labels. But Jackson was like Paige in that way: he was given the single gift of adulthood early—there would be no delay in him getting to be exactly who he was.